THE *Marriage* SOLUTION

STEPHANIE ROSE

THE MARRIAGE SOLUTION

STEPHANIE ROSE

That's What She Said Publishing, Inc.

The Marriage Solution

Cover Design: Najla Qamber Designs

Cover Photo: © Shutterstock

Editing: Lisa Hollett—Silently Correcting Your Grammar

Proofreading: Jodi Duggan

ISBN: 979-8-88643-927-4 (ebook)

ISBN: 979-8-88643-928-1 (paperback)

052923

For my alpha readers: Jodi, Rachel, and Lauren. Thanks for pulling me back when I fell off the rails in the first draft and helping me make Landon and Julie all they were meant to be. And for believing in me enough to give it to me straight, while not letting me give up hope.

For Jeannine: whose patience and great ideas saved my laptop from a fourteen-story demise off my terrace one sad afternoon. You're the real deal, lady.

For all the lupus warriors out there: Julie's life may change, but she still gets big love and dreams. Grab your spoons, and don't settle for anything less.

MESSAGE FROM THE AUTHOR

Julie's symptoms are based on my personal experience and that of a sensitivity reader who has a close family member with lupus. This book isn't meant to be read as a medical journal, and, as with all conditions—but especially autoimmune illnesses—the symptoms and treatments can cover a vast range.

For more information, please contact The Lupus Foundation at www.lupus.org

1

LANDON

"Please let me know if you need anything else during your stay. Welcome to the Bellagio," the hotel clerk said, her voice dipping to a soft purr as she handed me my keycard. She was young and pretty, I guessed mid-twenties at the most. "First time?"

"Thank you, and no, I've been here before." I smiled and grabbed the card.

"Then you've seen the sights. The gardens and fountains are beautiful."

I glanced behind me when I heard the click of someone's tongue against their teeth. Three guests leveled us both with the same impatient glare, and I didn't blame them. The clerk was cute, but I was with friends this weekend and I needed to step out of the way before her extra hospitality caused a lobby riot.

"They are, but thanks for the tip." I lifted my duffle bag and rolled my suitcase to the elevators.

"Weren't you supposed to beat me here?"

I smiled at the familiar voice drifting over my shoulder.

"Julie!"

I dropped my bags and lifted her up by the waist to twirl her around. "It's so fucking good to see you," I said as she squealed in my ear.

"You too." She smiled, her eyes crinkling at the corners as they met mine. I searched her face, trying to both register every detail and not be too obvious about it.

"Why are you looking at me like that?" She pressed her hands to her cheeks, peering up at me with a deep crease in her brow.

Julie and I had been best friends since college, and always stayed close despite the miles between us. This was the longest I'd gone without seeing her face since I'd known her. She looked the same as she had six months ago. Her cheeks were maybe a little fuller than they had been back in January, but she was still gorgeous. We usually FaceTimed a few times per week when our schedules permitted, but for the past few months, she'd refused anything other than phone calls.

I tried to make the trip up north every other month to see my father and always made time for Julie, but since my promotion to partner, I hadn't seen anyone.

"I missed your face since you've hidden it from me for all these months." I brushed a stray lock of hair off her forehead. "I thought maybe you'd grown a third eye or something."

She glowered at me, but I caught a flicker of something across her face, like maybe she really was hiding something that I couldn't see.

Her chestnut hair was shorter than I was used to, brushing the tops of her shoulders instead of falling down her back, but her brown eyes were still bright.

"Is something wrong? Nate isn't giving you any trouble about the house, is he?"

"No, nothing like that." She shrugged. "He was amiable about the house, and he didn't want to stay in the Bronx anyway. I was the one who wanted to stay in the neighborhood and didn't want to leave. He never even asked for his share of the down payment."

"That was the least he could do. I wish you would have just let me kick his ass."

She shook her head, pursing her lips at me.

"Kicking his ass wouldn't have helped anything."

"But it would have felt good. He never deserved you, Jules."

"It wouldn't have been a fair fight." Her lips twisted in a smirk. "Especially with all this new muscle," she said, squeezing my biceps.

"There's a new gym in my office building, and I stop there in the early mornings to work some of the stress off so I'm my sweet self by nine. And don't change the subject."

She shut her eyes and tilted her head. "It's fine. Hey, at least I didn't marry him. These things happen." She waved a dismissive hand.

Decent guys didn't "happen" to sleep with their assistants. Julie's ex-fiancé had always rubbed me the wrong way, and when she'd told me the reason they'd broken up, I was furious but not surprised.

"Yes, when you marry them and they cheat, it can get tricky. As you know, I speak from experience." I draped an arm around her shoulder. "Are you sure that's it?"

She shrugged without lifting her head. "It's supposed to be a fun weekend, Landon. Can we drop it for now?"

"So, something *is* wrong." I stepped in front of her. "Talk to me."

She adjusted her purse on her arm and lifted the handle of her suitcase.

"We have dinner at seven with Dean and Maria. We can talk later."

"No, we'll talk before. The restaurant is in the hotel. We can meet at the bar over there at six."

I motioned to the swanky bar next to the dinging slot machines.

A smile tugged at her lips as she narrowed her eyes at me. "All this worry is going to give you wrinkles." She tapped her finger between my brows.

"So then you can set me straight and tell me there's nothing to worry about."

Her face fell, making my gut twist even more.

"There they are!"

I'd know Dean's gruff Bronx accent anywhere—still just as thick as the first day I met him in economics class during our freshman year of college at Fordham University.

I was originally from Connecticut with no discernible accent, but I had picked up a little bit of one from the cluster of New York natives I was with all the time for four years. My father cracked up one Christmas vacation when I'd told him I was sick of someone "breaking my balls."

I'd been living in Charlotte since graduation, and while I hadn't acquired a Southern twang, I caught myself saying "y'all" sometimes, and I always got shit for slipping whenever we all were together.

"Here we are." I held out my arms as I came up to Dean. I laughed when he caught me in a bear hug, slapping my back and peering up at me with a wide, happy grin. For a guy who swore he'd never get married, he was bouncing with excitement as he backed away.

"Congratulations. Finally," I joked, heaving out an exaggerated sigh as I squeezed his arm.

"Finally seems to be our wedding theme." He laughed as

his dark eyes studied me. "I could say finally to you too. It's been months since we've seen you now that you're a big shot."

"Right." I snickered. "A tired big shot."

"Hey, Jules," Dean said as he kissed Julie's cheek. "We're so happy you made it."

Dean and Maria hadn't been dating or even friendly back when we were in school, always snapping at each other and falling into long, drawn-out arguments.

When he told me after graduation he hoped he'd never see her again, I knew he was full of shit. Three years later, they started dating and had been together ever since. We all figured they had a good Kurt Russell and Goldie Hawn thing going on until they shocked us with a wedding invite to Vegas.

"Thanks for making the time for this."

"I'd never miss it." I slapped his arm. "And I think a Vegas wedding suits the both of you."

"That's what we think." He lifted a shoulder. "A big wedding with a bridal party seemed dumb after being together for so long. The original plan was just to come here and do it ourselves, but a small ceremony with the people who matter most to us was a good compromise. It was nice not having to worry about my mother's cousin's daughter's five kids from Ohio or whoever else we'd have to invite to a big wedding, even if my mother keeps insisting they 'owe her.'" He held up his fingers in air quotes. "This weekend is for us and the ones closest to us."

He beamed at me, his eyes dancing and his grin so wide I couldn't help but smile back.

"I think it's great. I'm glad to be here."

"I appreciate you making the trip. I know what a busy fucker you are down there."

"Down there?" I snickered. "Maria finally making an honest man out of you is reason enough to drop everything."

"For real," Julie said. "I knew back in college you'd end up together when you pretended you hated each other."

"So did he." I lifted a brow when Dean glared back at us, but he didn't offer a reply of denial.

"Go get settled. Dinner is at seven tonight, and it's just us so we can all catch up. My parents are coming in later, and Maria's family is arriving today. But we can entertain them at the wedding tomorrow."

"I still can't get over a real wedding in Vegas." Julie chuckled. "I didn't think they had those."

"We have a coordinator and everything. Although, I wish we'd gone the Elvis chapel route instead of this intimate dinner thing. You guys are the only ones left now. Maybe one of you could make that happen."

"I'm good, thanks." Julie chuckled as she shot me a glance.

"Same," I said. "But you enjoy."

He flashed a tiny smile over his shoulder before shifting toward the elevators. "I'll see you all later."

"Please stop that," she said when she caught me staring, shaking her head as she exhaled a long sigh.

"Stop what? Looking at you?" I joked, my stomach sinking a bit when she didn't laugh with me.

"Stop worrying." She nodded toward me with her chin. "I look like shit from a long flight, so try to lose the crease between your eyebrows for the moment." She tapped the space again with her finger.

"I can't help it if I worry about you. And you don't look like shit. You're beautiful as usual, Jules."

"Right." She let out a humorless chuckle. "I better go change before dinner."

"You mean *drinks* and dinner," I said, raising a brow.

"Yes, nag. Drinks first. What room are you in?"

I flicked the card over in my hand to read the number on the holder.

"Uh...426."

"Ah, I'm 326. Try not to have any loud parties and keep me up."

"No promises, babe. It's Vegas."

"That it is," she sighed, dragging her suitcase toward the ding of the elevator.

All three were my oldest friends, but Julie was my family. Well, other than when my eyes traveled along her soft curves as she ambled toward the elevator. My best friend was beautiful, and I was human.

And I wouldn't be able to leave her alone until I figured out whatever she was keeping from me.

2

JULIE

I dreaded this weekend for so many reasons.

I was thrilled to see two of my oldest friends get married, and I'd missed my best friend—especially lately. A weekend in Vegas should have been something to look forward to, but I'd almost canceled the trip a million times before revving myself up to board the plane at LaGuardia.

Keeping the plot twists in my life a secret was a lot easier across the miles, but avoiding the subject had turned into unfair lies of omission. Telling Landon the truth would make it all official in a way I wasn't ready for.

I'd gone through enough changes to my physical appearance that he would have picked up on something, no matter how hard I tried to pretend. Hiding my face on camera for the past few months had allowed me to avoid the questions I didn't want to answer—and the looks of pity that would mean well, but would sting all the same. I loved him and I trusted him not to judge me, but I was still embarrassed for him or anyone to see me like that.

But I couldn't hide forever, and closing myself off from

the people I cared about was the opposite of what I needed right now.

I tapped my foot as I waited for the elevator to descend to the lobby. After dodging this conversation for months, I felt my heart race as the elevator seemed to inch down floor by floor, my impatience to just get it over with making me shift back and forth on my feet.

I spotted him in less than a second, a smile sneaking across my mouth at his wide shoulders, the muscles of his back working beneath his button-down shirt as he lifted his tumbler to his mouth. His head stuck out above any crowd because he was so damn tall, but with the new bulk added to his frame, he seemed massive.

He was still gorgeous, with his big chocolate eyes, model-worthy cheekbones, and chiseled jaw. But under that large frame of a man, he was a giant mush, and I knew he'd be worried sick about me after tonight.

I glanced down at the low-heeled sandals I'd bought for this trip. My joint pain had improved overall, but my ankles still rebelled against the skyscraper heels I'd worn for most of my life. I lifted one foot, stretching out my sore arch as I drew a small circle in the air with my toes, eyeing the under-one-inch wedge heel and rhinestones on the straps.

My concession of sexy shoes felt like another loss—another piece of myself that wasn't mine to claim anymore.

As if he could sense me behind him, Landon craned his neck to the entrance, a slow smile creeping across his lips. "I was beginning to think you were standing me up," he said, flashing a wide grin when our eyes met. "I'll buy you a drink, and you can tell me all about how I'm overreacting that something is wrong." He stood, motioning to the barstool next to him.

"It's only five after six. Relax. So how much crystal do

you think this hotel has?" I nodded to what appeared to be a rhinestone shower curtain lining half of the bar. "The blown glass in the lobby is gorgeous, but that's a little Vegas gaudy, don't you think?"

"I'd hazard that this hotel is one of the least gaudy on the Strip, but I guess they add flash where they can to stay on-brand. And with that dodge, now you really have me worried."

I took in a slow breath and leaned my elbows onto the counter, straightening when I caught a glimpse of myself in the mirror behind the bar. I hadn't realized my flowy silk blouse cut so low until I noticed my breasts plumping over the neckline. The extra weight was good, especially when dropping it so quickly had made my boobs sag like deflated balloons.

Full was good, and full meant healthy, but I hadn't gotten used to *full* quite yet. After all I'd gone through, it seemed vain to focus on the changes to my appearance when my insides could have been—and could be—a lot worse. It was difficult to get used to my new life when I didn't recognize myself anymore.

"Just talk to me. Please."

"What can I get you?"

I turned my head toward the bartender, uneasy under the scrutinizing heat of Landon's stare in my periphery.

"Just a ginger ale. Thank you."

"That's all?" His brows pulled together when I turned back to him.

"I haven't eaten yet and want to have my one drink with dinner."

"One drink? Why can you only have one drink?"

"Jesus, Landon. Do we all have to be drunk all day? This isn't like when we were here in college."

"No, but why can you have only *one* drink? Are you feeling all right?"

"I'm fine," I said, my reply clipped and cold enough to make Landon flinch.

"Hey, I'm sorry." I draped my hand over his. "I didn't mean to snap at you. I'm on medication and it's still new, so I'd rather keep it to one drink at dinner."

"Medication for what? Antibiotics?"

I cupped my forehead and rubbed my temple, shutting my eyes for a moment. My diagnosis was new enough to not seem that real yet, even though it had been a relief when the awful way I was feeling had been given a name. I'd been told I was lucky, but lucky was the opposite of how I felt every time I relayed this story.

"Remember in February, not too long after I saw you, I was sick in bed with a fever for a week?"

He held my eyes, bobbing his head in a slow nod. "I remember it took you a long time to shake it."

"I *didn't* shake it. I told you and my parents that I was feeling better, when I felt worse every single day. The fevers kept coming, then everything hurt so much I could barely climb the subway steps to go to work. Getting through a normal day was torture. My boss let me work from home half the week, which helped, but not much."

"I knew something was off," he whispered, shaking his head. His dark eyes were full of concern that tightened the ever-present knot in my stomach. "But you insisted you were just tired. Why didn't you tell me?"

"What could you do?" I shot him a sad smile and shrugged. "I was tested for every single disease they could think of, and it was all negative. I figured this was my life now until I saw a lupus medication commercial one day while I was in and out of sleep on my couch."

"Lupus?" He pinched his brows together. "I've heard of it, but I don't know what it is."

"I didn't really know what it was either, but some of the symptoms the commercial listed sounded familiar. I figured that was one thing they didn't test me for, so why not ask them to? Turns out, that's exactly what it was."

My gaze flicked to his, his eyes glossy as he barely blinked.

"Is it…is it serious?" His voice was a gravelly whisper, the sad fear in his eyes a reminder of why I hadn't had this conversation with him sooner.

"It's…chronic. But it has the potential to be serious. My immune system doesn't act the way it should, and it's something I'll have to live with and watch for on a permanent basis, but I'm happy it has a name." I forced a smile across my lips, my stomach sinking when Landon didn't smile with me.

"But I promise, now I really *am* better." I picked his hand back up and squeezed. "I found a good doctor, and once she put me on a treatment plan, I started to improve almost immediately. I'm on steroids now—low dose, but I started high, which is why you probably notice the big cheeks and wider curves." I glanced down at my body. "I didn't want you to see my face, especially at the beginning when I was on such a high dose."

I blew out my cheeks, trying to make him laugh, while holding back a wince at how that wasn't really an exaggeration of how I'd looked.

"I was a mess. My face is still a little full, but not so unrecognizable."

He dipped his head to meet my gaze, his jaw tightening as he narrowed his eyes.

"You didn't want me to see. *Me.* Did you think I'd judge you? You were sick and didn't tell me. For months."

"It wasn't that you would judge me. I didn't want you to see me like that. *I* didn't want to see me like that. I cringed every time I caught a glimpse in the mirror. And telling you would have made it all a little too real for me. But I am better. Well, a lot better than I was."

"What's wrong now?" His voice was low as he searched my face again, holding on to the tumbler so tightly I was waiting for it to break into shards in his hand.

"I get tired sometimes, so I have to rest even when I don't want to. Which, knowing me as you do, I hate. And if I get sick, it can take longer to get over it. Even a cold has the potential to be dangerous if I don't take care of myself. I'm learning to take things day by day."

I tried for a wide smile to make him relax, but his only reply was a slow nod.

"I'm sorry I didn't tell you. I didn't want you to worry, and I'm still getting used to it all myself, but I never should have shut you out. Please forgive me."

His eyes fell to the last drop in his glass as he swirled it around. Reactions to my news ran a wide gamut. I hadn't told many people, but some appeared grief-stricken, like my mother and Landon, and some just said "oh," shrugging it off as if I'd told them that I had a paper cut.

I didn't blame anyone for how they took my news, as I didn't know how to react to myself yet either.

"Where was Nate through all of this?" he asked through gritted teeth, his voice so low it was almost a growl.

"At the beginning, he was concerned, or appeared to be. Especially when it seemed like I was never getting better from this weird, unending flu. Then I started to improve after my diagnosis, and..." I took a sip of my ginger ale as

Landon's eyes thinned to slits in my periphery. "And I guess he lost patience and interest."

"He was fucking his assistant while you were sick?" He grunted out the words, his entire body rigid as anger radiated off him.

I shrugged. "I honestly don't know. It was a while—at least, it looked that way when I found out. But I'm not sure if this was happening all along, or if it came to be because he couldn't handle being with someone with an unpredictable, chronic illness who wasn't fun anymore."

I hoped it was the latter, that he was just a jerk who didn't take monogamy or commitment seriously, something I should have figured out when he'd taken so long to agree to set a wedding date. He'd grown more and more frustrated with me toward the end, always insisting that I looked fine and needed to snap out of it.

There were symptoms he couldn't see, like the fatigue that would hit me after a long workday or excruciating joint pain that I'd wake up with after being fine the day before. But I was up and out of bed, so I guessed he thought I should have been over it already, not realizing that chronic meant lifelong.

"It's a lot to take on."

"A lot to take on?" Landon's voice was so loud, the bartender's head whipped in our direction. "Jesus, Julie, please tell me you aren't making excuses for him."

"I'm not, just being real." When I rubbed my hand over his back in circles, every muscle clenched under the path of my palm. "But I need you to dial it down a little. I appreciate that your first reaction was to defend my honor, but I don't want you to spend the one weekend we get to see each other preoccupied with planning Nate's painful demise."

I managed to pull a tiny smile out of him when I arched

a brow. "I'm going to need you to perk up before dinner, and for the rest of this trip." I draped my arm over his shoulders and kissed his cheek. "Please."

He leaned into me and kissed the top of my head.

"If you say so. Just promise not to keep anything else from me. But you're okay now? Work is okay?"

"Well, about work...that's something else."

I poked the ice in my glass with my straw, seriously considering breaking the one-drink rule I'd made for myself and asking for a shot.

"Something...else? Shit, were you laid off?"

"That's a fun secondary issue." I barked out a humorless laugh. "A few weeks ago, my department was cut, and any creative work now is on an hourly project basis. Even though I was assistant creative director, my rate with those few hours isn't enough to live on. Don't take this one personally as it hasn't sunk in enough for me to tell anyone yet."

"I can understand that. Maybe you can take this as an opportunity for a break. Live off the severance and unemployment and regroup."

Now he was attempting to rub soothing circles on *my* back. It was good to see him in his usual problem-solving mode instead of sad and angry.

"I could, but after thirty days, I'll have no medical insurance unless I pay out of pocket. And since we bought the house last year, my savings are depleted and the mortgage falls solely on me. I've resolved not to think about that until I land back in New York."

I inhaled a long breath and let it out, trying not to think about how this little trip I'd forced myself to take would set me back.

"Julie, you need insurance. I mean, everyone does, but you can't—"

"Stop." I pressed my hand into his chest as his heart strummed against my palm. "I will figure something out. For now, we finish our drinks and go meet up with our friends and celebrate. Can you do that for me?"

He shut his eyes, nodding with a groan.

"Anything else you need to tell me before I order a round of shots for myself?" He wrapped his arm around my waist and drew me into his side.

"Nope. That was it." I breathed out a relieved gust of air and let my cheek drop to his shoulder.

"So that's why I look a little different to you." I swiped the hair off my shoulder, still expecting to find long tresses flowing down my back. After my hair thinned out, I'd cut it to make it seem thicker and fuller. I'd always hesitated to cut even a half inch off, but I had gotten a ton of compliments for my accidental new look. While I didn't hate it, I didn't feel like me.

I was a different me—a me I was still getting to know while I let go of who I used to be.

"But I'm still okay," I said, unsure which one of us I was faking enthusiasm for. But I ran with it. "Promise."

"You're beautiful. Now and always." His voice dipped into a soft, low whisper. "So cut that out."

From Landon, I could almost believe it. It had felt like such a long time since I'd felt beautiful or even vital. I'd taken life and the purpose I had in it for granted, and now it seemed that, no matter who I was with or where I was, I was still lost.

3

LANDON

"Well, we have a little news. Other than this." Dean nodded at Maria next to him.

"This?" Maria pinched her brows together. "My fiancé, the romantic," she said, pressing a dramatic hand to her chest.

Dean and Maria had invited us to dinner at a noodle restaurant in the hotel, as it was much more casual than the other options. Dean said he wanted to enjoy our company and not have to cringe if one of us got loud, which, most of the time, was him.

He looped an arm over her shoulder and pulled her close, dropping a kiss to her temple.

"As you know, we've been living in the same apartment for a while now."

"Just like you've been dating a while," I joked, cracking up when Dean narrowed his eyes.

"Right. Well, last week, we closed on a house in Scarsdale. The one I told you about with the huge deck and pool."

"It's got other good stuff too, but that's what sold Dean from the beginning." Maria gave Dean a playful eye roll.

"This is another reason why we didn't have a huge wedding. We wanted to put the money we worked so hard for where it counted." He picked up Maria's hand and brought it to his lips.

We used to tease Dean and Maria when they started dating about looking like brother and sister. The olive skin and almost black hair and eyes from their respective Italian and Puerto Rican heritages allowed them to resemble siblings, or at least family.

They'd been together for so long, I couldn't picture one without the other, and even though my divorce had soured me on marriage for myself, I loved watching them come full circle.

"I still remember your first date," Julie said, crossing her arms as she leaned back in her chair.

"You do?" Dean scoffed. "*I* barely remember it."

"You are so full of shit," I told him. He glared back at me from across the table. "You annoyed me for days with all the different options you picked and which one I thought she'd like the most."

"You did?" Maria shifted toward Dean, her jaw slack. "I didn't know that."

"Well, I was hoping that would stay buried. No such luck with these two." He narrowed his eyes at Julie and me.

"We've been friends long enough to remember it all," I said, a smile rushing across my mouth. Being with my oldest friends reminded me of a time when life was simple, with no worries beyond classes or what bar to hit later. We'd been young and sometimes a little stupid, but I missed the carefree, pure happiness I had been in such a rush to give up at the time.

"That we have," Dean mused. "For a long time. Although I can't think of the last time I saw you guys. Are we those people already? The ones who only see each other for weddings and funerals?"

"Adulting sucks," Julie said. "I miss the days of college when we'd just hang out without looking at a calendar first."

"Well, you guys are busy, I get it. Especially this one." Dean nodded to me. "This is why we need to keep up with the video chats." He turned to Julie. "You live ten minutes away, and we haven't seen you for months."

"We can start the video chats again," I said before Julie could reply. I knew she didn't want to talk about her new illness or her job loss, and although he'd mean no harm, I didn't want him to get on her for keeping to herself over the past few months.

After all she'd just told me, about being sick, her job, and her dick of an ex, my mind was going a mile a minute, trying to figure out a way to help her. As much as we talked, I missed a lot being so damn far away. The number of miles hadn't changed between New York and North Carolina, but after learning all she was able to keep from me for so long, the distance seemed even greater.

"There is a possibility of NameTech opening a branch in New York. They asked me if I'd be interested in running it, but nothing is definite yet. So, you may have to get used to seeing my face more often."

My firm had just gone through a merger when they'd recruited me out of college. My first boss had told me Name-Tech was originally a placeholder until they could figure out what to name the new company, and one of the executives thought it would be funny to keep it. Turned out, the interim name was sticky enough to gain recognition and for the company to double in size during my first five years.

"Really?" Julie's head whipped around, her eyes wide as they found mine. "That's another promotion, right?"

"It would be, but other than running the office, everything else would stay the same. It's not certain, so don't get too excited."

"No shit! That's great. And I could tolerate you if you moved back." Dean smirked around his beer bottle.

"I could too, I guess," Julie said, a smile lighting up her face in a way I hadn't seen since she'd spotted me in the lobby. I almost hadn't mentioned it because I didn't want to get anyone's hopes up—including mine—but I wanted this promotion for a lot of reasons.

I was never supposed to stay in Charlotte for long, but I'd gotten promoted and married, and I'd settled there when I wasn't looking. After my marriage had ended in less than a year, since my twenties, I'd transitioned into an easy bachelor's life, enjoying the city and the mild weather, in between working my ass off.

"We're just grateful that you both made it here now."

"We wouldn't miss it for the world. Although I'm surprised Mrs. Calabrese is okay with a Vegas wedding for her only son," I teased.

"That's another story," Maria said with a long sigh. "It's more wedding than you would expect in Vegas, but I'd like to think it's a little better than being married by Elvis." Maria raised a brow at Dean. "We wanted something nice that we could share with the people we love but keep it small and about us."

"I still think Elvis would have been cool. Maybe for our tenth anniversary we'll come back and have him renew our vows." Dean inched closer to Maria and kissed her cheek before glancing back at us. "The Elvis chapel I looked into had a greatest hits music package—"

"Yes, babe. I know," Maria said, rolling her eyes as she patted his hand. "I'm really sorry we can't walk down the aisle to 'Can't Help Falling in Love.'"

"Eh, it's okay." He shrugged and tugged her into his side. "As long as you're walking down it to me, I don't care what music plays."

"Oh my goodness, look at you guys." Julie bunched her shoulders and pressed her hands into her cheeks. "Who knew you'd be this adorable when you finally got married?"

"We should take a shot for every time someone says finally." Dean shook his head.

"That's a good way to get alcohol poisoning on your wedding day," I said, stifling a laugh when Dean glowered back at me.

"Yeah, don't do that." Julie waved her hand back and forth. "I'm going to head upstairs and pass out."

"Tired?" I asked, trying and most likely failing to keep the concerned edge out of my voice.

She lifted an eyebrow at me and exhaled a long breath.

"Just worn out from the long trip. Nothing more," she said, giving my wrist a quick squeeze under the table. "Thank you for a wonderful dinner." A small smile ghosted across her lips as she stood. "I'm touched I'm part of the small crowd of guests."

Maria nodded back with a watery smile.

"We love you guys," she said, her voice cracking as she rose from her seat to give Julie a hug. "Wow, marriage is making us both sappy."

"Nah, that's how it's supposed to be." I bent to kiss Maria's cheek. "So I hear," I said, throwing her a wink.

"Hey." I shot up and grabbed Julie's arm. "I'll walk you back."

"You don't have to leave early on my account."

"Dinner is over, right?" I looked back at Dean. "Nothing until tomorrow?"

"Nope. Our day starts earlier in the morning than yours, so we're about to head out too." He stood and dragged me into a hug. "You know," he whispered in my ear before he pulled away, his eyes drifting over my shoulder, "I always thought you'd end up with Julie."

"I *am* with Julie. We're best friends."

When I followed his gaze, I found Maria and Julie laughing and huddled in their own secret conversation.

"I always thought you'd be good together."

Julie smiled when she caught my gaze. She was gorgeous, then and now, and if she hadn't been dating a friend of mine when I'd met her in college, I wouldn't have veered that easily into the friend zone. We always gravitated toward each other, but other than a drunken almost-kiss the night of graduation, I'd never pushed for more. She was too important to me to risk losing.

And now, she was sick.

"If you're not too tired, how about going for a walk?" I asked Julie as we left the restaurant.

"Where?"

"Just around the hotel. We can check out the fountains, maybe. You've seen the water show, right?"

"Yes, a while ago." Her eyes flicked to mine before she stepped in front of me. "Please stop worrying," she said, reaching up to squeeze the back of my neck.

"Who said I was worrying? I asked if you wanted to see the water show."

"You are a lousy liar. I am okay, and I'm happy to spend the weekend with my best friend, but he needs to stop eyeballing me."

"It's your fault," I said, making an exaggerated perusal of

her body. "We're friends and all, but that top is something else."

She slapped my arm when I waggled my eyebrows.

"The top is tighter than when I bought it, like everything else lately. But eh, it's Vegas." She shrugged. "And stop deflecting. You know what I mean by eyeballing."

I stepped closer, holding her narrowed eyes as I grabbed her hand.

"Yes, I'm worried about you. My best friend just told me that she has a chronic and potentially serious disease and may not have health insurance to take care of herself. And when you get home, I'm probably going to randomly FaceTime you sometimes and text you enough to be annoying until I can trust you when you say you're *okay*, which may not be for a long while."

"Like you're going to have time to do that," she said, squeezing my hand back as her eyes filled with tears.

"I'll make time," I said, pressing my lips to her forehead. "For you."

She buried her head into my chest, her shoulders drooping with relief as she lowered the mask long enough to sniffle in my arms.

I dropped a kiss to the top of her head, holding her flush to my body as she cinched her arms around my waist.

"It's okay, Jules," I whispered, rocking her back and forth. "I've got you."

I'd do anything she needed to keep her well and safe. I only wished I knew how. The fear and the helplessness made me want to crawl out of my skin.

Maybe we weren't *together*, as Dean had suggested, but Julie was always with me, and I refused to think of a future when she wasn't.

4

JULIE

Landon kept hold of my hand as we meandered through the hotel lobby, gripping on to it as if he thought I'd run away. I was still recovering from the swell of emotion as I'd cried into his chest. As much as I tried to push my problems out of my mind, they'd sneak up on me. The pain in Landon's eyes when he confessed how worried he was did me in before I could stop it.

"When will you know about New York?" I asked when we arrived at the fountains. I lifted my hair off the damp nape of my neck. It was a warm Vegas night, the sweltering July heat still in the air even with the cool spray drifting off the water.

"Maybe in a couple of weeks. Like I said, it's all just rumblings now, but it would be nice. A lot more work, which I have plenty of already, but proximity to the important people in my life may make it worth it." He nudged my side as we came up to the railing.

"Would I even get to see you if you moved back? You need some balance. The hours you put in aren't healthy."

He nodded, resting his elbows on the railing.

"Trust me, I know. As much as I enjoy my job, some days I feel like it's killing me slowly."

"And you're not getting any younger," I teased, smiling when he raised a brow at me.

"Oh, I know that too. I even have some gray dotting my beard these days." He rubbed his jaw, a smirk curving his lips and teasing the dimple in his cheek under his cropped stubble.

I'd spotted the gray bristles when he'd lifted me for a hello hug, but they only made him that much more attractive. I had to laugh as my eyes roamed his face. We were both almost forty, but he seemed to be getting hotter with age, while I seemed to be falling apart.

"I'm really proud of you. You're a partner. At least one of us is using their business degree to their advantage."

The water was mostly still and quiet, unlike the constant, turbulent thoughts running through my head about my future.

"Don't say that. You'll be okay. You're talented and will find something soon, I'm sure."

"I know something will come up eventually, but the thought of job searching and interviewing again exhausts me."

"Exhausted? You're sure that you're feeling okay? There isn't a part three to the story you told me earlier?" He eased closer and draped his arm across my shoulders.

"No part three. One new reality was enough to deal with. I didn't need a second so soon."

"I know," he whispered into my hair and planted a kiss on the top of my head. I breathed him in, smiling at the familiar spicy cologne he'd worn since college. He drifted his hand down my back, looping his arm around my waist to pull me closer.

"I'd take it all away if I could."

His sad smile cut right through me when I lifted my head.

"I'd bet you'd try too." He laughed when I nudged his side.

"For you, you're damn right I'd try."

The lights dimmed, and Andrea Bocelli's "*Con te Partirò*" blasted through the speakers as the water danced to the tune of his voice. Even though I'd seen it before, the water show was still just as breathtaking. My eyes followed the tall crests around the fountain and the ebbs and flows that came together for a beautiful performance.

A lock of hair blew across my eyes when I turned my head. Landon tucked it behind my ear and cupped my cheek, running his thumb back and forth along my jaw.

The warm breeze kicked up as Landon and I stood together, frozen and barely blinking as our eyes stayed locked.

He framed my face, a smile twitching at his lips. The graze of his thumbs back and forth across my cheekbones sent a shiver rolling through me. This was Landon, my best friend for most of my life, yet I couldn't look away. My mouth went dry as I tried to swallow, reaching up to grab his wrists.

"Eyeballing me again?" My voice came out like sandpaper as I tried to get my bearings. After Nate had discarded me like the damaged goods I felt like, it was hard not to see that every time I looked in the mirror. My self-esteem and self-worth had taken a hit. Not to mention, the loss of a job I loved and the question of whether I could continue to do it—even if I had been able to keep it—screwed with me on a constant basis now that I had nothing else to do but ponder and worry.

"Maybe," he said, his raspy whisper traveling down to my toes. I'd never heard his voice dip so low, and I couldn't decipher if it was anguish or need dripping off his words. "You're beautiful. Don't ever hide from me again."

My gaze snagged on his lips, the perfect mouth I'd always teased him about. My mind went back to the night in college we'd almost kissed. He'd had more to drink than I had but sobered first before our lips touched.

We'd blown it off at the time and laughed whenever we'd reminisce about it, but nothing in this crazy moment was funny. The deep rasp of his voice, the heat in his eyes, I wasn't sure if I could believe what I was seeing, but my vulnerability was leading me—leading *us*—into dangerous territory. We inched toward each other, my eyes still on his mouth as a pull that came out of nowhere pushed us together like a couple of lost magnets.

I had enough complications to keep me up at night. Falling into a kiss with my best friend was one I didn't need or think I could handle.

"You're pretty smooth." I cleared my throat and sputtered out a nervous laugh. "I can see why the women love you."

I pressed my hand to his chest, putting enough distance between us to catch my breath as I shifted away and brought my attention back to the fountains. The water slowed and the music faded as I tried to get my racing pulse to ease. I dropped my hand to escape the thump of his heartbeat against my palm.

"You're the only one. Most get fed up with me pretty quickly." He looped his arm around my shoulders, yanking me to him for a moment before he let it drop.

"I doubt that," I said, gulping in short spurts of air when I heard how breathless I sounded.

"The long hours I keep aren't conducive to relationships. It's why I'm not really the marrying kind, I guess."

"Such a heartbreaker," I teased, drawing a chuckle out of him as he lifted a shoulder.

"I try not to be. I'm honest. You're the most important woman in my life, so as long as I still have you..." He searched my gaze, one side of his mouth curving up.

"Always." His lips spread into a wide smile at my reply. "Whether you like it or not. Would you mind if we called it a night? I'm afraid if I don't turn in soon, I'm going to crash big-time and I'll have to drag myself through tomorrow." I held up a hand when I spied the deep crease in his brow. "Again, I'm fine. I just need to get some rest after the long trip."

"All right, I'll believe you." He stuffed his hands in his jean pockets and pivoted back toward the hotel.

I was wired enough not to be able to sleep for a couple of hours, and I hoped I wouldn't have to pay for it tomorrow. My request to cut the night short had less to do with getting rest and more with shaking off whatever that was between Landon and me.

I'd lost count of the arguments Nate and I had fallen into over Landon. I'd get a side-eye from Nate anytime Landon would call, and he'd be just this side of asshole when Landon would come to visit. The last straw was when I'd extended a business trip to Charlotte in January to visit him, and Nate had flat-out accused me of having a years-long affair, insisting a man and a woman could never be close friends for that long without it turning into something else. Looking back, it was hard to tell if it was jealousy or projection because of the affair *he* was having at the time.

Of course I noticed how attractive Landon was, but I never was tempted to be unfaithful or even thought about crossing those lines with him at all—until whatever was in the desert night air almost made me lose my mind and myself.

My almost-kiss tonight with Landon was most likely a cross between a fabrication of my imagination and nursing my bruised ego from feeling scorned and unlovable. I never doubted that Landon loved me, but the way his eyes had bored into mine as he called me beautiful made the tiny hairs on the back of my neck stand straight up.

My body and my mind couldn't be trusted. I'd sleep this off and forget about it, although I couldn't deny enjoying the momentary distraction.

We headed to the elevators in a comfortable silence, even if I tried to ignore Landon's eyes on me in my periphery. I wasn't sure if it was him still trying to find something wrong, or if he was having the same confusing battle with himself.

"You don't have to walk me to my room. Stay, play some slots."

"Nah, I'm not a gambler, you know that. I'm a little tired myself." Landon pressed his hand to the small of my back as I stepped on to the elevator, a move he'd made a million times before and shouldn't have triggered a jolt of heat down my legs from his touch. I needed to crawl into my fluffy hotel bed and reset my brain.

He held the door open when the elevator dinged on the third floor. "A pretty girl shouldn't walk anywhere alone in Vegas."

"Oh please," I said as I fumbled in my purse for my keycard. "The Southern gentleman thing is adorable, but nothing is going to happen to me."

"I live in the South, but I'm still from Connecticut." He held out his hand until I gave him the keycard. "But yes, I'm a gentleman, and I wasn't kidding about that top." His eyes flicked to my chest as the lock beeped. I had to laugh at his wry grin as he held the door open.

"You're ridiculous," I said, grabbing the card. "See you tomorrow."

"See you tomorrow." He kissed my cheek and turned back to the elevators. I allowed myself a minute to watch him leave, tearing my eyes away when they traveled up his strong legs and lingered on the perfect swell of his ass.

I went inside, locking the door behind me before I fell back against it, pressing the heels of my palms against my eyelids.

I was scared, confused, and starving for a man's attention to satisfy a silly quest for validation. That had to be it.

I stripped and pulled on my pajamas, washing my face with ice-cold water to snap out of whatever had just come over me, hoping the shock would cool off the fantasy enough to keep it out of my dreams.

5

LANDON

I had such a shitty night of sleep, I wasn't even sure if I'd gotten a full hour. Between tossing and turning, I couldn't help myself and Googled lupus on my phone just to learn a little more about what Julie was dealing with. I didn't anticipate spiraling down a rabbit hole of horrors. Most sites listed it as a "very treatable disease," but the bullet points of potential complications tortured me enough to keep my eyes open for most of the night.

Julie seemed embarrassed by the weight gain, but she was still as beautiful as she always was. So much so that when I wasn't obsessing over symptoms she might be experiencing that I couldn't see, I was trying to figure out what the hell had come over me by the fountains.

When she'd cried in my arms last night, I'd wanted to hold her as close as possible and shield her from this sickness that I didn't understand and didn't know how to fight. I'd been married and had my share of failed relationships, but I meant it when I said she was the most important woman in my life, which made all I'd found out about what could happen to her plain fucking terrifying.

What would I do without Julie? It was a question I never wanted to ponder past the hypothetical, and that desperation had almost made me lose it enough to kiss her last night.

We knew each other well enough to flirt and tease back and forth without it meaning anything. I trusted Julie to show her everything about myself and not have to mask any kind of weakness. I'd thought it was the same for her until she'd hidden her illness from me for months. I was still angry but understood her reluctance to worry me after I'd spent the wee hours of the morning freaked out by my own research.

Julie had meant everything to me for most of my life. She was the first one I wanted to spill any good news to, and when things went wrong, only she would do.

Everyone else had tried to be there for me when my mother had passed away right after graduation, but I'd only wanted Julie. She'd stayed in our spare room the weekend following the funeral after I asked her not to leave because she was the only one who could soothe me just by being there.

I wanted to return the favor so badly, to be the person she leaned on to get her through this, and that compulsion had kept me up most of the night—along with Google.

When she'd leaned into me, peering up at me with those troubled chocolate eyes, my gaze had fallen to her mouth, and for a dangerous instant, I'd forgotten she was my best friend and just wanted to taste those lips and kiss her troubles away, if only for the moment.

I scrubbed a hand down my face as I waited for Julie in the lobby. Worry and helplessness over being so damn far away from her once we left Vegas had my mind wandering to crazy places, and I needed to get it together.

"Geez, Clark. Rough night?"

I pivoted around to find Julie behind me, her arms crossed as she stalked over. Her smoky eyes danced as they found mine, her chestnut waves swaying back and forth over her shoulders as she shook her head at me.

"Did Vegas get the best of you last night after all?" she asked as she smoothed the lapels of my suit jacket. "Or did you Google?"

A sheepish smile pulled at my lips.

"You got me. I met a showgirl by one of the craps tables, and the night got away from us." I swept my gaze up and down her body, trying to be quick enough not to be obvious. Her off-the-shoulder green dress clung to the curves she had no reason to want to hide. I had to fight the urge to peek at the mid-thigh slit teasing her long legs.

"This dress is also a little tighter than when I bought it, but—" she shrugged as she glanced down her body "—I think I can get away with it."

"You more than get away with it. You're breathtaking."

"Thank you." A blush stained her cheeks as a slow smile curved her lips. "And you're pretty handsome for just coming off a bender." She kissed my cheek and curled her hand around my bicep. "Do *not* Google. Believe me, it doesn't help. I promise to be honest with you from now on, and you can go by what I tell you. Okay?"

"Okay," I agreed, but I couldn't promise. I was known at work for researching everything to death, especially with a new client or company venture. I didn't like surprises and felt better when I was prepared.

This was the first time I'd looked something up in an attempt to beat it and came away with more questions than answers.

"And about last night, by the fountains. I know it got weird for a minute, and I'm sorry—"

"Stop," she said, pressing her hand to my chest. "It was an emotional day, for both of us. And after feeling ugly and useless for the past few months, I know there are worse things than a gorgeous man almost kissing me. So don't worry about that either."

I tucked a lock of hair behind her ear and cupped her chin. She looked just as healthy as she ever had, and I wanted to forget what she'd told me as much as she wanted me to. I'd try as hard as I could for a day.

"We have a wedding to go to." I crooked my arm. "You really do look beautiful."

"Back at you." She slid her arm against my elbow. "The shoes aren't so nice, but tiny wedges are all I can get away with. At least only one person this morning asked why I was limping."

I looked away and clenched my eyes shut in an effort to reset myself, even if it only lasted for a few hours.

"We aren't going to worry about any of that. At least for tonight." I led her across the lobby floor toward the chapel. "Think Vegas weddings have cake?"

"God, I hope so." She dropped her head to my shoulder as we strode across the shiny marble. Not worrying was easier said than done, and I'd have to somehow take her word for it about how she was feeling. I resolved to try to enjoy my best friend's company without worrying about what would happen to her after we parted ways in the morning.

When we arrived at the chapel, it didn't seem like a Vegas wedding at all. The simple white chairs were draped with purple flowers and framed a white aisle runner with an ornate purple design. It was elegant and simple without flash, perfect for Dean and Maria.

I spotted Dean pacing back and forth near the end of the aisle. He breathed out a long exhale when he noticed us.

"So, how do I look?"

Dean motioned down his body as we walked into the wedding chapel. He wore a black tuxedo over his broad frame, and I couldn't remember the last time I'd seen him out of jeans. Dean worked in jeans and boots at the construction company he owned and hated dressing up. I smiled, remembering the argument he'd had with Maria at a friend's wedding for constantly smoothing the inside of his collar because the tie was "choking him."

It was a big contrast to the man I was looking at now. Bouncing with excitement and showing off his suit as he waited for his bride.

"You clean up very well," I said, squeezing his shoulder. "I'm so damn happy for you."

"Me too," Julie said and kissed his cheek. "Your bride is going to be blown away."

"Thanks," he whispered, a soft grin spreading across his mouth. "Is it dumb that I'm a little nervous? We went this route because it was easier than a big wedding, but my stomach is doing flips the closer it gets to one o'clock."

"Not at all," Julie said, shaking her head. "That means you're excited. And you should be. This is going to be a great day."

"I hope so." Dean rubbed the back of his neck. "Thank God we only have twenty guests."

"Hey, you better take your place at the end of the aisle." I pointed to the large purple vases at the front of the room. "It's almost one."

"I guess it's time. Maria was out of the room before I woke up, so I haven't seen her yet."

"I bet she's just as jittery. We'll see you after." Julie squeezed his hand.

"Congratulations, man," I said, pulling him into a hug. "Thanks for asking me to be here."

"Thanks aren't needed," he said as he let out a long exhale. "I'm honored you came. Although now I wish you'd brought a flask I could borrow."

I chuckled, slapping his arm before Julie and I went to find our seats.

"I hope this is a quick ceremony," Julie leaned in to whisper to me. "His palms are soaked."

"I know," I said, chuckling as Dean swiped his damp brow. "I don't think I've ever seen him this nervous. I hope he doesn't pass out before he says I do."

"I don't remember you being that nervous when you married Shayla."

I shrugged. "That's because our wedding was a runaway train driven by her mother. I wasn't a groom as much as I was a participant."

"Yes, I remember that." She nodded. "It was my first Southern wedding. Her family pulled out all the stops. It was an awesome wedding, though."

I nodded. I had to concede that it had been a great, well-coordinated wedding. But when it came to the marriage, things didn't fit as easily. We were young, and Shayla had been more into the party than the actual marriage after. After months of fighting, and her boyfriend coming to my office to confess their affair after she broke it off with him, she didn't fight me when I asked for a divorce.

Everyone craned their necks to the back of the room when the music started. I watched Dean's expression fade from trepidation to tears when he spotted Maria coming down the aisle. She was stunning in a simple white dress as she walked to Dean on her father's arm. As much shit as I gave them for waiting so long, I wished they'd have the happy, long life they deserved.

Julie squeezed my arm when they were announced as husband and wife, and the tiny room erupted with thunderous applause.

"It's nice to celebrate something. For a change." She shot me a smile as we stood from our seats and followed the other guests to the dining area.

"It is," I agreed, looping my arm over her shoulders. "My mother used to say the bad times make the good times better, so there are plenty more celebrations to be had. Sometimes things get sucky before they get good."

"Sucky?" She burst out laughing. "That's an odd word, yet sadly appropriate." She slid her arm around my waist as we walked.

"And I'll be here through all of it," I said. "That's a promise. If that helps." I flashed her a smile.

She laughed, dropping her head to my shoulder.

"It does. It helps a lot."

6

JULIE

"So what are your plans after this?" Dean's grandmother asked us from across the table. "I'm hitting the craps tables if you'd like to join me."

Dean and Maria had placed Landon and me at a table with his family for dinner. We'd spent the summers at Dean's parents' house while we were in college since they had a huge in-ground pool. His grandmother lived in the downstairs apartment and always insisted that we call her Nana. We all got the biggest kick out of her no-nonsense attitude, and she never minded hanging out with the college kids who invaded her backyard.

"And they are never going to see you coming, Nana," Landon teased.

A blush bled into her ninety-year-old cheeks, deepening the rouge already there. She looked no more than seventy and had a built-in strobe light on her cane. She was vibrant and full of life, something I wished for when I became her age, even if I questioned if I'd even get to *be* her age.

Having a chronic disease with scary possibilities was an

introduction to mortality. And if I did get the opportunity to grow old, what would my body do to me by then?

When patients younger than me would walk into my doctor's office with the assistance of a cane, I always had to look away. Lupus took on many different forms and trajectories, but it was new enough to loom even on the days I almost forgot about it.

I'd told Landon that I took things day by day to keep up with all the changes, but I could only handle life a little at a time because I was still afraid to look too far into the future.

"You are such a cutie. Why are you still single? Same for you." She pointed a bony finger at me. "Such a pretty girl. You two would make nice-looking babies. That is, if you move fast since you're not getting any younger."

Landon choked on a mouthful of bourbon as we both burst out laughing.

"Ma," Dean's father groaned, glaring at his mother with a deep frown. "That's none of your business." He looked so much like his son, with the same height and crooked nose, but he had a full head of salt-and-pepper hair instead of black.

"I'm old. If I only talked about things that were my business, my life would be pretty damn boring." She scoffed, pursing her lips as she glanced toward the dessert table. "Why don't you go talk to your wife, maybe tell *her* how she should mind her own business too since she's spent today moping around her son's wedding because it wasn't the one *she* wanted."

Dean's mother hadn't cracked a single smile all day except when she forced one for the family picture, obviously still not happy that her only son had rejected the huge wedding she'd wanted him to have.

If I did make it to Nana's age, I hoped I had the guts to

speak my mind like she did, because saying whatever the hell you wanted seemed like a lot of fun.

"Come on, Ma," Mr. Calabrese said as he rose from his seat. "We can dance to some Sinatra before you hit the tables."

She fought a smile before giving her son a slow nod.

"Fine." She took her son's extended hand and padded to the small dance floor, giving Landon and me the arch of her brow before dancing with her son to "The Way You Look Tonight."

"Feel like dancing?" Landon asked me. "Although we may get Nana's hopes up."

"Sure, we can give her a thrill." I pushed off the table and took Landon's hand. The wedding was winding to a close, the dessert table already half empty as the small handful of guests filtered out.

"I still can't believe they did it." Landon nodded to where Dean and Maria were chatting with the officiant, Dean's arm around Maria's waist.

"I actually think it's kind of nice they waited so long, so they could come here today without any doubts or reservations because they know each other so well."

"Do I hear a little regret in that sentiment?" Landon asked, bringing our joined hands to his chest. When his lips curved in a wry grin, I almost forgot his question.

He was stunning as hell in a suit. The jacket stretched across his broad chest and cinched his tapered waist. As much as I tried to put last night out of my head and assured Landon that it was no big deal, I'd noticed him more today than I usually did. As in noticed him as Landon the gorgeous Adonis of a man and not the Landon who was my oldest and closest friend.

I tried to reason away the new feelings with the same

excuse I'd given him. It was an emotional weekend, and we hadn't seen each other in a long time. Aside from my news and our friends getting married, we probably just missed each other. We'd start video chatting more, as I was sure Landon meant it when he said he'd constantly be checking on me once we went home, and the next time we saw each other wouldn't be this intense.

I melted into his chest as Frank Sinatra sang about thinking back to tonight when the world turned cold—as in when I'd board a plane heading back to New York and would have to try to figure out my life. Right now, I felt protected and beautiful in Landon's arms. I'd simply try to let it feel good without questioning why it shouldn't.

"Hey guys, I don't want to make you uncomfortable, but my grandmother is staring at you," Dean whispered from behind us.

Landon and I stopped dancing and turned around.

"That's because she told us we'd make good-looking babies, so she may think she set us on our way," Landon joked.

I laughed, trying to blink away the intrusive picture in my head that I didn't need right now.

"She told the wife and me the same thing," Dean quipped, turning his head when Maria wrapped her arms around his waist.

"I've overheard Dean call me 'the wife' for years, although it didn't sound very romantic then." She crinkled her nose as he peered down at her.

"How does it feel to actually be 'the wife'?" I asked, a grin spreading my mouth as I looked between them.

"This doesn't change much of our daily lives, yet it changes everything at the same time. I can't explain it."

The pure joy in her eyes caught me in the throat.

"No, I think you did a great job of explaining it," I said, swallowing when I heard my voice crack. "I see it in both of you."

"Mr. and Mrs. Calabrese, we need you for a moment." The wedding coordinator, a thin woman in a business suit with red hair pulled into a tight bun, crooked her finger at Dean and Maria.

"I guess she means us and not my parents," Dean said with a shrug. "Excuse us."

"I've never seen you cry at a wedding before," Landon mused as he studied me.

"I didn't cry, but I did get a little choked up at seeing how happy two of my oldest friends are today. Your eyes were watering during the ceremony," I said, squinting at him as I came closer. "Don't deny it."

"My contacts were bothering me. You saw no such thing."

I laughed at his narrowed eyes.

"Do you want to go somewhere after this?" I flicked my watch to check the time. "It's too late for a show, but we could walk around. I hear the botanical gardens in the lobby are nice."

"That sounds good to me. My flight isn't that early tomorrow." He curled his arm around my waist and drew me into his side. "As long as you feel up to it."

"Don't do that."

His brows drew together after I stiffened and pulled away.

"Don't do what?"

"Don't treat me like your sick friend. I know you mean well and you're worried about me, but for the rest of tonight, can I just be Julie to you? Your best friend who wants to get as much time as she can with you before you're a face on a video screen for the next few months."

His face fell before he pulled me flush to his body, bending to bury his head into the crook of my shoulder as he wrapped his arms around me.

"You're always Julie to me," he whispered into the top of my head. "We'll do whatever and go wherever you want. I'm not in a rush to miss you either."

"So then—" I pushed him back, flashing him a smile so he would relax "—you can take me to the gardens and buy me some gelato since the cake slices were so paper-thin. I promise I won't push it, and I'll call it a night if I get tired. But until then, maybe we can just pretend I won't have to." I shrugged.

Landon nodded, shutting his eyes for a moment.

"I'll do whatever you want."

"Sorry about that—is everything okay?" Dean asked with a concerned frown pulling at his mouth.

"Oh, fine," I said, inhaling a quick breath through my nostrils as I straightened. "This one is just a big softy at weddings."

Dean's brow pinched as he looked between us, nodding slowly as if he wasn't sure what he'd seen but didn't quite believe what I'd said.

"The coordinator said it's time for everyone to get out, so looks like you're the last ones to go." He smiled and wrapped us both in a hug. "Thank you. Let's not go so long without seeing each other again."

"You have my word that we won't," Landon said. "Especially if I end up back north."

"Back north?" Dean snickered. "I'll see *y'all* soon." Dean shot me a smirk. "I'll go get the missus and head up to the honeymoon suite. Wait here. You can walk out with us."

"Are you going to tell them?" Landon whispered as Dean jogged over to Maria.

I nodded at Landon without turning my head.

"I'll tell them the next time we're all together. I just didn't want to do it now. This is a happy weekend for them, and I didn't want to put a damper on it. And—" I shrugged and exhaled a long sigh "—it was nice to be around people who don't know yet. Once they do, things change."

"*Nothing* changed with us after you told me." He stepped closer, leveling me with a glare, his dark eyes almost disappearing as they narrowed to slits. "Besides me still being a little mad at you for not telling me much sooner. And that I'm probably going to annoy you a lot more often once we're both home. So *you* don't do that."

"Yes, sir." A smile ripped across my mouth as Landon darted his eyes away, agitation radiating from his shoulders.

Since Landon had twirled me around in the lobby yesterday, I'd been more myself than I had been in months. I'd try to take that home with me and accept that while I was different because of my illness, I didn't have to become it.

Maybe the only one who was letting it define me was me.

7

LANDON

"Last chance to join us," Dean's grandmother said as she hobbled over to me outside the chapel on her son's arm as I waited for Julie to come out of the restrooms.

"I appreciate the invite, but craps tables aren't my thing," I teased and kissed her cheek. "Win big, Nana."

"Damn right, I will." Nana patted my chest. "So handsome. Julie needs to wake up and marry you before I do."

I nodded, knowing that if I reminded her that we were just friends, she wouldn't believe me.

And after a day of fighting to tear my eyes away from Julie, I wouldn't have been too convincing.

"Does your wife want to join us, or is she still moping around?" she asked Dean's father. The poor guy inhaled a deep breath as he ran a hand down his face.

"I'm not moping, Ma."

Our heads whipped around to Dean's mother, her huff now more sad than irritated, as it had been throughout the day. She swept her brown hair off her shoulder and smoothed her black dress as she glowered at her mother-in-law.

"I just wanted to have a big wedding for my only son. I guess that makes me a bad person." A soft sigh fell from her lips as she trudged over to us.

"Your only son had the wedding he wanted, and you were able to be there. That's all that matters, and this day is about *his* happiness, not yours. So, lighten the hell up, for Christ's sake." Nana huffed before scanning the casino floor. "That one feels lucky." She pointed at one of the tables with her cane. "We'll head there first."

She yanked her son's arm so hard he almost fell over. Dean's mother followed, defeat in her every step across the patterned casino carpet.

"I feel like she's going to be out a lot longer than we are." Julie came up behind me as we watched Nana rest her cane against the edge of the craps table and drop the chips from her purse onto the felt.

"Longer than Dean's parents are probably ready for."

Julie's laugh was easy and relaxed, and I'd try to do what she asked and enjoy her company without worrying about her once she was home. I agreed that it had been an emotional couple of days for a lot of reasons, but having her in my arms as we danced felt good. Putting what almost happened between us out of my mind was proving to be more difficult than I expected it to be, especially with her looking so damn gorgeous tonight.

Julie had always been gorgeous, and I'd never beaten myself up for noticing. But that was because I hadn't been tempted to cross a line like I was last night. I'd need a few more days to reason my way out of it, and although I hated the thought of parting ways tomorrow, maybe a little distance between us would give us the space we needed to cool off.

"This hotel is so pretty," Julie mused as we strode through the hotel's botanical gardens, passing the batch of red-petaled tulips and daisies. The flowers were framed around an indoor fountain, with tourists meandering through each display and bumping into one another, focused on the flowers and not where they were going.

"It is," I agreed. "Nice hotel for a wedding. Although watching them be married by Elvis like Dean wanted would have been something."

She nodded, her arms cinched around her torso as we moved past more rows of flowers.

I dug into my pocket and pulled out a penny, motioning to the little boy across from us tossing coins into the fountain.

"Penny for your thoughts?" I asked, holding out my hand to show her the penny in my palm.

"Maybe I should make a wish. Couldn't hurt, right?" She took the penny, rubbing it between her fingers. "Should we find a slot machine after I throw this to see if it worked?"

When her shoulders shook with a chuckle, my gaze fell on the cluster of freckles on her collarbone. My wish was to figure out how to make her see how gorgeous she still was and that she never had to hide from anyone. Although the way I'd been tempted to remind her of that last night was off-limits.

"We could. Like I said, I'll take you anywhere you want to go." I came up to her, holding her eyes as they searched mine. "Just don't make me join Nana at the craps tables. I'm not built for that."

She shoved my shoulder and stepped closer to the edge of the fountain, closing her eyes before tossing the coin into the water. My eyes followed the ripple of the coin as I made my own wish.

"I'm sorry," Julie said, her whisper so low and almost drowned out by the running water.

"Sorry for what?"

"Well, for a few things," she said, easing closer to me. "I'm sorry for lying to you all this time, and I'm sorry that I can't get out of my own head and I keep taking it out on the people closest to me."

"You've had a lot going on. It's okay to be pissed at the world about it."

"I guess. You want to hear something weird?"

"Always."

Her eyes flicked to mine, a sheepish smile dancing across her lips.

"When we were sitting at the table tonight, all I could think of was how I wished I could be like Dean's grandmother. To get to be that full of life at her age."

"Everyone wishes they could be like Dean's grandmother." I chuckled. "After managing so many different personalities at work and having to choose my words so damn carefully, I'd love to be able to just say whatever comes to my mind and not have to put a filter on it."

"Right? But more than that, I wished for the chance to at least *get* to her age. My doctor told me that I'm improving, but my blood tests say that lupus is still active. I feel like it's this monster waiting to pounce when I'm not looking. She assured me that's common with a new diagnosis and I'll get used to it." Her gaze drifted to the other rows of flowers in the distance. "Everything about my life feels...temporary. I can't explain it."

I couldn't fathom anything related to Julie as temporary. I had a lot to get used to about her illness too, like keeping myself in check before I hovered over her and pissed her off. But picturing her not in my life someday? I'd never get used to that or even be able to bring myself to imagine it.

"I know it's hard not to think that way, but nothing is temporary. Just different." I brought her into my arms before I could help myself. It was always easy and familiar between us—hugs and kisses on the cheek were passed back and forth without them meaning anything but a friendly show of affection. Now, touching her made me pause and register where every inch of her skin touched mine.

"I hate that you live so far away," she murmured into my chest. "I'm used to it, but now—"

"I know what you mean. Our goodbyes are usually a little sad, but this one may be painful."

I slid my hands down her arms as she laughed.

The fear of losing her or what could happen to her was messing with my head. I was sure I'd torture myself with all these confusing feelings on the entire flight back to North Carolina, and hopefully, I would figure out a way to deal with them once I landed.

"I'm always a phone call or a text away." I draped my arm around her shoulders as we walked. "And you will get back on your feet soon. You're good at what you do."

"And I'm almost forty. Creative directors are getting younger every day and would work a lot cheaper." She heaved out an audible sigh. "At least I'd have insurance if I had to take a pay cut at a new job, but my friends in the job market are all saying it's taken them months to find something. I hate to have to choose between prescriptions and groceries, and I *really* hate how that's not an exaggeration."

"First of all, that wouldn't happen because I wouldn't let it."

"No, I am not taking money from you." She stepped in front of me and shook her head. "Ever."

"I think you're panicking a little. It's understandable but not good for you. Especially now." I angled my head to meet her gaze. "And if it came down to it that you needed money to eat and stay healthy, I'd find a way to give it to you, whether you liked it or not."

She glared at me before her lips twitched into a smile.

"You're relentless. What would I do without you?"

"You won't have to find out. No matter what happens, I'm right here, Jules."

She nodded, a gloss shining in her eyes before I looked away.

"Unless I happen to run away with someone. Nana told me while you were in the bathroom that if you didn't marry me, she would."

We shared a laugh as I leaned my forehead against hers.

"You have good insurance, right? Maybe we could see if that Elvis chapel is open."

When I didn't laugh with her, she squinted at me. I stopped walking as a crazy idea barreled into my head.

"Why don't we?"

She jerked her head back, her eyes saucer-wide as she gaped at me. The words left my mouth in such a rush, it shocked me too, but I didn't take them back.

"I was making a joke. Landon," she breathed out, pressing her hand to her chest as it heaved up and down. "We can't get married just so I could have insurance."

"If you had insurance that you didn't have to pay for and your doctor visits and medications were covered, could you get by on unemployment for a little while as you looked?"

Julie's eyes darted back and forth, a deep pinch in her brow.

"Landon, come on. We can't—"

"That was a yes or no question, Jules." I shifted to face her and grabbed both of her hands. "I have excellent insurance with my job, and you could relax a little and take care of yourself if your medical expenses were covered, right?" I gripped her shoulders as desperation ran through me. "We're right here. Let's just do it."

"You're serious about this, aren't you?" Her eyes grew wide when they met mine. "I cannot marry you just so I can take your insurance. Look," she said, grabbing my face. "I love you for wanting to do this, but I can't let you."

"Why? All I'd be doing is filling out a form when I got back to work."

"And won't they take more out of your paycheck for a wife? Stop it, Landon. This is nuts." She shook her head and shifted away from me.

"I make a great salary, and I wouldn't miss it." I spun her around. "You'd really be doing this for me. Because I didn't like that crack about choosing between groceries and medications. I'm not going to watch you get sick just because you're stubborn."

"Okay, let's say I agree to be your fake wife in the name of insurance fraud. And you meet someone and have to explain you're married, but it's just for convenience?"

"It's no one's business but ours. If I met someone, it would be a long time before marriage was even a consideration, if ever. And if she didn't understand how much you mean to me, if for some reason I did have to tell her, then I wouldn't want to waste my time with anyone like that anyway."

She draped her hand over her eyes, still shaking her head.

"And this only has to be until you get on your feet, for

maybe a couple of years, if that. If you find a job or meet someone you decide to marry, we'll divorce just as secretly." I lifted one side of my mouth, trying to relax her, but she waved her hands and shook her head again.

"I'm not close to dating anyone, much less thinking of getting married. But this feels like I'm taking advantage of you."

"I told you, I wouldn't miss the premium out of my paycheck, no one has to know, and again, we are right here. It's almost like fate."

"A fated fake marriage."

"Yes," I said, bobbing my head in a slow nod. "I can't take this away from you. I'd love to wave some kind of wand and you wouldn't have to worry about being sick ever again, but I can't. But this—" I grabbed her biceps, gripping them tighter until she turned her head toward me "—I can fix this."

"A marriage fix?" She huffed out a humorless laugh.

I lifted a shoulder. "More like a marriage solution."

"But," she sighed, pressing her fingers into her temples. "Won't word get around at work that you're married?"

"I don't care if it does or it doesn't. I'll tell HR that I got married and need to add my wife to my insurance plan as soon as possible. They're supposed to keep it private, but if they don't—" I shrugged "—it's no one's business beyond that."

"Landon," she said, picking up my hand and holding it in both of hers. "I adore you, but I cannot let you do this."

"I adore you too, that's why you need to marry me. Since you told me about all of this yesterday, I've been going crazy trying to think of a way to help you and dreading going back to Charlotte and worrying about you all the damn time. If we do this, I can help you."

I cupped her cheek when she stilled, holding her gaze as she barely breathed or blinked.

"Think of it as a favor to me. Let me do this for you so *I* can relax. I'm already going to text and call too much and drive you crazy."

I kept hold of her hand and dropped to one knee. A group of women by the opposite row of flowers gawked at us in my periphery. Getting down on one knee wasn't necessary, or even appropriate for the type of proposal this was, but I was desperate. And with the crowd gathered around us, I hoped embarrassment would force her to say yes, and I'd hold her to it after.

"Get up," she said in a loud whisper as she scanned the space around us and noticed all the heads swiveled in our direction.

"Nope," I said, popping the p as a grin split my mouth. "Julianne Marie Robison, I love you, and I want to take care of you." Her face softened before she clenched her eyes shut. "Please marry me."

8

JULIE

What was crazier about this disaster of an idea? The fact that Landon thought of it in the first place, or that I was giving it serious consideration?

I had other financial concerns besides health insurance. Nate didn't want his part of the down payment back, but when we'd bought the house, I'd put in most of it anyway. The mortgage was enough to eat up most of my salary and would gobble up my severance before I could even blink. What I would get from unemployment wouldn't even make a tiny dent in my monthly payment, never mind the other utilities.

But if I took Landon's offer, I could look into freelance jobs or concurrent part-time ones without having to worry about a chunk being taken out for hefty insurance premiums. I wouldn't exactly be comfortable, but I could manage and breathe a little.

Marrying my best friend purely in the name of convenience was one thing. Marrying him while I was so attracted to him lately? That made me take a serious pause. My vulnerability and displacement had me latching on to Landon like a life preserver for the past couple of days, which was probably the catalyst for how drawn to him I was now. While that would most likely turn out to be a temporary thing due to circumstance, making him my husband while I was so *aware* of him felt dangerous and a little reckless.

But this wouldn't be a forced-proximity situation like all the fake marriage romances I liked to read. He'd be in North Carolina, and I'd be in New York. Our daily lives would still be just as separate, and the only thing we'd have to share would be an insurance plan.

Then why did the entire notion of marrying Landon as if it were a business transaction leave me with a feeling of ominous dread in the pit of my stomach?

"Get up. There has to be another way."

"Fine," he said, still camped out on the floor in front of me. "Then tell me another solution that is this simple and fast?"

"Landon, this is *not* simple. In fact, it's got the potential to be a disaster if we're not careful."

"Why? Don't you trust me?" A flash of hurt pulled at his features.

"I trust you more than anyone."

"Then what's the problem? I won't let you make yourself sick." He gripped my hands tighter. "We're adults and going into this for practical reasons and with our eyes open. We can handle it."

Maybe since he'd been married and divorced, the offer didn't have the same value to him as it did for me. My long engagement never made it into marriage, but calling someone my husband had weight to it, even if it wasn't true in the traditional or even real sense.

But I didn't know another way. At least not one I could think of. I was squished between an impossible rock and an unavoidable hard place.

"There is no one else I'd contemplate committing insurance fraud with, but I can't ask you to do this."

"You aren't asking. I'm offering. Pleading with you, actually." The corner of his mouth curved up. "Now, are you going to make an honest man out of me tonight or what?"

Pretending to marry Landon didn't feel honest. It would be legally legit, but we were in a weird space right now. I felt a new pull between us that unnerved me, but I was about to agree to accompany him to an Elvis chapel to become husband and wife. The whole thing was batshit crazy.

Yet, Landon had a point. I'd packed for this trip with a knot in my stomach from the guilt over traveling to Vegas when I should have been grasping on to every penny and feeling frustration at how difficult life had become every time I'd thought things were getting better.

My eyes fell to where my hand was still trapped in his. If there was anyone in this world I could trust, it was Landon. I knew he'd move heaven and earth to keep me safe and healthy, and I'd seen the worry on his face all weekend since he'd pulled my confession out of me. As hard as I tried to step back and look at all this from a practical perspective, this still felt like taking advantage. I'd refused the idea of Landon giving me a loan, but I was giving serious thought to marrying him instead.

My head spun so much it ached.

"We don't even live in the same state. Won't that tip them off?"

"Tip them off? We aren't committing a crime," Landon said, laughing as he squeezed my knee.

"Technically, we kind of are. It's insurance fraud. And I

don't think I could be covered under you since we live in separate states. I'd have to find a doctor in North Carolina."

"Jules, I am sure people get married every day for lots of reasons outside of the conventional. We won't have to serve time, I promise. If anyone investigates us, we'll send them to Dean's grandmother, who would say she saw it coming."

He chuckled, and despite the nausea rolling around my stomach at what I was about to agree to, I smiled back.

"And we have remote employees all over the country who have local doctors. I am sure HR would work with me to find a plan that covered you in New York. I do have a little pull."

I had to laugh at his crooked grin. He wasn't backing down, making it impossible to say no, and I only had a little more fight left in me before I agreed. When the astronomical prices of out-of-pocket monthly doctors' visits, blood tests, and medications would flash in my mind, the panic would squeeze my chest. The mere idea of letting go of all that worry because of agreeing to this crazy scheme was already bringing me tangible relief.

If Landon were ever in trouble, I would do anything for him without an ounce of hesitation. If it were within my means to help him, I wouldn't waver for a second. If I took away the weird moments of the past couple of days between us, this really was just a friend helping a friend.

At least, that's what I would tell myself during the million times I'd panic afterward if we went through with this.

"Okay, we can talk about this. Can you just get up so people stop staring?"

A victorious grin split his mouth as he popped up from the floor and pointed to the bench behind us.

"I think Dean said the chapel was close."

I followed and settled next to him as he poked at his phone screen.

"So you really want to go the Elvis route for this?"

"We're in Vegas, right?" He shrugged without looking up. "Might as well have the whole quick-marriage experience." My jaw dropped when he winked.

"You really think this is no big deal? You're going to marry me tonight, and it's just something we're doing? Like ordering takeout?"

He set the phone on the bench between us and lifted his head. "Actually, looking back to when I did this the last time, I'm a lot more sure of the woman I'm walking down the aisle with now. And while my intentions may be a little different for after, you've already got me for life, regardless of whether we're married or not."

He grabbed my hand and laced our fingers together.

"So, this is actually a pretty simple decision for me, knowing that by signing a paper and filling out a form, I'm keeping you healthy. Plus, it would be kind of fun to check out the wedding Dean really wanted."

"Too bad we can't tell him about it."

"This is the chapel Dean told us about." He turned the screen to face me, ignoring what I'd said. "It's a few minutes from the Strip and open all night."

"Is that the officiant?" He was in a full white jumpsuit with thick sideburns and oversized sunglasses.

"One of them, I guess. My mother would have gotten a kick out of this. She loved Elvis." His grin shrank to a wistful smile.

"I didn't know that. I don't know if she'd be thrilled about you not marrying for love."

"Who said I'm not? I can promise you on this our wedding day, that I have never loved a woman as much as I love you." He kissed the top of my wrist. "And that is why you're going to let me do this."

He snatched the phone from my other hand and scrolled to the bottom of the screen.

"It's legit? Like we can really just walk in, get married, and it's legal?"

"Looks like it," he said as he kept scrolling. "We'll walk out with a marriage license, and you will be Mrs. Landon Clark. I mean, in theory." His lip curled as he shot me a glance. "You have your driver's license on you, right? I'll get us an Uber, and we can be there in fifteen minutes."

"I do." I grimaced when his head shot up.

"You do? Meaning, yes, you'll marry me?"

"Meaning I love you too." I swallowed, trying to ward off the burning in my nose. "And unlike the other time I was planning to do this, I trust you completely." My pulse kicked up as I sucked in a long breath and slowly let it out.

"So, yes." I took a deep breath and offered up a silent prayer that this *solution* wouldn't blow up in both our faces. "Yes, I will marry you."

9

LANDON

As it turned out, with a few more clicks of research, we couldn't simply walk into the chapel and get our license. We had to stop at the Clark County Marriage Bureau, which, as luck would have it, was less than twenty minutes from the hotel and was open until midnight. We picked it up, jumped back into an Uber, and headed on our way to make this fake marriage official.

"It doesn't even look real," Julie mused as the car pulled up to the chapel. It looked like a tiny white schoolhouse except for the exaggerated stone-covered steeple along the side. The neon sign in front flashed "Wedding Chapel" in bright orange as a low stream of instrumental Elvis songs played from speakers we couldn't see.

"Are they actually playing 'It's Now or Never'?" Julie cracked up as she stepped out of the car, setting her hands on her hips as she surveyed the outside. "No pressure, right?"

I laughed and grabbed her hand.

"For some. Maybe for others, it's needed encouragement. Not backing out, are you, Robison?"

"No, Clark. I'm good." She peered up at the buzzing neon sign. "I feel like we've walked on to a movie set."

"This is all real and legit, like I told you. Well, real and legit in the sense—"

"I know." Her smile faded when she dragged her gaze to mine. "I'm ready if you are."

I stepped onto the tiny porch and held the door open for her to step through.

"Aren't you two precious?" the clerk at the front desk told us as she looked us over. "Come in," she said, waving us in. "I'm Mandy, and I'll get you all set up." She clasped her hands under her chin. "And already dressed up. We have button-downs for the guys who come in a little too casual. But you are both picture-perfect!"

As far as authenticity went, the Now or Never Chapel of Bliss was on point inside and out. I wasn't sure if younger patrons appreciated Mandy's resemblance to a young Priscilla Presley, with her bright pastel eye shadow and teased blond hair, but the man who was set to marry us was all Vegas Elvis, complete with the exaggerated curl of his lips when he spoke.

Even though he wasn't here, and I had no idea if we'd ever tell him what we'd done, I convinced Julie to choose the Greatest Hits package in Dean's honor.

"Okay, so we have all your information," Mandy chirped after we handed her all the forms. "Time to get the show on the road!" She handed Julie a fake bouquet of lilies. "Do you want to walk down together or have your hunk of burning love wait for you?"

We snuck a glance at each other, both of us stifling the same laugh.

"I'll take my hunk with me to the altar." Julie slid her

arm into the crook of my elbow, peering up at me with a soft smile. "Ready, doll?"

I narrowed my eyes at her suggestion for a pet name. She didn't seem as freaked out as when I first suggested it, and I was hoping she'd fly home with a little relief, knowing that, at least, her medical expenses were covered.

"Absolutely, darlin'. You can lead the way."

"Darlin'?" she whispered to me when Mandy turned around. "My God, you even said that with a Southern drawl."

"I'm from the South now, remember? It was that or sugar plum, but darlin' seemed to fit better for reasons I can't explain." She burst out laughing when I shrugged.

"Okay. I'll meet y'all down there," Mandy sang as she jogged down the aisle, maintaining a good speed in her spiked heels and grabbing a microphone while she fiddled with a control panel.

Despite my efforts to convince Julie this wasn't a big deal, as we made our way down the aisle to "Can't Help Falling In Love," my heart sped up with every step. I was marrying Julie, and regardless of why and where we'd be this time tomorrow, it meant something more to me than just a way to help her through her financial struggles.

But as I'd just gotten her to relax and go along with it, I kept the surge of odd emotions to myself.

"Dean would be so jealous," I joked as we inched down the aisle. My voice was a strained whisper as this game of pretend seemed a little too real for a minute.

Mandy wasn't a bad singer as she crooned about what wise men say. I'd marry Julie a million times if it meant that I could help take care of her, even when we were miles apart. Maybe this was a hasty decision, but I stood the fuck by it all the same.

Nothing was a guarantee, but at least having medical insurance would help prevent Julie from getting sick again —or sick*er*. The notion of Julie sick at all was still sinking in, and she furrowed her brow at me when the thought made me hold on to her tighter.

"Who has the rings?" our Elvis officiant, Hal, asked us as he smirked at Mandy.

"Here you go." Mandy handed us the plain silver bands we'd picked out when we arrived. This little chapel had thought of everything.

"Landon, do you take Julianne to be your wife?"

"I do," I replied, my words clear and strong as I held her gaze and slipped the ring on her finger.

"Julianne, do you take Landon to be your husband?"

A slow grin curved her lips as she slid the ring on my finger. "I do," she said, with more determination than I expected, and kissed my cheek.

"Thank you," she whispered, her eyes wet when she pulled away.

"Now, hold on. I'm about to close," Hal bellowed. "By the power vested in me by the fabulous state of Nevada, I now pronounce you husband and wife. And we don't hand over the paperwork without a good kiss, so you may now kiss the bride."

I felt Julie stiffen next to me.

"Could they do that?" she mouthed to me.

As much as I'd laughed at Julie's suggestion of insurance fraud, at this stage of the game, we didn't need any obstacles in getting that signed license. Maybe Hal was one of those true love advocates who would give us a problem if he thought we were faking.

I'd speak to HR first thing on Monday morning to get

her on my insurance plan as quickly as possible, but we needed that damn marriage license.

I slid my palm over the nape of her neck, giving her what I hoped was a reassuring squeeze to get her to look up. She nodded when she lifted her head, and before we lost the moment—and I lost my nerve—I pulled her flush to my body and slanted my mouth over hers. Julie dropped the bouquet in shock before she melted into me, opening her mouth on a sweet sigh when I flicked the seam of her lips with my tongue.

I cradled her cheek, holding her in place for as long as I could have her. The kiss was full of hunger and an odd rush of relief as I went through with what I'd been so tempted to do last night. Her hand sifted through my hair as I wove my fingers around a fistful of hers, enjoying every second before I let go and we had to go back to this not being real.

"Well, I know who is in for a good wedding night tonight," Hal quipped.

When Julie and I broke apart, he regarded us with a shake of his head, his belly still jiggling with a hearty laugh as it pushed against the seams of his jumpsuit.

"Congratulations! You both are going to be so happy," Mandy gushed as she looked between us. "I have a good feeling, and my feelings are never wrong. Time for another picture!" She pointed her tablet at us. "Get nice and close."

"*Another* picture?" Julie's nose crinkled at Mandy.

"Oh, I got a good shot of that kiss." She waggled her eyebrows and scooped the bouquet off the floor before handing it back to Julie.

Julie's brows popped. I laughed, my heart still hammering against my rib cage as I pulled her into my arms.

"Do you want that one?" Julie asked, peering up at me with a smirk.

"I don't need a picture of something that's permanently burned into my brain."

Her smile faded as she sank her teeth into her bottom lip, her tell when she was anxious. I pressed my thumb to her chin to release it as I held her hooded gaze. "Good wedding memory."

"The best," she whispered as she grazed her hands down the front of my jacket. A dazed smile broke out on her swollen lips, and my best friend had never looked so beautiful.

My best friend who was now my wife. As fake as it all was supposed to be, every second my lips touched hers was too real to deny.

"What a lovely couple," Mandy said, beaming at the screen after we turned our heads. "I'll print those out as we sort your paperwork."

After Mandy scurried away, I searched Julie's face. My gaze fell on her flushed cheeks and the mouth I could still taste, taunting me already. Her brow furrowed as she eyed the bouquet in her hands, her breaths coming as quick as mine as her chest heaved up and down.

"That was..." she said as she took tiny breaths of air. "Wow."

"I would completely agree with that."

We laughed as we both sobered, the spell between us this weekend coming to a head right after we'd become husband and wife.

"Are you okay?"

"I am. Maybe a little shocked. I can't believe we did it," she whispered, gazing up at me with wide eyes as a slow smile spread across her lips.

"We sure did." I picked up her hand and laced our fingers together. "We got two weddings this weekend for the price of one," I joked as I pretended the Earth hadn't fallen off its axis from that incredible kiss.

"We did," she said, giving me a watery smile. "I don't know how to thank you."

I framed her face and shook my head. "You don't. I'd do anything to keep you safe. I love you. Wife."

She hiccupped a laugh through her tears.

"Right back at you, husband."

The tension eased from my shoulders at her easy smile.

"What do you say we find something to eat? Have our own wedding celebration."

I couldn't let her go just yet. Marrying her and just heading back up to our respective hotel rooms until we had to depart for different destinations felt wrong, no matter how fake the marriage was supposed to be.

"I spotted a taco truck outside." Julie jutted her chin to the front door. "We can ask if they have a bride and groom special."

"If not, we'll make one. My wife deserves the best."

She shook her head. "This is on me. I think I can splurge on tacos for us. Think of it as a wedding gift."

I laughed and draped my arm across her shoulders.

"See, that means we have a good marriage—give-and-take. You needed insurance, I could use a taco."

She burrowed into my side as we gathered up our license and photos. "Right, seems like an equal exchange."

"We'll take care of each other." I pulled her tighter, pressing a kiss to her forehead as we made our way to the entrance. "Thank you for letting me take care of you."

10

JULIE

Landon and I ate our wedding feast of tacos on the concrete bench outside the chapel, looking everywhere but at each other. The only sounds between us were the occasional crunch of shells and crinkling of the paper across our laps. I followed him with my eyes as he stood and padded to the trash can next to the entrance to dump his empty paper bag. We never let anything dangle unsaid between us, but I didn't know where to begin.

"So, are we going to talk about this, or just sit here in silence until we go back to the hotel?"

"They're good tacos." I shrugged, taking the last bite of my heavenly chicken taco, chewing slower than usual to buy myself a few minutes to gather the right words. Our practical fake wedding was now the culmination of a confusing weekend, and tomorrow we'd fly back home and try to make sense of it all.

"Did the kiss freak you out?" He leaned forward on the bench, his mouth curving in a tiny smile.

"No," I answered too quickly, swallowing the last bite whole as Landon's dark eyes bored into mine.

"No?" His brow furrowed as he studied me. "Because I can admit I'm a little freaked out."

"Well, maybe a little," I conceded and scooted closer to his side of the bench. "I doubt he could have really held up the paperwork if we didn't kiss, but I don't know what rules Vegas wedding chapels have. As ridiculous as the place is on the outside and inside"—I craned my neck to the buzzing neon sign—"maybe they don't take kindly to fake marriages."

"My mind went there too. To come all this way and get called out at the end would've been frustrating as fuck."

"Yes, talk about a letdown." I shot Landon what I hoped was an easy smile.

"But that's not what's freaking me out."

"What do you mean?" I squinted at him while I wiped a napkin across my mouth.

"I *wanted* to kiss you. Yes, I didn't want any trouble getting the license, but Hal didn't exactly twist my arm."

I could still feel the scratch of his stubble against my chin and how soft his lips had been as they'd moved against mine. When my tongue had wrapped around his, the sexiest groan had erupted from his throat and liquefied my knees.

"And I didn't fight you." I shrugged, a smile sneaking across my mouth at his sheepish grin. "Of course, you're an overachiever at that too."

He kissed with a passion and determination that made my toes curl, and while I could reason away the sudden attraction as emotional attachment, there was no way to ignore the heat pooling between my legs after that kiss.

I'd dropped my fake bouquet at the exact moment it had all become too real.

"If that's your way of saying you thought it was a great

kiss, I totally agree." My cheeks heated at the deep rasp of his whisper. "I'm not going to lie. I've had...more than friendly thoughts of you before, especially when we first met. In fact, if you hadn't been dating Dale freshman year, I would have asked you out."

My eyes grew wide. "Seriously?"

"Definitely." He grinned as he gave me a slow nod. "I used to live for those skinny jeans you wore to class every day. Then, they paired us up for that weird philosophy project, and talking to you became the highlight of my day."

"Mine too." I moved closer and dropped my head to his shoulder. "And the rest is history, I guess."

"I guess," he said, resting his chin on the top of my head. "I was afraid to ask you out after you broke up with Dale because we were already best friends at that point. Other than the drunk almost-kiss after graduation, staying in the friend zone wasn't that difficult. I'm not sure why it's been so hard to stay in my lane the past couple of days."

"I noticed you too. Even when I was going out with Dale."

He reared back as his brows shot up. "Really?"

I exhaled with a groan. "The entire female population of Fordham got whiplash whenever you walked by. A good number of the guys too. I remember when you played on Dean's softball team that summer in Pelham Bay Park and practiced in a tank top. I think even the squirrels drooled."

His head dropped between his legs as he laughed.

"Were you one of the squirrels?"

"Maybe." I lifted a shoulder. "It's been a little bit of a struggle for me to stay in my lane too."

"Losing you wasn't an option then. And now..." He let out a long sigh, rubbing the back of his head. "You asked me not to worry and promised me that you're okay, but ever since you told me, all I can think of is what would I do without you?"

"Landon, stop," I looped my arms around his neck when his voice cracked. "Yes, it has scary possibilities, but I'm not going anywhere. I may have to deal with new limitations and I don't know what to expect, but please don't think like that, okay?"

He nodded, rubbing his eyes. "Maybe that's why it's been a little weird. I really don't have an answer."

"Like I keep telling you, it's been an emotional trip."

I kissed his cheek, breathing him in one more greedy time, even though we were back to rationalizing the pull between us.

"And we'll video chat, and hopefully you'll be in New York soon and we can see each other a lot more. Would it make you feel better if I told you that I'm breathing so much easier right now? That I'm very grateful I have an amazing best friend who made sure to find a way to take care of me before we went home?"

I spied his shoulders jerk with a chuckle.

"I love you. And when I find skinny jeans in my new size, I'll wear them every day if you move back to New York."

He laughed, burying his face in the crook of my neck and pressing his lips to the sensitive spot behind my ear. His breath fanned hot on my skin, and I had to cross my legs to ward off the tingles between them.

I eased back and sucked in a quick breath as I straightened. Having the sudden hots for my new fake husband would not be practical or in the least bit helpful.

"I love you too, Jules." He rose, grabbing the empty taco bag off the ground. "We should head back. I can buy you some wedding gelato if they're still open."

"That sounds like a great idea." I stood, wincing at the tightness in my legs and arms. My elbows were sore, the first joints that protested if I pushed myself too hard. I was feeling the aftereffects of a busy weekend and the crash of post-fake-wedding adrenaline. I looked forward to a long, hot shower to loosen everything back up before I went to bed.

"What's wrong? You're limping." Landon clutched his phone as his eyes roamed my body. When he'd done that next to the Bellagio fountains last night, his gaze had been full of heat. Although I hadn't known what to do with it, I hated the panic drifting over his face now.

"I'm worn out. Nothing a couple ibuprofens and a hot shower won't fix. I'll have some gelato with my new husband and head back up to my room." I squeezed his arm. "It's okay. It happens."

He frowned as he tapped his screen to order an Uber. "The car should be here any minute. I'll get you back, and you can go up to the room and rest."

"I can manage for gelato. It is our wedding night after all."

He didn't answer as he strode to the street and waved the car over. Landon needed a minute to get used to what had become a reluctant normal for me. I hoped the more we talked and saw each other, the less upset he'd be.

He held the door open after the car pulled up, easing me inside before he shut the door. I watched him as he made his way to the other side of the car, tension in his gait that hadn't been there before or since I'd first told him about my diagnosis at the bar. It had dissipated while we celebrated Dean and Maria's wedding and even during our fake one, but seeing rather than hearing about my symptoms seemed to upset him even more.

I wished for the days of our younger years, or the last trip I'd taken to Charlotte to visit him. We'd barhopped in the city until three a.m., laughing and eating omelets in the diner by my hotel before I went back to my room. I'd been tired when I'd gone home, but I'd been invigorated instead of wiped out.

It was only six months ago, but it already seemed like a different lifetime.

"We should be back soon. Are you okay?"

"No."

"What's wrong? Are you in a lot of pain?" He cradled my cheek as his eyes searched my face. "What do you need?"

"For you to do what you promised. To believe me when I tell you I'm okay. Your handsome face is going to be covered in wrinkles before you land back in Charlotte, and you'll drive yourself out of your mind if you don't try to relax over this."

"I am trying. It's hard, but believe me when I say I'm trying."

I nodded, taking in the masculine beauty of his profile as his gaze drifted out the window. His chest heaved up and down as his jaw ticked. I drifted my hand across his shoulders, grazing my palm back and forth and squeezing his neck.

When he swiveled his head, he smiled at me. It wasn't his usual easy smile, but his jaw relaxed a bit as his eyes held mine. I eased closer and brushed his lips with a light kiss. The kiss didn't ignite as it had at the chapel, but it had a sweet relief to it. Landon didn't pull away, giving my lips one more quick peck before we broke apart.

This was as far as we could take it. When we arrived back at the hotel, we needed to retreat to the friend zone and put this weird yet wonderful weekend behind us.

But I couldn't resist taking one more kiss.

"Happy wedding day," I whispered, resting my forehead against his.

He chuckled and pulled me into his chest.

"Happy wedding day, darlin'."

11

LANDON

After I walked Julie back to her hotel room, I packed and tried for a night of sleep that I knew wouldn't come.

Julie was probably right. My fear over what could happen to her made the inhibitions and boundaries we'd set for ourselves all those years ago harder to uphold. That almost-kiss in our early twenties scared the hell out of me because I knew once my lips touched hers, I'd be in a constant battle with myself not to take more.

Like the one I was fighting now.

But after tomorrow, this interlude, or whatever you'd call what had happened between us, would end. She'd go back to the Bronx, and I'd fly back to Charlotte. I'd be able to see her face more often, and maybe that would take the power out of whatever had come over us here.

But either way, I was a big boy and would handle myself. I wouldn't ruin a friendship I'd counted on for most of my life just because my hormones got the best of me. I still hoped to move to New York eventually, but maybe the miles between us would be a good thing for once, at least for a little while.

But as far as not worrying about her as she'd begged me to do last night, that was going to be the bigger struggle by far.

Julie looked great, and while I had to force myself not to fixate on symptoms I couldn't see, watching her limping and in obvious pain as she climbed into the car illustrated all the fears I'd had. All the terrifying complications I'd learned about on my phone until the wee hours of the night started to turn in my head, and I'd never felt more helpless and useless.

She'd fallen headfirst into some shitty luck over the past few months. Knowing she could keep her health insurance now was a big relief, but that was only part of her recent troubles. No matter how hard I wanted to try, I couldn't save her from all of it.

Even if I was up most of the night wishing I could figure out how.

I picked up my suitcase and headed downstairs. My flight wasn't until noon, and I wasn't meeting Julie in the lobby for another hour, but I was itching to leave the room after the mostly sleepless night I'd had. Too much alone time meant too much time to think, and Julie had asked me to try not to obsess over this. I couldn't promise, but maybe a cup of coffee would clear my head before she saw me and realized how much I wasn't listening so far.

I settled into one of the fancy armchairs in the lobby and sipped from the paper cup in my hand, laughing to myself at the guests who were just stumbling in from the night before. I'd been to a few conferences in Las Vegas over the years and had dragged myself back to my hotel room in the early morning light. At the last one a few years ago, my friend Will and I made the same walk of shame back to our rooms at Mandalay Bay after a night of fake names and decisions bad enough to cause the stench of regret the next morning.

Will had joked on the plane back home that he hoped neither of us had gotten married and didn't remember it.

I almost had to laugh at the irony. The one Vegas weekend I was stone-cold sober, I ended up leaving with a wife.

"What are you doing up so early?" I jumped at the sound of Maria's voice behind me. Her dark curls were piled up on top of her head, one falling in front of her face as she came closer. "I thought your flight wasn't until later."

"It's not, but I was restless. How are you feeling this morning, Mrs. Calabrese?"

She smiled as she stuffed her hands in the front pocket of her hoodie.

"I keep looking over my shoulder for my mother-in-law when anyone calls me that. I feel amazing, actually. I came down to get us some coffee before heading out for the day. Now that the wedding is over, we wanted one day with just us and not having to entertain anyone. As much as we love all of you."

I smiled, her joy so infectious that I forgot my worries for a minute.

I held up a hand. "No offense taken."

"Maybe we'll go see Elvis so Dean can have the Vegas wedding experience he originally wanted." She chuckled until she realized I wasn't laughing with her. "Everything okay? You looked a little tense there for a second."

"No, I'm fine," I said, waving a hand, trying to blow off the moment I'd flinched as a bittersweet secret memory had flashed in my mind.

"Did you guys have fun last night? I wondered if Nana convinced you to come with her to the craps tables."

"No, I told her I wouldn't be able to keep up."

She chuckled with a slow nod. "That lady is the best. She seemed stuck on you and Julie when we spoke to her last night."

"Stuck on us?"

Maria grinned. "She said you were a beautiful couple and needed to admit you were in love already. I told her that's just how you guys are. You're close but just friends."

"We are." I nodded, flashing her a smile when I noticed the defensive edge in my voice. "She told us to hurry up and get married because we weren't getting any younger."

She burst out laughing. "Sounds like Nana. Although..." She pursed her lips as she narrowed her eyes at me. "I always kind of hoped you'd get together. Every time one of you would break up with someone, I'd tell Dean, maybe it'll happen this time." She shrugged. "Just me being a sap again, I suppose, wanting my friends to fall in love and ride off into the sunset."

"Focus on your own sunset. And Julie and I will always be together, even if it's not the way you guys hoped for."

"Look at the beaming bride. I'm surprised you're up so early."

I swiveled my head toward Julie's voice. Her hair was pulled back in a messy bun, loose hairs falling over her delicate cheekbones as she giggled with Maria.

"How was your night?" Maria asked as she looked between us. "Do anything good?

"Nothing," we both answered too quickly.

Maria stepped back, arching a brow.

"Are you sure *nothing* is all that happened?"

"We went for a walk in the gardens and got some gelato,"

Julie said, shooting me a quick glance. "Nothing too exciting."

"We better get going," I said, lifting Julie's carry-on bag off the floor.

"Landon," Julie sighed and pulled at the strap already on my shoulder. "I can handle it."

"I'm a Southern gentleman now, remember?" I arched a brow at her. A smile twitched at her lips before she conceded.

"Enjoy your honeymoon," I told Maria and kissed her cheek. "My regards to Elvis if you go."

Julie's eyes widened in my periphery. I gave her a tiny shake of my head.

"I will," Maria said before hugging us both goodbye.

"You're not going to carry me on to the plane too, are you?"

"Well," I said with a shrug, "I did forget to carry you over a threshold last night. We should try to keep the traditions where we can, right?" I nodded to her rolling suitcase. "Do you need me to—"

"Remember what I said last night? Yes. Yes, I do."

She grabbed the handle of her suitcase, pursing her lips at me before turning toward the entrance of the hotel. "I appreciate it, but I can still do things. Like roll a suitcase."

"I know you can, Jules. I'm just a pain in the ass who wants to help you as much as he can while he has the chance. You can carry all the bags you want when I'm not around. How's that?"

She turned back, regarding me with a sad smile.

"You're too good for this world sometimes."

I stepped up to her and tapped her chin with my knuckle. "What are best friends for? You lead the way."

I followed her outside to the taxi line, averting my gaze

so I wouldn't be tempted to scrutinize the way she was walking this morning. She seemed well rested and mobile, the opposite of me as I stifled a yawn. Julie eyed me as I climbed into the back of the cab behind her but didn't call me on the shit I probably looked like.

"Looks like my flight is on time. How's yours?" Julie asked as she scrolled through the airline app on her phone.

"Seems like mine is too," I said after checking my phone. "I'm at gate ten."

"I'm at gate twelve." She looked up with a wide grin. "Glad we booked the same airline. We get an extra few minutes together before we head in different directions."

"That's lucky. I thought for sure we'd be at opposite ends of the airport."

She lifted her head, her brown eyes bright and shining as they met mine. "It sucks when you have to go just when I get used to having you around."

"You may have to get used to me being *around* on a regular basis if I move. Hope that won't be a problem."

"It would be the best problem." She cuddled into my side and dropped her head to my shoulder. I shut my eyes and rested my chin on top of her head, enjoying the last moments of quiet together until the car pulled up at the terminal.

A prolonged goodbye wouldn't be any less painful. Watching her board the plane, especially if I caught any discomfort as she made her way inside, wouldn't set me the least bit at ease. But she didn't want me to hover, and I couldn't do any more for her at the moment. Just stay in constant touch and hope her health continued going in the right direction.

"Sundays when you don't have work on Mondays still seem weird. At least I don't have to worry about heading back right after vacation," Julie said as we waited for her flight to board. "Hopefully you can get some sleep on the plane. Doesn't look like you had much last night." She elbowed my side, her eyes narrowing into a scowl.

Once we'd arrived at the gate, we'd found out my flight was scheduled to depart a half hour after hers due to a delay, so I would have to watch her take off. I always hated saying goodbye to her, but as I suspected, this time, it was bordering on excruciating.

But I couldn't tell her that or show it. I'd deal with the still confusing-as-fuck feelings on my own time.

Our heads jumped up at the boarding call for New York.

"Well, this is me."

I turned as Julie stood from her seat and hung the strap of her carry-on bag on her shoulder.

"Oh wow," she mused as her gaze caught on her hand. "We never took our rings off."

I peeked at my left hand, and sure enough, the plain silver band gleamed back at me.

"Maria must have been too high on newlywed bliss to realize," I joked as my eyes fell on her ring when she grabbed the handle of her suitcase.

"I guess so." She lifted her head, a soft smile pulling at her lips when her eyes met mine. "I'll keep it on until I get home. I wouldn't want to lose my fake wedding ring by sticking it in my pocket."

"I guess I will too. So I don't lose it." I tried for an easy smile, the thought of pulling it off my finger too sad for me to ponder or understand.

"I better go before they take off without me," she said with a nervous laugh.

I nodded without a word and pulled her to me, cinching my arms around her as tightly as I could.

"Hey, you'll see me soon. Maybe not in person for a while, but I promise I won't hide my face anymore." Her chuckle vibrated against my chest as she drifted her hand up and down my back.

"You better not." I searched her glossy gaze as all the words I wanted to say got trapped in the back of my throat. "Text me when you land. Have a good flight."

"You too," she said, planting a kiss on my cheek. I was tempted to turn my head to catch her lips, but I kept my gaze forward.

"Talk to you soon, doll."

A laugh escaped me when my lips found her forehead.

"Talk to you soon, darlin'."

I kept my feet rooted to the floor as Julie made her way to the front of the line, scanning her boarding pass and disappearing into the jet bridge.

I always missed her the second we parted ways, but this gnawing in my chest as she left was new. There were a shit-ton of reasons why it seemed as if a piece of me was leaving on that plane, but none that I was ready to face.

12

LANDON

"So, talk to me." Will, one of the VPs and the closest friend I had in Charlotte, settled onto the couch in my office after our Monday morning meeting dispersed.

"About what?" I asked, swiveling my chair away from the computer and wishing I could escape all the work that had piled up because I had the audacity to take off on a Friday.

"Your weekend in Vegas? Tell me all about the showgirl you brought back to your room." He waggled his eyebrows.

"I don't think they call them showgirls anymore."

"Hot cocktail waitress, singer, whatever. Please, dude." He dropped his head back and groaned. "I was knee-deep in the Barnes project and need to live vicariously through your exploits this weekend."

"I hate to break your heart, but there were no exploits. I was there with old friends, and there was no time for any debauchery."

"You could have snuck off for a night. Come on."

Will was five years younger than me, and while he worked hard, he played even harder. I still liked a good time, and I couldn't function at my job if I didn't blow off a little steam once in a while, but I hadn't wanted to be anywhere but with Julie this weekend. Something Will wouldn't have understood, and something I was even still making sense of, given that she'd been on my mind since the airport.

"No, I couldn't have. I'm sorry to disappoint you." I almost laughed at the sadness pulling at his features. "I have work to do, and so do you."

"Yeah, I can tell you wasted a weekend in Vegas since you have such a grumpy-ass attitude."

"Again, don't you have work to do?" I asked on a sigh as I reached for my tumbler of coffee.

"So you were at the wedding the whole time? What were you, a third wheel?" He snickered, still not budging.

"No, my best friend Julie and I hung out while the couple went off on their own. I wasn't a third wheel, but I didn't go off and do anything I'd be ashamed of upon my return."

"What a waste," he said on an exaggerated sigh. "Wait, Julie's the hot brunette, right? The one who visited you in January?" He leaned against the doorway of my office, not getting my not-so-subtle hint to leave. "And the one with the long legs who could wear the hell out of a skirt."

He wasn't the first friend to mention how hot Julie was, and it wasn't the first time Will had brought her up since he'd met her.

However, this was the first time I'd wanted to clock him in the jaw for it.

"Yes, that's Julie," I said, pain shooting up the side of my head from the tight clench of my jaw.

"Damn." He crossed his arms, letting a whistle seep through his teeth but still not moving. "How do you hang out with her so much and not hook up with her? You're, like, made of steel or something."

"She's my best friend. That's how. Bye, Will."

"Okay, geez," he said, pushing off the wall. "I know when to take a hint."

"No, you actually don't."

"Fine," he grumbled. "I'll see you later."

I had to laugh when he gave me a mock salute before turning to leave.

I didn't plan on telling anyone other than HR that Julie had been upgraded from best friend to fake wife, but Will's interrogation had me on edge, even if I didn't have far to go.

I'd emailed HR once I got home on Sunday, explaining I had gotten married over the weekend and needed to add my new wife to my insurance plan as soon as possible. Everything was supposed to stay confidential, but a partner traveling to Vegas for a weekend and coming back married would get around the office soon enough.

Julie was so worried about what I'd say to another woman I was dating about our fake marriage, and that was still among the least of my concerns. Once I confirmed that she was covered and there would be no interruption to her care or medications, I didn't care who found out or what they would say.

"Hey, Landon. Sorry to interrupt. Oh hey, Will."

"Nice to see you, Bonnie," Will crooned at Bonnie, one of our HR managers, as he lingered in my doorway. Bonnie was in her sixties, with the company since before the merger, and always had a sweet, motherly way about her. She wore big, rimmed glasses that often dangled on a chain around her neck and didn't dabble in office gossip. I'd breathed a sigh of relief when she'd called first thing this morning to tell me she was taking care of my request personally and—thankfully—hadn't said anything other than congratulations.

"So much paperwork for a Monday morning," Will noted, eyeing the thick folder in Bonnie's hands.

"Go. Back. To. Work."

Will was a good friend, but I had to fight the urge to push him into the hallway to get him to leave.

"It's a tragedy to go to Vegas for a weekend and come back this tense." He shook his head before he finally headed out.

"I took care of everything in the system, but it will take a while for Julie to get her insurance card. She should be able to use the group ID number in the meantime, but here's a paper she could show a doctor or pharmacist to process."

"Thanks, Bonnie," I breathed out, the relief already palpable, as I plucked the folder from her hands. "And thanks for getting on this so quickly," I said, lowering my voice in case anyone was out in the hallway.

"Of course. I hear we're probably losing you soon when that New York branch opens." She regarded me with a sad smile. "Good to be closer to your wife, though, I'm sure."

"Nothing is definite yet, but yes. It would be good to be close." And it would be, just not for the reasons Bonnie was probably thinking. Or maybe it wasn't that different, because being away from my "wife" had made me a grumpy bastard from the time I'd gotten out of bed this morning.

"I'll let you get back to your day. Again, if you or your wife have any questions at all, please let me know." She squeezed my arm before heading out the door. "And congratulations again."

"Thank you," I said, holding in a cringe at the swiveled heads I'd noticed behind her. Since my promotion to partner and a lot of staff moving between offices, with the exception of Will, I considered most of the people I worked with as friendly acquaintances. I still didn't care who knew, but I didn't feel like explaining anything. I couldn't tell the truth of why we were married, but no one needed an in-depth explanation if they asked. I got married. My wife was in New York. End of story.

I made it a point not to date anyone I worked with, but most of the women I'd met over the years had been through coworkers. I doubted I'd get the same requests to meet a single friend of someone once word got out that I was married, but not only did I not care about that, I had no interest.

That realization was what had me the most on edge and snapping at Will and probably anyone else who would pry about the details of my weekend trip.

I'd deal with my fucked-up head later. In the meantime, I welcomed the distraction from the mountain of work I was about to dive into.

Before I set my phone on Do Not Disturb, I shot Julie a quick text.

Me: *Good morning, wife. Looks like you're all set. I'll email you the paper you can use for doctors' visits and prescriptions until your insurance card comes.*

Julie: *Thanks, doll. Can you talk, or are you busy?*

I pressed the call button and brought the phone to my ear without thinking twice.

"Hey, I'm sorry to bother you on a Monday."

"Are you okay?"

"Landon." Her soft sigh filled my ear. "I'm fine. I wanted

to thank you before you got too busy. And maybe I have a little husband separation anxiety."

A laugh fell from my lips and relaxed me. Maybe that was the root of my agitation this morning. Julie and I had gone through an intense couple of days, and both of us were still acclimating to all that had happened. And almost happened. Our wedding kiss still lived rent-free in my head and replayed on a loop whenever I closed my eyes.

"I may have a little of that. What are you doing this morning?"

"Meeting with a freelance creative recruiter on Zoom in about an hour and figuring out what top to wear so my boobs don't take over the conversation."

"They are pretty loud."

"Tell me about it." Her easy laugh was literal music to my ears. "I'll let you go be a big shot. I just wanted to thank you since I wouldn't have been able to consider this if you didn't wife me up."

"*Wife* you up?" I snickered. "Is that what the kids say now?"

"I think. I'm too old to know. And maybe I texted you because I wanted to hear your voice."

I rolled away from my computer and leaned back in my chair. Her voice soothed me right back, especially when I noticed some energy in it. The consuming worry had been in the back of my mind since she'd told me about her diagnosis, and I didn't expect it to ease anytime soon. The lilt in her voice eased some of the frayed nerves I'd left Vegas with, if only for the moment.

"My voice is all yours whenever you want to hear it. Can I call you on my way home?"

"Sounds good, doll."

A smile ran across my mouth. I went from lusting after

her in person to mooning over her from a distance—and both needed to stop.

"Good luck, darlin'. Not that you'll need it."

"Oh, I need it," she said with a chuckle. "But thanks."

After four meetings and hours of catching up on email tasks, I felt the crick in my neck tell me I was done. My tired eyes read 4:45 in the lower right of my screen, and I was just about to text Will about a quick drink after work when a call came through from reception that someone was here to see me.

I opened my calendar and scanned the meetings for the day. There was nothing after three, and I had no clients scheduled until later in the week. I stood, wondering who would just drop in at almost five on a Monday.

"I never thought I would have to ask to see my son."

My head whipped around at my father's voice.

"Dad, what the hell are you doing here? Is everything okay?"

A slow grin spread across his face before he pulled me into a hug. We spoke a few times per week, but it had been months since I'd seen my father in person. I'd planned to make a trip over the next couple of weeks but never expected him to beat me to it.

"Everything is great. You were too busy to come to me, so I came to you. Let me look at you." He grabbed my arms and pushed me back, scanning my face. "You look good, kid. Tired but good. Must have been some wedding."

I shrugged, ignoring the odd twinge of something in my gut when he said *wedding*.

"I'm tired from a long day, but..." I trailed off, studying him right back. "I didn't expect you."

"Because that's how you plan a surprise. Does a big executive like you have time for dinner with your old man?"

"Always. There's a decent bar and grill across the street if you're up for that."

"Sounds good to me." He squeezed my shoulder. "You look different."

"Different?" I squinted back at him.

"Well, you're bigger." He crinkled his nose and pinched my bicep. "But something else. You can tell me at dinner. Come on."

I grabbed my jacket and keys and locked my office door behind us. My mother used to tease us about how alike we always looked, like a before and after version of identical twins. We both stood out above any crowd at well over six feet, and when I wasn't weight lifting my problems away, he had the same frame and build as me, even at almost seventy.

The big difference between us was his hair, now a lot more salt than pepper, but I'd noticed the dots of gray along my temples multiply over the past year.

He'd been to Charlotte before, but this was the first time he'd ever visited me at the office, and he'd never come without giving me a heads-up first. We made small talk as we made our way to the restaurant, and I replied with short answers, all the while trying to figure out the real reason for his visit. I didn't doubt he missed me, but something was up.

"I have some news," he said after we found a table.

"Ah, I had a feeling." I set down my menu and leaned back. I expected good news, judging by his beaming smile and the gleam in his dark eyes. At least, I hoped it was good since I couldn't handle more bad news, this time from the other most important person in my life.

"There's someone I'd like you to meet." He raised a brow, awaiting my reply as the waitress breezed by the table to take our order.

"I've never been here before," Dad said and jutted his chin to me. "I trust him enough to get what he gets."

The waitress laughed as she turned to me.

"Cheeseburger deluxe, medium, with the IPA on tap."

I handed her the menus and turned back to my father when she walked away.

"You came all the way here to tell me that you have a girlfriend?"

My mother had been sick for a year, but to us, it still seemed as if she'd died suddenly. Dad and I had been catatonic for weeks after. Julie had pulled me out of it, but Dad had kept mostly to himself those first few months and didn't take his wedding ring off for years.

"You're sure it doesn't bother you?"

My father searched my gaze, his brows knit together as he thanked the waitress when she brought our drinks.

"Why would it bother me? You deserve happiness, Dad. And Mom would totally agree. It's about time you dated someone." I grinned as I lifted the glass and took a healthy pull. Even though it had been a long time, the thought of my father with someone other than my mother was still something I would have to get used to, just like I had to keep reminding myself that my best friend was my new wife. I took a second and longer swig at that reminder.

"I've dated," he said, lifting the glass to his lips. "This is fantastic. Is it local?"

"It is. It's a company called Lady Luck. That's usually what's on tap here."

Julie had loved that beer when she'd tasted it the last time she came to visit me, and now that we had gotten fake married in Las Vegas, the name had a weird resonance.

"Anyway, like I said, I've dated. I just didn't tell you."

"Oh," I said, more to myself than him. I should have realized that, but the thought gave me more pause than I expected. "You could have told me."

He shook his head.

"I'd only tell you if I met someone worth introducing to you. The women I dated were nice but no one I wanted to meet my son."

"Sounds serious."

His slow grin more than confirmed how serious it was.

"It is. I..." He darted his eyes from mine for a moment. "I want to ask her to marry me."

I sputtered a mouthful of beer and set down the glass.

"That's...that's amazing, Dad. Congratulations."

"Well, I didn't ask her yet. I wanted to come down here first."

"What, to ask my permission?" I coughed out a laugh.

"To tell you in person, I guess. I didn't expect this to happen either, but everything in its own time, right?"

"Absolutely. Now I really can't wait to meet the woman who has you this happy and unshaven."

"Thanks, son." He rubbed his almost full beard. "That means a lot. Anything good you can tell me? Other than you're ruling the place?"

"I'm not ruling the place. Not quite C-suite yet."

"Seem pretty damn important to me. You're doing so well down here. I miss you, but I'm glad you're happy."

"I won't be here for much longer. They're opening up a New York branch. It was all speculation until today. They haven't made a formal offer yet, but they want me to run it. Soon, you won't have to miss me that much."

"Wow, that is great news." Dad's smile grew even wider. "I bet your friends will be thrilled. Julie, especially. How's she doing?"

"She's sick."

All the elation evaporated from the table as Dad fell back against his seat with wide eyes.

"What's wrong? It's not...like your mother?"

"No, not that. Thank God, but it's still serious. She has lupus. She's been sick since January and now she's feeling better with treatment, but it's still there."

"I worked with a woman with lupus. It's tough. I'm glad to hear she's feeling better. Is she still able to work?"

"Yes, but she was just laid off."

"Shit. That poor kid. And when you're laid off, insurance is an arm and a leg. I'll make a call when I get back home and see if I can help her."

"A call?"

"Remember I did this for a living? I worked in health care and insurance. I wasn't an executive like you, but I still have some friends." He arched a brow and rested his elbows on the table. "There's coverage she can get that's good and at a low premium, but you need to know where to look and who to speak to."

"She's got insurance."

"Well, that's a relief. Is it part of her severance? I know that our layoff packages had that included for a while—"

"I married her, Dad."

Until I blurted it out, I'd had no idea how much I'd needed to tell someone. Or maybe I needed my father's advice or approval, or some kind of assistance to drag me out of this torturous headspace I'd wandered into.

When he looked up, his face was stoic. No shock, no anger, no hurt. His non-reaction unnerved me.

"You married her? In Vegas? After Dean and Maria got married?"

"Yes. So she can have my insurance. I put the paperwork in today. She has a big mortgage to pay on her own, so now she doesn't have to worry about paying for insurance because she's covered under me."

Dad was silent as the waitress brought our food over to the table.

"We're still friends. It's just an arrangement."

"An arrangement," he said slowly, his eyes narrowing as they met mine.

"Yes, she's in New York. I'm here, for now. I couldn't let her go home with no insurance. I'm still worried sick about her, but at least she has that."

"That's noble of you, and I know the two of you have always been close, but what happens when you both start seeing someone else? A marriage of convenience can't be easy to explain."

"Dating is the least of my concerns. All that matters to me is Julie, and I don't care about anything or anyone else."

"I know, son," he said, examining me as a tiny smile drifted across his mouth.

"You seem like you have something else to say."

He shook his head, his eyes flicking to me as he picked up his burger and took a bite.

"I don't," he mumbled into his napkin. "I'll wait for your brain to catch up to your actions."

"I don't know what that means."

He stilled as he was about to take another bite and set the burger back down on his plate.

"When we talk about your mother, we don't speak of that time right after she died. I was a mess, and you took care of everything. Something I'll never forgive myself for."

"Dad, it was fine—"

"No, it wasn't. Your mother would have kicked my ass, but that's not the point of the story. I couldn't help you like I should have, but I'd watch you, wondering when you'd finally cry. Family even pulled me aside to ask why you hadn't shed a tear. I knew it was because you didn't want to make me feel worse by seeing you upset, but I didn't really answer any of them. Julie stayed at our house the weekend after everyone went home."

"I remember," I said, memories flashing through my mind of how I didn't let her go for ten minutes once she came in the door, but I didn't say a word to her or anyone.

"When I'd finally snapped out of it a little and went downstairs to find you, you were sobbing in Julie's lap. She was the only one able to get through to you and the only one you wanted. I was always grateful to her for that."

"So, you get it. We're best friends. I help her the way she helps me."

"Oh, I get it, son." He nodded, a sad smile pulling at his lips. "But you don't."

"Not you too." I let my head fall back against the booth. "We are *friends*. And I did this for her because I could, because I wanted to."

"I will drop it. And I am glad you were able to make sure she has insurance. But keep in mind that the universe only gives you so many tries." He held up his hands. "But we're here to celebrate, not argue. When do you move back?"

"They want to move fast. So maybe in a couple of weeks, they'll send me up just to look for an apartment and check out the office space. It's a small office. We'll all mostly be remote for a while."

"When you come up, we'll all have dinner and you can meet Darlene. Bring my daughter-in-law."

"Sure," I laughed and picked at the fries, mulling over what my father said. "She'd love to see you."

Was that why I couldn't get Julie out of my head? Why everyone else always assumed we were together when we weren't? My brain was fully aware of my actions. I'd married Julie because I loved her. Because I couldn't imagine my life without her.

"Are you all right, son?" Dad asked me around a mouthful of burger. "You look like something just slammed into you."

"I'm fine," I said, clearing my throat as I reached for my beer, taking a long gulp before the next puzzle piece slid into place, and I had no choice but to see the whole picture.

13

JULIE

"I never thought I'd be so happy to be on a Zoom call."

I laughed, both at my friend Kaitie's beaming smile in her video thumbnail and how sadly true it was. The meeting with the recruiter went well, and for the first time since the layoff, my professional life didn't seem as bleak. I planned to pay bills this afternoon and balancing my checkbook would probably suck that joy right out of me, but it was nice to be hope*ful* instead of *less* for once.

As I was gathering my portfolio and references to send to the recruiter as a follow-up, my former boss had texted me to see if I was available for the next few weeks to work on a project with our old team. It was part time, but the hourly rate was decent, and we would all work remotely. I'd texted back yes before I'd even finished reading his message, so grateful to grasp back a tiny piece of normal, even if it was temporary.

The positive shift in energy today had a smile plastered on my face too. I welcomed the new purpose and distraction from thinking about my fake husband and dissecting why I swooned over his "Good morning, wife" text. We'd been texting each other good morning on most days for years, and Landon and I didn't swoon over each other.

But we also hadn't done a lot of things before this weekend.

I'd need more than a single night's sleep to acclimate to it all, although I was hopeful that would do the trick. For the moment, I'd attribute the butterflies during our phone call this morning to an aftershock of kissing for the first time and getting fake married.

The kissing affected me more than the notion I had a husband in North Carolina that no one knew about. We agreed the marriage was an arrangement, and it was all a joke until I had the best kiss of my life after I said I do.

After my colleagues and I were briefed on the project, we all spent the rest of the time catching up. Kaitie and Sierra were my favorite designers to work with. I had been their supervisor at our old job, but we were friends and had a good dynamic when we'd worked together. I missed the days of drinks after work before I'd become...who I was now.

I'd decided to stop using the word *sick* after I came home yesterday. Sick was what I'd been back in February. Now I was just different. But different didn't have to mean less.

I needed to stop living behind the boundaries I'd created for myself. Yes, I had limits and new things to worry about, but none of that applied today. I'd do my best to push that off to the side until it did.

Healthwise, I felt great and more like myself than I had in a long time. I was thrilled to be able to work from home, but seeing my coworkers again gave me wistful memories of overpriced Manhattan lunches and gossip over Starbucks runs.

"Sorry, I'm late!"

A new thumbnail popped up, and Elyse's face filled the screen. I stifled a groan as I caught Sierra's quick eye roll. Elyse was also on our old team and a decent designer, but she was just so...much. She always had drama and an issue that she had to come in late or leave early for but would brag about the little work she'd managed to do. I'd snapped at her when I was feeling really ill to just do her job without telling everyone how great she was at it, and I'd had to endure a long call with HR afterward about managing different personalities and how some were more sensitive than others.

"I told Frank I'd join you guys later since I had a call about another job. I just can't keep up with all the interviews after posting to only one site last week! I mean, I'm so grateful, but it's tiring."

Before Elyse joined the call, we'd been discussing how job searching online felt like shouting into a void where no one could hear you. But of course, her résumé was the golden key that unlocked all the opportunities.

When she'd talk about the breaks she'd get or accolades at work from executives, I'd wanted to believe she was lying. But as my grandpa used to tell me, fortune didn't always reward the worthy, so you needed to make your own luck.

I was recovering from a bout of crappy luck courtesy of fortune, but thanks to the positive turn my Monday had taken, I was in a generous mood and indulged her despite myself.

"That's fantastic," I said with as much enthusiasm as I could muster without being nauseated. "I assume Frank filled you in. We were just discussing how to divide and conquer."

"Yes, and he already told me what I'd be doing. Just wanted to check in with you guys." She scooted closer to the camera, a bright light offscreen illuminating her saccharine smile.

"We're all doing well. I was about to tell Julie how fantastic she looked," Sierra said as we shared an on-screen grin. I appreciated her compliment and change of subject.

"Sierra is right," Kaitie said. "I know you weren't feeling well for a while, but you look healthy and gorgeous now."

"Thanks, ladies." My cheeks heated a bit at the compliments, and it felt good to allow them to sink in. I'd gone up two clothes sizes, but I'd seen health, not a moon face, when I'd put on my makeup this morning. I was easing back into light morning workouts, but the extra weight didn't bother me anymore.

Fixating on the physical changes of lupus seemed shallow, but when I was feeling terrible, seeing the visible effects on the outside made it even more devastating. Now that the insides were mostly sorted out, the outside didn't look so bad to me.

Of course, maybe my boost of confidence could have come from when I'd caught Landon checking me out a few times with a more than friendly appreciation. Wherever it came from, the sun was shining brighter in the Bronx today, and I was rolling with it.

"You do look a lot better," Elyse said as she pursed her lips at the screen. "What was it, a bad flu?"

"No, flus eventually end." I huffed out a laugh. "I have lupus. It's an autoimmune disease, but with treatment, it seems to be under control and I'm feeling well these days. I just need to learn to rest more or I pay for it after, but it's a process."

"I'm so sorry," Sierra said, concern creasing her brow. "Autoimmune diseases can be so rough, and I'm so glad you're feeling better."

"Me too," Kaitie agreed.

"I have lupus."

We all flinched at Elyse's statement.

"You do?" I asked.

"Oh yes. I get tired a lot and need a ton of rest. So if I'm a little late for the first part of the project, you'll get why."

I hoped she wasn't the type of person to fake a serious illness for attention, and there were degrees of disease. It seemed convenient that she had the same condition I did, and after never mentioning it before when we'd heard her lament for a half hour over a possibly infected hangnail when we were in the office, I couldn't help being skeptical.

No one really knew anything about lupus unless you had it or knew someone who did. It was elusive enough to fake without too much effort. She still looked great—her skin was glowing and her red hair seemed just as thick as the curls cascaded down her shoulders, but appearances meant nothing for symptoms that no one could see. It was the argument I'd had with Nate more times than I cared to recall. I looked fine, so why wasn't I fine?

"If you're going to be late, just let us know," I said. The freedom of a freelance job meant that while I had to be civil, I didn't have to placate. I wouldn't dismiss anyone for not looking sick after being dismissed myself, and I would give her the benefit of the doubt despite my suspicions. But if I pulled my weight, truthful diagnosis or not, so could she.

Lupus was still the monster lurking around the corner, but I was grateful for all it had taught me so far about people, patience, and the order of importance in life.

Elyse changed the vibe of the call enough for us to end it quickly after going over the project details. My fingertips tingled with the possibility of creating again. That was the best part of my job, even on the boring projects. Turning a client's request into a tangible thing I made from scratch made me feel alive, and to get a glimpse of that again, even for a part-time project, was nothing short of wonderful.

I hoped to do that with my house. After Nate left, my goal was to decorate it the way I'd originally wanted to, maybe even make my own wallpaper borders. But I didn't want to get too attached to it if I had to move. Things seemed to be heading in the right direction today, but it wasn't something I could count on long-term. Rent for an apartment would be a more manageable expense and would make the most sense, but I couldn't bring myself to contact a real estate agent yet.

Instead of using my spare bedroom, I'd made an office out of the alcove next to my kitchen. It was my favorite part of the house and what had sold me after viewing so many listings. Nate had wanted to move out of the city, but I liked the neighborhood I'd grown up in and the easy access to public transportation to travel back and forth to my office in Manhattan.

I peeked out my screen door and found Oliver, my neighbor from across the street and my friend Karen's husband, cutting the grass in my yard. Karen was one of the few who'd seen me in my early days of illness and one of the few who knew about my diagnosis. Nate had helped at first around the house when I could barely move, but once I looked better, he had constant excuses as to why he couldn't do more at home, not really *being* home much toward the end anyway. Karen would often stop by for a "visit" and clean my house.

She was a new friend, only moving on to the block last year, but our lack of history made it easier for me to confide in her. She cared about me and worried about me but wouldn't be so quick to shut down my fears for the future because she couldn't handle thinking about it. She simply listened and encouraged without sugarcoating it or offering a solution to make us both feel better, like my mother tended to do and I was sure Landon would if I told him how dark my fears would get on tough days.

Her manner was something I appreciated more than I could ever express.

In addition to being a safe space to talk to, she was an occupational therapist, and her suggestions for kitchen utensils when my hands were too painful to work and ways to stretch and move my body when every joint was screaming at me were a godsend some days.

I waved through the mesh screen when he spotted me and sat back down at my desk to shoot his wife a text.

Me: *Your husband wandered over here again.*

Karen: *Good. Keep him.*

Me: *This is nice, but he doesn't have to keep doing this. At least let me pay him.*

Karen: *I'm sure cutting your grass is the highlight of his morning. He can escape the retirement to-do list that I make for him every day.*

Oliver was a recently retired cop, and judging by the smile on his face when he'd spotted me, I guessed he really was content to be away from his house and his wife's list of chores.

Karen: *And you are not paying him. Don't offer again, or I'll get pissed.*

Me: *But I've got a job now. Sort of. Freelance project for a bit.*

Karen: *That's great! I'll be over this week with some wine to help you celebrate.*

Karen: *And you're still not paying him.*

Downloading all the files and setting up my part of the project took up most of the afternoon, and before I knew it, it was after eight. I climbed up my stairs with a little disappointment at not hearing from Landon, but he was always pulled into last-minute meetings and left work at all hours. It would probably be more of the same if he moved back, but knowing he was close would put me more at ease.

Because he was my best friend. Not the fake husband I was lusting over half the time and talking myself out of any non-friend feelings for the other half.

Instead of lying on the couch and passing out until I trudged to bed at two a.m., I brought my laptop up to my bedroom to find a movie to watch. I'd still pass out, but at least this time, I would already be in bed. The energy I had today was too precious to burn out.

My phone buzzed with a text right after I'd settled under the covers.

Landon: *Sorry it's late. FaceTime?*

I glanced down at my tank top and shorts. I slept in a bralette under my shirts, loose enough to be comfortable but still kept my fuller-than-usual breasts from flopping around as I tossed and turned. I sifted my ponytail holder out of my hair and combed my fingers through the tangles.

Landon had seen me at much worse, as he'd been the

one to hold my hair back as I'd puked on more drunken nights in college than I wanted to think about, and looking pretty for him shouldn't have mattered.

Me: *Yes.*

I texted back with one hand as I applied tinted lip gloss with the other, and I would deal with how disgusted I was with myself later.

My laptop chirped as soon as I straightened against my headboard. A happy rush of air whooshed out of me as Landon's face filled my screen.

"I'm sorry it's late. I was going to call you on the way home, but I had news I wanted to tell you in person."

"Oh?" I scooted under the covers and brought the screen closer. I recognized the black headboard in Landon's bedroom from the last time I'd visited, so he was in bed too.

I was in bed with Landon.

Jesus, I needed to stop this.

He'd removed his contacts and adjusted his black wire-framed glasses as his mouth curved into a smile. He hated his glasses, but I always thought they brought out his sharp jaw and cheekbones. I hadn't seen him in glasses in a while, and with the sparkles of gray I spotted in his tousled hair, they brought him from handsome to unfairly stunning. His broad chest stretched the gray Fordham University T-shirt he'd had since we graduated. I was impressed that it hadn't fallen apart, especially as his new muscles pulled at the old seams.

Not that I noticed. Or kept noticing.

"I think it's good news, or it looks like it." I crinkled my nose and let out a relieved breath when Landon laughed.

"It is, and it's in two parts. The first one, the New York

branch is a go, and they gave me an informal promise of an offer today."

"Holy shit!" I gasped. I'd hoped he was moving back, but the confirmation was still a happy shock. "Landon, that is so great. Congratulations."

"Thanks." His crooked grin killed me. I wished I could leap into the screen and launch myself into his arms. "I'm honestly a little nervous. It's the same job, but running the office, even if it's small and will be mostly remote at first, is a little scary of an idea."

"You are going to be amazing." I crossed my arms and rolled my eyes. "Like you always are at everything."

"Am I?" His lips curled into a smirk.

"Are you fishing for compliments?" I cracked up at his slow shrug.

"I'm having a needy moment. You're supposed to be my best friend, and that means it's your job to blow smoke up my ass when I'm feeling low."

I narrowed my eyes with a groan. I didn't remember Landon getting anything less than an A- in college, and I'd lost count of his promotions after graduation. His needy moment was cute, even if I was annoyed he'd brought up thoughts of his ass.

"You are the smartest, most successful person I know, and the New York office is only the beginning."

He pursed his lips, leaning against the headboard with the back of his head resting on his hand. Landon usually took that position during video chats, but it had been a long time since we'd had one. Even though I used to tease him about his sex god pose, I wasn't used to it anymore, or the fantasies it sparked of me climbing on top of him and tasting the lips I couldn't seem to forget—along with his groan during our kiss that still vibrated through me whenever I'd allow myself to think about it.

Distance was supposed to put a stop to this, not fan the flames. I'd need to figure out a way to compose myself now that he was going to be close enough to touch.

"That's it?" he teased.

"Well," I said with a long sigh. "My job as your best friend is also to keep your ego in check enough that your head isn't too big to board the plane back to New York."

His chest rumbled with a laugh.

"I'm proud of you. I always am, but you still find ways to amaze me."

His grin shrank to a soft smile, and even across the miles, the air still sizzled between us.

"Better?" I asked, arching a brow as I leaned into the screen.

"Yeah," he said with a gravelly whisper. "That was good."

"Okay," I said. "Hit me with part two."

"My father is engaged. Or he will be when he gets back to Connecticut."

"Wait—" My jaw dropped as I adjusted the laptop over my thighs. "Your father is there? And he's getting married? Do you know who she is?"

"Her name is Darlene, and he's in love enough to grow a beard."

"Oh my."

"Exactly. He wouldn't ask her until he told me, so as I was leaving work today, I had a surprise visitor. He told me over dinner."

"Wow, that's a big day. How do you feel about it?"

He shrugged. "I'm happy for him. It's still odd to think of him with anyone other than my mother. Or to know that he's been dating women all this time. He said he didn't want to tell me unless he met someone worth introducing me to."

"Seriously? I hate to break it to you, but your father is a silver fox. I am sure since you left Connecticut, he's dated plenty."

"Ugh, Jules." He scrubbed a hand down his face. "Don't call my father a silver fox."

"A few more gray bristles in your beard and you're heading in that direction, buddy."

"Oh yeah?" He ran his hand over his jaw, brow arched, shooting me a playful scowl. Our friendship was built on teasing back and forth, but the way his dark eyes narrowed at me gave tonight's teasing a much different connotation.

"Like you don't know. Anyway—" I cleared my throat when I noticed the rasp in my voice "—when does New York happen?"

"I'll be up in a few weeks to hopefully sort out an apartment and the office space we're renting. Dad wants you to come to dinner with us to meet Darlene, so I'll let you know what weekend I'll be up."

"He does? I love your dad. I'd be happy to meet her, and yes, I can clear my schedule of doing nothing that day for you."

"I appreciate it," he said. There was the crooked grin again. "How did the recruiter go?"

"Very well, and my old boss contacted me this morning about a part-time freelance project. So things are looking up, finally."

"That's awesome, Jules. See, I told you."

"You did."

"You're feeling okay?" His cocky smile softened as his brow furrowed. The poor guy would always be worried, and I'd made it worse by lying for so long. I would have felt guilty at the way he chewed on his bottom lip if it weren't so hot.

"Yes. Great, actually. I got a ton of sleep yesterday and had a wonderfully productive day. The girls on my old team even commented on how good I looked."

"You're beautiful, Jules. I think I told you that too."

He was the beautiful one. Not only because of his perfect face. He had a big, gorgeous heart he'd pretend was closed but always opened wide for me—every time. Maybe if I'd let him in from the beginning, when I'd first become sick, I wouldn't have taken so long to get the confidence to try to be myself again because he would have pushed me to get there. He loved old me and new me unconditionally, and I'd always felt the same way about him.

As much as I didn't want to see him in this new light—the one that made me not only miss him but made me jealous of the computer across his lap because I wanted to be *that* close to him—it wouldn't turn off.

"Back at you, doll," I teased, getting a chuckle out of him as he shifted on the bed.

"I like seeing your face on-screen again," Landon said, moving his laptop closer.

"Try to give me a little more notice next time. I'll wear the good pajamas."

"I see nothing wrong with *those* pajamas." His eyes flicked to my chest as a flush ran up my neck. I was overattuned to body parts that felt hot or clammy, but this heat had nothing to do with lupus and everything to do with my hot best friend.

"I better get some sleep. I'm on a good energy streak of one day, trying to go for two."

"Yes. That's important. I'll text you in the morning."

I set the laptop next to me and turned on my side.

"I admit I got a kick out of my 'Good morning, wife' text."

His wide grin probably matched the one making my cheeks ache.

"Noted. Sweet dreams, darlin'."

I flipped the laptop shut and rolled onto my back.

Before he moved to New York, I needed to find a way to stop falling for my fake husband.

14

JULIE

Landon: *It couldn't hurt to try it, right?*

I groaned, scrolling down to the end of Landon's text with *another* link to an anti-inflammatory diet plan. His new hobby over the past couple of weeks was to search for superfoods or natural supplements that could possibly combat symptoms from autoimmune diseases. This was better than torturing himself with research on lupus complications, but he was driving us both a little nuts.

Landon didn't know how to be helpless. He hated the unexpected and wore himself out researching every potential problem because he'd always insist there was an answer somewhere. That was what had gotten him ahead in his career so quickly. Being told no or that something was impossible to him was issuing a challenge.

There was no magic cure, only maintenance. While he was smart enough to know that a cure didn't exist, it wasn't in him to sit and do nothing about it. I knew this came out of love and I tried to be patient, but I'd poke him with my fork tonight if he scrutinized every piece of food I put in my mouth.

> **Me:** *This is a vegan plan. We've been over this. I cut out a lot of dairy already, but after all I've been through, I don't want to lose bacon too.*

"Why do you have that face?" my mother said as she sat across from me at my dining room table.

She'd lived around the corner from me in the same house I'd grown up in until a couple of years ago. My stepfather, Sean, had found a condo in an over-fifty retirement community about an hour away in Hudson Valley, New York. When I'd been really sick, she'd stayed here most nights until I'd forced her to go home or asked Sean to pick her up. Even after I began to feel better, she still made the drive once per week to *spend the afternoon with me* or, really, to check on me.

Watching me get sicker with no cause or cure for those few months had taken a toll on her. I let her fuss over me when she'd visit, even if it meant biting my tongue for half the time she was here.

Sean had managed to convince her to take a vacation to their time-share in Florida three weeks ago, and then I'd started my freelance job. This was the first afternoon we'd both had free for almost a month. The last time I'd seen her was the day before I left for Dean and Maria's wedding.

And mine.

She'd probably be relieved I had good insurance that I didn't have to pay for, but I didn't know how to make her understand the dynamics of my fake marriage since I didn't quite get it myself.

"Landon keeps sending me anti-inflammatory meal

plans and natural remedies, and he's driving me a little crazy."

She picked up her mug of tea with a soft smile. "That doesn't surprise me. He was always a nice kid."

"He's not exactly a kid." I set my phone aside and shot my mother a wry grin. "We're all almost forty."

She waved a hand at me. "You're all kids to me. And don't be so quick to dismiss natural remedies. I saw something on TV about—"

"Mom, I'm going to stop you right there." I draped my hand over hers. "I already take enough vitamins and supplements to choke a horse and am trying to eat as healthy as I can. Despite what you see on TV and what Landon finds in the far corners of the web, I'll stick with what my doctor tells me."

"It wouldn't hurt to ask your doctor about the possible benefits of a different diet plan. My friend's son went vegan —I think that's the right word—he cut out all meat and dairy, and she said he's never felt better."

"He has lupus?" I raised a brow. I had to laugh at her frustrated inhale.

"He has some kind of inflammation...somewhere."

"That's all Landon has been sending me. Vegan diets that fight inflammation." I crossed my arms. "You both fell down the same hippie rabbit hole. You should check in with each other and consolidate your efforts."

She scowled at my chuckle.

"So, why don't you at least try it? It can't hurt."

"And you both try to sell it the same way." I turned my phone around to show her the screen.

"You can't blame us for worrying about you."

A twinge of guilt poked at my gut as a concerned frown pulled at her mouth.

I couldn't control if people worried about me, and while I appreciated it, it frustrated the hell out of me. I wanted to find my bearings and get back to my life before I had to plan around a chronic illness. Pushing me toward a special diet, or my mother grabbing the dishes out of my hands and washing them before I could even stand up, only reminded me of the limitations I was trying to forget.

But I wasn't the only one afraid of what the future held, and I had to find nicer ways both to set the people I loved at ease and keep them in check. I picked up my phone and scrolled through all the links and screenshots of articles Landon had sent, more guilt washing over me at all his efforts.

Me: *I'm doing all the right things, I swear. I'll talk to my doctor about this, but for now, you need to relax, doll ;)*

Me: *And promise me you won't give me a dirty look if I butter my dinner roll tonight.*

"Sorry, Mom." I reached across the table and squeezed her hand. Her short blond hair was almost white, but that was the only sign of her age to me. Her skin was still flawless, the creases by her eyes her only noticeable wrinkles. I'd always been jealous of her blue eyes, but my brown ones came from my father. He'd passed away when I was six, and fuzzy memories and photos were all I ever remembered.

My mother had stayed single until she'd met Sean when I was twelve. He was more like an uncle than a father to me since I was almost a teenager when we met, but I'd liked him right away. He always treated my mother like a queen, and after all those years as a struggling single mom, she deserved it. They were one of those super couples everyone was jealous of, even in their late sixties.

Landon: *Can't blame me for wanting you healthy, darlin'. I promise I'll back off at dinner.*

"Hmm."

I raised my head from my phone screen and met my mother's scrutinizing gaze.

"Hmm, what?"

"It's just nice to see you smile like that again."

I touched my cheeks on instinct, unaware how wide my grin was while I sparred via text with my best friend.

Another source of constant frustration was how I melted every time Landon called me *darlin'*.

"You must be happy that Landon is moving."

I nodded, ignoring the way she eyed me over the rim of her mug as she took another sip.

"We always kept in touch, but it will be nice to see him in person more than a few times a year. Hopefully. He's a textbook workaholic, but he promised us he'd push for more balance once he's settled here."

Mom darted her eyes around my kitchen and bobbed her head in a slow nod.

"He's still single, right?"

"He is," I sighed, leaning back in my chair. It technically wasn't a lie since Landon and I were only married on paper. This wasn't the first time my mother had made a subtle suggestion about Landon and me possibly being more than friends, but I'd usually shut her down quickly.

It had been easier to dismiss the idea of Landon and me as lovers instead of friends when I hadn't been trying to shake these not-so-friendly feelings for him. Now, intrusive visions of us together blossomed in my brain faster than I could reason them away. While I complained about the natural remedies he'd been trying to push on the daily, I loved knowing that I was probably on his mind as much as he was on mine.

I loved *and* hated it, as having Landon and his annoyingly adorable self close by was going to get dangerous if I didn't get rid of these new feelings. We'd always spoken often, but since Vegas, we talked all the time. Whenever we'd FaceTime, we'd stay on for an hour or more, talking about nothing, with more than a little flirting back and forth.

I'd hang up equal parts happy, dizzy, and panicked.

"He cares about you a lot," Mom said, pulling me out of my Landon musings.

"I care about him too," I said, clenching my eyes shut for a moment when I caught the defensive edge in my voice. "We've been best friends for years."

At the core, we'd always be best friends. But best friends shouldn't have the urge to slip their hand down their panties one late and shameful night when the memory of kissing the other best friend flashed in their mind.

Once upon a time, I'd giggle thinking of having sex with Landon and blow it off as ridiculous. Now, nothing about it was even a little funny.

"Is it so bad if it turns into more?" Mom asked.

"Yes. No. I mean..." I raked my hand through my hair and dropped my head onto my table. "I love him. Too much to make things complicated and end up losing my best friend. I couldn't function without him in my life."

Mom's eyes narrowed as she tilted her head.

"Which one of us are you trying to convince?"

"Both?" I allowed, giving her a sad smile and wimpy shrug when I lifted my head.

"If you want my opinion, which you probably don't—" she rose from the table and came over to where I'd buried my head again into the crook of my elbow "—I think you have Landon for life, whether you take a chance on more or not. But a risk could mean something wonderful." I peered up at her hopeful smile. "I'm just saying."

I laughed to myself as she set her mug in the sink. My mother was trying to convince me to be more than friends with my fake husband. There was either a sad or poetic irony to what my life had become in such a short time.

"I'll head out so that you can get ready for dinner. Where is Landon's father taking you?"

"Somewhere by the Seaport downtown." I pushed off my chair to walk her out. "I'm trying to figure out what to wear."

"Ah, dress warm. It's always colder by the water," she told me as she shrugged on her jacket. "The air is starting to get a chill from the fall."

"I will take a jacket." I opened my front door and leaned against it.

"Have a good time," she said, clutching on to my elbow as if it was an order.

I laughed and nodded. "I will, Mom." I waved to Sean after he pulled up to the front of my curb. "Safe drive back." I kissed her cheek while she worried her bottom lip between her teeth as if she had a lot more to say. For this one time, I was relieved she decided to head to her husband's car instead of giving her daughter another lecture and a nudge.

After they drove away, I headed upstairs to get ready. I'd treated myself to new clothes this week. I needed shirts that buttoned for client presentations and job interviews once this project ended, but I couldn't resist a sleeveless gray suede dress with an empire waist that celebrated my new curves instead of bunching up in all the wrong places. I was thrilled when I stumbled upon a cute pair of flat, knee-high boots comfortable enough to walk in deep in my closet. It was only mid-September, but the temperature was supposed to drop enough for me to get away with suede and boots for a night.

I stepped up to my bathroom mirror, smiling when I spotted a deeper contour of cheekbones. New me was starting to look like the old me, and I didn't mind the slight difference as much.

This was a night out with my best friend and his father, men I'd known for half my life. The flutters in my belly were most likely from the simple joy of slipping on a new dress and feeling pretty for the first time in what seemed like too long to remember.

I'd been afraid to look forward to things, but now that I was starting to gather the pieces of my life back, I'd found something else I was afraid to look forward to, or to want as much as I did.

Landon was my person and always the highlight of my days, just like when we were in college. Something was happening, and everything was about to change. Or maybe it already had.

15

JULIE

"What's Darlene like?" I asked Landon as he drove down the West Side Highway toward downtown Manhattan.

"I only met her briefly last night. They were both just finishing up dinner when I got there, but I spoke to her for a little bit before she went home," Landon said with a shrug as he kept his eyes on the road. "She seems nice. I get the feeling she either lives there or just about. The bathroom is loaded with stuff I know doesn't belong to my father. I told Dad that she didn't have to leave just because I'm staying there for a few days, but he waved me off without a straight answer."

"Wow. How long have they been together?"

"A few months, at least in the serious sense since this is the first time he's brought her up to me. She's younger than he is, but not younger than us. That would have been a little weird." His face twisted in a grimace.

"Good for him. And good for you for taking this so well. I know this is a little tough."

He smiled when I massaged his neck.

"I don't know about tough. I never liked the thought of Dad being alone, and I worried about him when I moved, which was why I tried to travel back and forth whenever I could." He shot me a wry grin at a red light. "Although from what he alluded to about dating, he was probably glad for the empty house after I was gone."

I laughed at the arch in his brow.

"I think, while Mr. Clark wasn't a monk, he didn't have a revolving door either. He has that sweet goodness that you do. I can't see him ever being a jerk to the women he dated."

"I have a sweet goodness?" He flicked his eyes to me as we turned into the restaurant parking lot, his mouth curving up.

I turned my gaze to the Hudson River, trying to channel the tranquility of the slow ripples in the water and blink away my fixation on my best friend's mouth.

"What I meant was," I said, turning back to his smirk, "you're both good guys. It sounds like Darlene makes him happy, and I'm very glad."

"Me too." He nodded. "Thanks for coming with me tonight."

"Of course. It was so nice of your father to invite me. I haven't seen him in so long, he may not recognize me."

"You're just as gorgeous as always." His eyes roamed my body for a split second, enough for the heat in his gaze to singe my skin. "Especially in that dress."

My cheeks heated as I pulled at the hem of my dress. It hadn't seemed so short until I sat down.

"It's shorter than I wanted." I reached for my purse, looking away to bring down the uptick in my pulse from the husky dip in Landon's voice. "Sitting down makes it drift up my thick thighs. Hopefully the tablecloth is long," I joked as heat ran up my neck.

That was also something new. Maybe this was the voice he used with women who weren't me, and although I'd watched him date other women for as long as I'd known him and had attended his wedding, the thought triggered a jolt of jealousy.

"I treated myself, even though I should still be saving every cent while I'm working on this project." I let out a nervous laugh as I stepped out of his car.

I adjusted my purse strap and straightened my black denim jacket after I closed the door, gulping in a couple of breaths to clear my head. The one person in this world who never made me nervous was Landon, and I hated being this flustered in his presence.

"Ready?" I asked and gestured to the restaurant entrance.

He nodded, his long legs eating up the distance between us in two steps. He wore a black jacket over a button-down gray shirt and black pants, and thanks to the memory of his ass in pants just like that in the hotel hallway at the Bellagio, I was looking too forward to the moment he turned around.

"I would have asked you to come with me anyway." Landon framed my face. "You're my person." He grinned, his smile wide and beautiful, as he held my eyes.

"Same," I said, clearing my throat after I croaked out my reply.

"You look beautiful tonight—and healthy. So I won't ask you how you're feeling today and nag you."

"You don't nag me..." I trailed off when he raised a brow. "Maybe a little. But I love that I have a best friend who takes time out of his busy corporate executive life to send me links for special diets."

A slow smile crept across his lips and stole a little air from my lungs.

Landon had never taken my breath away before the events of the last couple of months, but maybe that was because I was never driven to look at him so closely. Once I had the motivation to direct my focus, everything about him was amazing enough to both astound and confuse me.

"I always have time when it comes to you. And I'm glad that in a few weeks we can see each other in person more. Not that I don't enjoy FaceTime, but not the same."

"Me too." I grabbed his wrists to give him a gentle nudge before I pushed him away, but I didn't. Neither of us moved, our feet stuck on the concrete of the parking lot as our gazes stayed locked.

"And thank you," I whispered. "It's been a long time since I've felt beautiful and healthy. So, tonight is nice for a lot of reasons."

"Yeah, it is," he said. And there was that husky whisper again. Was this a side effect of my weakened immune system? Did I lose some kind of innate resolve when it came to Landon? Yes, I'd always thought he was attractive but I had never been so distracted by his mouth or his eyes or where his skin touched mine.

My insides went soft like jelly as I wished for that superpower back.

I kissed his cheek, breathing in the familiar scent of his cologne and letting my lips graze his stubbled jaw as I pulled away.

"So, let's find your father and eat. And remember what I said. No stink eye if I order meat or dairy."

He laughed when I narrowed my eyes. The air became lighter between us when he dropped his hands. Still charged, but easier to breathe and hopefully get through dinner.

"I think this place is known for seafood," Landon said as

we made our way to the entrance. "Fish has Omega-3, and that's good for—"

I stepped in front of him and pressed my finger to his lips.

"Stop. I may get fish, or I may get a steak. And you're not going to say anything either way."

He smiled against the pad of my finger, and all I wanted was to grab the back of his neck and taste the soft lips I couldn't stop thinking about.

This was going to be a long dinner.

I did my best to shake it off as we strolled into the restaurant. I spotted Landon's father right away, sitting with a stunning brunette at a table by the window.

They were huddled together, his arm draped over her shoulders as she laughed at something he said. I turned my head and snuck a smile at Landon. It was a little strange for me to see Mr. Clark with anyone, too. When I'd met Landon's mother while we were in college, she was already sick, but she had such a wonderful spirit. She was a sweetheart, just like her son, and I used to wish someone would look at me the way Mr. Clark always looked at his wife.

"There they are." Mr. Clark stood and made his way around the table to greet us. "I'll introduce you ladies after Julie gives me a hug."

I laughed when he opened his arms.

"It's so great to see you, Mr. Clark," I said as he pulled me in for a hug. "Thank you for inviting me tonight."

"First of all," he said as he pushed me back. "Like I always tell you, stop calling me Mr. Clark. You're old enough to call me Gavin."

I shook my head. "I don't think I am."

He chuckled and looped his arm across my shoulders. The close resemblance Landon shared with his father always spooked me. They had the same sharp jaw and dark eyes and were both over six feet tall with broad shoulders. The Clark men were genetically blessed.

Darlene beamed next to him, her hazel eyes shining. Her dark hair was cut into a short bob with sideswept bangs, and she wore a green sweater dress over her slim frame. I agreed with Landon about her age. I guessed she was in her early fifties at the most with her flawless olive skin.

"I'm so glad to finally meet you," Darlene said, extending her arms. "I'm a hugger, and we're pretty much family."

I laughed and hugged her back, my chest pinching a bit when she called us family. I guessed I was family to Landon and his father on a couple of levels. Landon and I had been friends since we were in college, and according to the marriage license no one knew about, I was her fiancé's daughter-in-law.

I'd considered Landon my family for almost two decades, which made how attracted I was to him lately all the more confusing and frightening.

"I'm so happy to meet you too," I said after we pulled away. I caught the sparkle of her engagement ring when Mr. Clark drew her into his side and she drifted her hand down his chest.

"And congratulations. I'm so happy for both of you."

"We're happy for us too," Mr. Clark teased. "Now that introductions are over, come sit." He motioned to the empty seats across from where they were sitting.

"Gavin and Landon told me that you're a very talented graphic designer," Darlene said after she handed us the menus already on the table. "I used to be a copywriter for an agency for many years. Is agency life still as awful as I remember? I mean, I always loved the work. The hours, not so much."

I nodded in agreement.

"My old agency was like that sometimes, especially after I was promoted to creative director. I've been working on a freelance project now, so I agree about loving the work and hating the hours."

"I did freelance for years and loved it. I would work on a few different projects from different clients at once, and the variety and flexibility were amazing. Insurance can get expensive when you're freelance, but I never went back to full time after that."

"I like hearing that you made a good living in freelance." In my periphery, I swore Mr. Clark had given Landon a conspiratorial glance, but it was probably the mention of insurance making my mind play tricks on me. "Gives me some hope."

I nodded a thank-you at the waitress when she set down our water glasses.

"From what I hear, you're very talented and don't need to hope so much. Start getting feelers out, and soon you'll have to refuse jobs because you're too booked."

"Landon is a little biased," I said, angling my head to meet his gaze as he perused the menu. "But that would be nice."

"It's not that I'm biased. Well, not completely," Landon said, draping his arm across the back of my chair. "I still have the sketches you gave me in college. To be able to create that kind of amazing detail without any real training is pure talent."

"I was always jealous of the designers." Darlene sighed and closed her menu. "I can string words together, but stick figures are my only artistic talent."

I chuckled, scanning the menu, before I whipped my head to Landon after what he'd said sank in.

"You still have sketches I gave you almost twenty years ago?"

His brows pulled together as he nodded. "Why would I throw them out? The only reason I didn't frame them was because they were an odd size and I didn't want to cut them. So they're rolled up in my home office. Or former home office, after I head back to Charlotte to pack it all up."

He grinned and went back to the menu, as if what he'd just said hadn't cracked my chest open. I brought my water glass to my lips and took a long sip, hoping the cold liquid sliding down my throat would soothe me enough to calm me down.

Did not taking a risk for something amazing make me a fool, or would I be a fool for taking a reckless chance and losing the most important person in my life? The question was enough to paralyze me.

"Ready to order?" the waitress chirped next to our table.

"Yes," Darlene said, opening her menu. "I'll have the salmon, please."

Mr. Clark nodded at me.

"I'll have the bacon-wrapped scallops." I shot Landon a wry grin as I handed back the menu. "Good compromise?"

"Perfect," he whispered, squeezing my shoulder. "That sounds good. I'll have the same."

"Steak, medium." Mr. Clark passed back his menu. "I'll be different."

The waitress smiled as she scribbled everything down.

"Anything to drink?"

"Pinot grigio, please." I said, hoping that didn't come out as desperate as I felt for a buzz to dull the anxiety of uncertainty.

"Beer, whatever you have on tap, please," Landon told

her, flicking his eyes to mine with a smirk. "See? Compromise isn't bad," he whispered.

"I told you as long as I can keep my bacon, I'll be fine." I nudged his side.

"I promised I'd lay off tonight, and I will." He kissed my temple, "No eyeballing if you butter your bread."

Conversation was easy, or easier, after that. Darlene was sweet and funny, and Mr. Clark was obviously head over heels for her. I was so full, I picked at my dessert when it came, but the entire meal was delicious, even if I had to work to get the first couple of bites down.

"Excuse me for a minute. I need to run to the restroom. Don't let them take my dessert," Darlene told Mr. Clark, pointing at her chocolate mousse cake.

He held up his hands. "I'll guard it with my life, babe."

She shot him a playful scowl before grabbing her purse and heading to the back.

"Darlene is really great," I said when she was out of earshot. "When are you getting married?"

"We were thinking of going to Lake Tahoe. Neither of us wants a big wedding. Maybe you both can join us if you have the time."

"I'd love to, Dad. Tell me a date, and I'll make it work."

"Me too," I said, unsure how I would afford it and a little afraid to attend another wedding with Landon, considering the effect the last one had on us.

"That would be wonderful," Mr. Clark said, grinning as he looked between us.

"Shit," Landon hissed when he dug his phone out of his pocket. "This is my boss. I have to talk to him about the rental space lease. I'll be quick." He stood and jogged outside.

"I really hope he means it when he says that he'll have

balance at work when he moves up here." Mr. Clark shook his head at Landon's departure.

"I think it's just busy with the move. He promised me the same thing, so I have no problem getting on him if he's still working at all hours."

"Good. He only listens to you anyway." His smile shrank as he leaned in closer to the table. "You look beautiful. How are you feeling?"

I smiled back before my stomach sank.

"You know?"

He nodded. "About your diagnosis? Yes, Landon told me when I went to visit him."

"He's been worrying himself sick about me, but I'm feeling okay. Resting as much as I can but feeling a lot better than I was."

"I'm very glad to hear that. I was worried about you too when he told me. I was going to call in a favor at my old job to set you up with affordable insurance until he told me how you were already covered."

My eyes widened over the rim of my cappuccino as I was taking a sip.

"You know that too?"

"I do," he replied with a slow nod. "But that wasn't the shock you may've thought it was."

"Really? Your son proposing a marriage of convenience for the sake of my medical insurance didn't shock you?" I sputtered out a nervous laugh.

"Julie, sweetheart—" he reached across the table and took my hand in both of his "—when I asked Landon why he asked you to marry him, he told me that nothing matters to him more than you do." He gave me a wistful smile as he held my gaze. "You mean everything to him. You always did."

"He means everything to me too. Your son is amazing. He always has been."

Mr. Clark's smile deepened as his shoulders shook with a chuckle.

"You two," he sighed, shaking his head. "What you have is as rare as it is wonderful, if you only opened your eyes." He patted my hand and let it go when his gaze drifted over my shoulder.

"Sorry about that. I tried him earlier, but he was at an all-day conference and is out of pocket for most of tomorrow." He looked me over with a furrowed brow. "Feeling okay, Jules? I'm only asking because there's still chocolate cake on your plate."

His mouth pulled into the crooked smile that haunted my dreams and now sliced me in half.

"I'm good, just full. Dinner was fantastic."

I smiled at Mr. Clark. He nodded back, acknowledging more than just a "You're welcome."

After Darlene came back to the table, we finished our desserts and said our goodbyes. The drive home was quiet, and I made myself yawn a couple times so that Landon would think I was tired, not freaking out in the passenger seat.

"You never told me about how the apartment hunting went yesterday," I said as I watched the lights from the skyline blur across my window.

"Oh, that's a funny story. Remember Marco from Fordham? He works for a building management company. I can put apartment searching on hold for a few months while I sublet an apartment on the West Side."

"You're letting Marco find you an apartment?" I turned my head and gaped at Landon's oblivious face.

He shrugged. "Marco wasn't a bad guy."

"Maybe not, but he's kind of a flake. I'm friends with him on Facebook, and I feel like I see a post every month announcing his new job somewhere. What happens to your apartment if he job-hops while you're staying there?"

"I'm sure I'll have to sign something that I can't be thrown out if he leaves." He reached over the console and squeezed my knee. "Now who's worrying? I'll be fine." He lifted his hand, the graze of his thumb still shooting a jolt right up my thigh.

Best friends didn't have jolts between them.

The visceral reactions were becoming too potent to ignore, but I kept denying them all the same.

He pulled up in front of my house and shut off the engine.

"You don't have to walk me in. I'm okay, and you have a long drive back to your dad's."

"Don't be ridiculous." He clicked the locks open and climbed out, shutting the door behind him as he came around to the passenger side. He beat me to opening my door as I was moving a little slowly. Going out at night was becoming easier, but I felt like a sad Cinderella, my joints telling me cut my night short when I didn't want to.

Landon's brow furrowed, but he stayed silent as he reached for my hand and helped me out of the car.

"Thank you for coming tonight. My dad loved seeing you." Landon kept hold of my hand as we made our way to my front stoop.

"Don't thank me. I was happy to be there. I like Darlene. I don't know if I can afford Lake Tahoe, but I'd love to see them get married."

"Jules, Lake Tahoe would be on me. He'd want you there, and so would I." He held his hand out for my keys.

"I can manage a lock." I pursed my lips as I dropped them into his hand.

"I know you can. I just like doing things for you." He unlocked the door and held it open for me to walk through. I turned on the light as his father's words rattled around in my head.

What you have is as rare as it is wonderful, if you only opened your eyes.

I was tired enough to go right to sleep but smart enough to know it wouldn't be peaceful.

"Safe travels back to Charlotte." I roped my arms around his neck and dropped my head against his shoulder.

"I'll be driving back up with all my stuff even though I'm leaving most of my furniture, so this will be the easy part of the trip." His soft chuckle settled in my belly as I melted against him. Right or wrong, I wanted to be close to him and was too tired in body and soul to fight it.

"Hey," he crooned, drifting his hands up and down my back. "I'll be back before you know it. And for good. Get some rest, darlin'," he whispered into my hair.

I was too tired to ask about why he'd told his father or relay what Mr. Clark told me Landon had said about me.

"See you soon, doll." I kissed his cheek, spotting the corner of his mouth lift as I inched back.

I watched him drive away, and I shut and locked the door behind me.

My eyes were wide open. What we had was rare and wonderful—and terrifying.

16

LANDON

"Hey, man. I'm really sorry. I can put you up in a hotel for a night. There's one not too far from here."

I held in a groan as I kept my weary eyes on the road. The last thing I wanted to do was check in to a hotel tonight and have to leave in the morning. I should have known that Marco's offer was too convenient to be true. Marco was every bit the flake that Julie had said he was, but I had been desperate enough to overlook it and hope for the best.

The one time I didn't overprepare screwed me in the end. I'd asked for a form to sign to sublet the apartment for the next few months, but I was so focused on closing everything up and packing before I left Charlotte, I'd forgotten to follow up. I'd headed up here on good faith, and right as I pulled onto the New Jersey Turnpike, Marco called to let me know the family who was subletting had moved back in earlier today.

And without a form, and since they were in already, there wasn't anything he could do—at least not for a place to sleep tonight.

"I'll figure out something. Thanks anyway, Marco."

I ended the call, not wanting to hear any more excuses that would just piss me off. I'd been in the car for over ten hours today and just wanted a place to sleep. I only knew of one hotel close by to where the apartment building was, and I didn't feel comfortable sleeping there, let alone parking my truck with everything I owned in the lot.

I had two choices. I could either drive an extra hour and a half to Connecticut and disrupt my father's life with his fiancée, or turn onto the Cross Bronx Expressway and be at Julie's in half the time. Before everything had shifted between us the past couple of months, it would have been a no-brainer, but staying in her house—alone with her for a few nights—had me uneasy.

I loved Julie. Not only as my best friend, but loved as in was head over heels in love with her. Maybe I had been all along, and I'd managed to compartmentalize it enough for the sake of friendship all these years, but now, I wasn't unsure of my feelings or what I wanted. After I'd blurted it out during dinner with my father that night, it was an epiphany I couldn't deny or take back.

Julie had broken me when she'd told me in Vegas how she thought of her life as temporary. I could never think of her in those terms, but wasn't life temporary in general? Hesitating now seemed not only pointless but wasteful. Maybe the New York office was fate setting us on a path to each other when the time was right. Or almost right.

We'd be amazing together, and I was sure Julie felt the same way. But I knew she was a couple steps behind me in what she wanted to do about it. Judging by the way she looked at me lately, I could tell she was still back in the terrified and confused stage.

I wasn't totally free from the fear, but I wasn't the least bit confused.

I wanted to make my best friend mine, but it had to be done in baby steps. Staying with her while I hunted for a permanent place to live, however long that would take, I feared would set us back instead of moving us ahead to where I wanted us to be.

But at eight p.m. on a Wednesday night, I didn't have any other choice. I'd be a big boy and handle myself, even if the woman I wanted more than anything was in the same house and close enough to touch. I called her and hoped for the best.

"Hey, are you okay? I was starting to get worried."

I smiled at Julie's relieved sigh over my car speakers. I'd told her I'd call once I got to the apartment, which I'd expected to be a lot sooner.

"Traffic set me back a couple of hours, but I need a favor. Can I stay with you for a few days?"

I checked the screen on my dashboard to see if the call had dropped after a long few seconds of silence.

"Jules?"

"So, Marco flaked out?"

"He did, and you can tell me all about how you told me so later."

"Of course you can stay as long as you want."

"Thank you. I'll try not to bother you while you're working."

"I work from nine to three and in the alcove by my kitchen. You can have my spare room. I have a futon and a desk in there. I think it's comfortable. Nate stayed in there a lot."

"He did?"

"Yes, when I was first sick. He told me that I got up too many times during the night and he couldn't sleep."

"Jules," I said, gritting my teeth as I white-knuckled the steering wheel. "Please don't tell me anything else about that douche while he's close enough to kill."

"Aw, take it easy, tough guy. What I'm saying is that it's a nice room, and you can have it all to yourself. Feel free to set up whatever you want in there for as long as you want. How close are you?"

"Just got onto the Cross Bronx Expressway."

"Ah, so I'll see you in another six hours."

I laughed as, sure enough, I merged onto a slow-moving parking lot.

"I'm so sorry to put you out like this tonight. And it's already late, but I'll be there as soon as I can."

"You aren't, and you should know that. You get here when you get here. Try to relax, and I'll see you soon."

Relaxing was always easier said than done for me, but now I was tense for more reasons than just figuring out a place to stay. It had taken me almost twenty years to figure out that I was in love with Julie, and once I did, our lives together made too much sense. My failed marriage, her broken engagement, and all the people we'd been with who never seemed to work out. There was a reason we were the only constant in each other's lives, but up until Dean and Maria's wedding weekend, I'd thought we were just lucky to have a deep friendship that stood the test of time.

Maybe it was the thought of losing her that had jolted me awake. Other than when I'd first laid eyes on her back in our freshman year of college, I'd never allowed myself to look at her as anything other than my best friend. Sure, I always thought she was beautiful, but it was as if a switch flipped between us that night by the fountains, and I couldn't go back.

After years of dates and relationships I'd taken at face value, I finally understood why. Julie was endgame for me. I'd never been so sure about anything in my life. Nothing and no one else mattered, but I needed to find the patience to let her catch up to where I was. That had been my plan until I'd had to ask to live with her for an undefined period of time. I wouldn't be able to hunt for apartments while I set up the office and staff for at least the next few weeks.

When I decided on something I wanted, slow was not my preferred speed. And I'd never wanted anything as much as this. As much as her.

I was running a lifelong marathon for this woman without realizing it, and I wouldn't fuck it up now, when we were so close to the finish line. Julie and I belonged together, and I'd do whatever I had to in order to make that happen—including wait until she was ready.

Two hours later, I parked in Julie's driveway. Her Bronx neighborhood was more suburb than city, other than the sounds of the six train as it pulled in and out of the above-ground station two blocks away. Her street was still and quiet at ten p.m. on a Wednesday night, amplifying the ding of the train doors opening and closing as I fished my suitcases out of my truck.

I was still displaced without a permanent place to live, but heading to Julie's doorstep felt like I was finally home. I hadn't been unhappy in Charlotte, but I'd spent a lot of time and dollars traveling back and forth over the years. On the long drive, I'd dissected the past almost-twenty years in a million different ways in my head, and the one constant through it all was Julie. It had taken longer than it should have to realize why, but I wouldn't dwell.

The only important thing was that I was here now.

The front door locks clicked open as I set my suitcases on her stoop and reached for the doorbell. In what seemed like slow motion—or maybe I was just that damn tired—Julie opened the door and leaned against the jamb. Her hair was tied in a messy bun on top of her head, and she was in a hoodie and leggings, a wide smile rushing across her lips when our gazes locked.

Fuck, she was beautiful.

"Welcome home," she said, running into my arms.

I lifted her up by the waist and laughed when she wrapped her legs around me. I buried my head into the crook of her neck and tightened my hold around her. Even though I was exhausted and stiff from the long drive, I didn't want to put her down or let her go.

Nothing felt as right as when Julie was in my arms, and now, I finally knew why.

"Happy to see me?" I lifted my head with Julie still wrapped around me. I had less than a minute before my joy in having her this close moved lower and became all too noticeable.

"Eh," she said, shrugging as she roped her arms around my neck. "It's still sinking in that you don't have to leave. I mean, that you don't have to go anywhere until you find an apartment." She cleared her throat and smoothed back a lock of hair when it fell into her eyes.

"Nope, staying put," I whispered, a promise to both of us that she didn't pick up on yet, but she would soon. I'd never leave her again.

"Everything okay, Julie?"

Our heads pivoted to the voice across the street. I made out an open window with soft light in the background, but I couldn't see the face of the dark figure behind it.

"All good, Mrs. Perez." Julie raised her arm in a wave, her other one still wrapped around my neck.

Julie turned back to me, a smirk tipping the side of her pretty mouth. "You should probably put me down before any other neighbors think I'm being assaulted," she whispered.

"Why?" I held her with one arm and tucked a loose hair behind her ear. "I'm enjoying my welcome."

She held my eyes, taking in a slow breath through her nostrils as her smile faded. Instead of putting her down, I yanked her closer.

"Check us out," I whispered. "I can finally carry you over a threshold." I went through the open door with her in my arms, her eyes wide and still on mine.

"Fake marriage complete," she said with a nervous chuckle. "Although, I don't know if that counts."

"Says who?"

She smiled and gave me a slow nod. "I guess there are no rules."

"Not with us," I rasped, kissing her cheek before I slowly set her down. Dragging my bags from Julie's stoop, I shut and locked the door behind me.

"Everything is set up for you," Julie said, rubbing her hand against her chest as if she were calming herself down. When I'd set her down on her feet, my body had slid against hers as I'd pulled away, like an accidental caress. I bit back a smile at the blush bleeding into her cheeks.

"I set out clean sheets and towels in case you feel like taking a shower tonight. I even wrote the Wi-Fi password on a Post-it by the desk, so you should be all set."

"Thanks. This is a great hotel."

She laughed, crossing her arms as she leaned against the wall. "I work in the morning. I'll set up coffee for you, and you can help yourself to whatever you want for breakfast. Dunkin' and a great Italian bakery are in walking distance if you feel like venturing out. Do you have to go into the office tomorrow?"

"No, the space won't be ready for a few days. Are you sure I won't bother you if I work out of your spare room?"

She shook her head. "I told you. I like working from the alcove. The light is good, and now that my neighbor tends to my yard, the view out the window is nice." Her eyes darted around the room before they came back to mine, a tiny smile pulling across her lips. "I like having you here. So it's not a bother or hassle. Stay as long as you need to."

"You're a lifesaver, Jules." I slung one of my bags over my shoulder. "And go ahead and tell me I told you so. I know it's eating away at you."

"No, I'm good. I'll wait until you've gotten a good night's sleep and can appreciate it. Do you need help bringing anything inside?"

"All I need right now are my clothes and my laptop. The rest can wait in my truck. That is, if you think it's all safe in a Bronx driveway."

"Hey," she said, poking my shoulder when I laughed. "I can say things like that, you can't. But yeah, good policy in general to take your valuables inside," she said on a yawn. "I'll follow you upstairs."

I shook my head and nodded up the carpeted staircase. "Ladies first. Lead the way."

Letting her go ahead of me was less about being a gentleman and more about the view of her ass in those leggings. I'd have to keep myself in check while I was here, but it was a relief not to feel the need to talk myself out of it when the air charged between us or tear my eyes away from the soft curves that she still tried to hide.

I couldn't be obvious, but the guilt over sneaking a peek had lifted once I'd realized I was in love with her.

"It's not very fancy. I had a lot of plans for this house that got derailed for...reasons." She sighed and motioned to the futon. "I left you a blanket too. Nate took the TV, so sorry about that."

I nodded and dropped my bags on the floor, still fuming whenever I thought of him staying in here because it was too much to take care of Julie when she was sick.

"He can keep it if it means he stays away from you." I shot her a scowl over my shoulder.

"He's gone and never coming back, so stop having dreams of beating him up." She shook her head.

"I don't think I can do that. And I don't watch much TV anyway. I'll have to drop a star on Yelp for this place, but I can manage."

"I understand." Her gaze drifted over my shoulder. "Now that I look at it, I hope your legs can fit on the futon. I thought it was a big enough size, but—" she looked me up and down "—maybe just for most people."

"I'll be fine. I'll take a shower and turn in. Go to bed." I took her face in my hands. "And thank you. I'll buy you breakfast for your troubles."

"You aren't any trouble. I told you." She reached up to grab my wrists. This seemed to be our default stance since our fake wedding whenever the air got too heavy between us. I'd frame her face, locking my gaze to hers instead of roaming down her body and battling the temptation to taste her mouth again. She'd clutch on to me but keep me at a distance.

These were the moments that would be hard, when I'd have to fight with myself not to take more because I wanted everything for us, but for her, I'd find a way.

"Sweet dreams, darlin'," I rasped, almost grazing the corner of her mouth when I brushed my lips over her cheek.

"Get some sleep, doll," she replied in a throaty whisper.

Julie and I had slept in the same places before over the years, though knowing she was so close all night would be torture, but I'd find the patience to get through it. Somehow.

I grabbed a T-shirt and shorts and headed for Julie's bathroom. I hadn't made a stop in almost five hours, and my neck and shoulders were jacked. I let the hot water sluice over the tight muscles of my back as I pressed my hands against the tile. I inhaled a long breath through my nostrils and caught a whiff of the open bottle of Julie's body wash on the shelf. She always smelled like vanilla, even in college. I'd teased her about smelling like cookies ever since we first met, when I'd wanted nothing more than to take a bite, even though she was dating my friend and off-limits.

Of all the regrets I had in life, letting someone else have Julie would always be at the top of my list.

My mind ventured to dirtier places, like Julie in this shower, naked and wet, suds dripping down her body. She had no idea how gorgeous she was, back then and especially now. My cock hung heavy between my legs as I wrapped my hand around my shaft and wished for her.

I'd start at her neck, learn all the sounds she made as I ran my lips lower, over those beautiful, full breasts until I captured a nipple between my teeth. My cock jerked as I imagined her nipple pebbling on my tongue as she whimpered my name.

"Like that, darlin'?" I panted out as my hand moved faster, imagining her gorgeous body quivering with need as I made her forget about Nate and every other asshole who'd come before me. Because she was mine. She belonged to me, even if she didn't know it yet.

I pictured sinking to my knees, hooking one of her gorgeous legs over my shoulder as I licked my way inside her. I'd kiss and suck every delicious inch as she'd unravel in my arms. I wanted to do everything to her, and once I had my hands on her, I knew I'd never get enough.

"Fuck," I grunted out as I pumped faster. I'd tell her to come on my tongue, and then once she did, I'd sink deep inside her and fuck her until neither of us could move. "Julie," I whimpered as my balls ached for release and my body cried out for the woman two doors away, the one I'd loved for my entire life but had only just figured out now. "My Julie..."

I came in long spurts, the rush of the shower washing it away as if it had never happened. I gulped in breaths of air as my heart hammered against my rib cage. The small amount of relief took the momentary edge off, but nothing would ever come close to the real thing.

Being clueless about my feelings for Julie would have served me a hell of a lot better while I was staying in her house. I'd never believed "the one" existed until I'd married her—and then I'd realized that she'd been there all along.

17

JULIE

When I told Landon to stay here as long as he wanted, I knew that having him two walls away from me would have me on edge, but I was confident that I could handle it.

That was, until I heard him jerk off in my shower and everything went to a higher and even more unbearable level.

The groan echoing from my bathroom reminded me of our kiss, only this time deeper, almost guttural. I wasn't sure if a fantasy brought on by wishful thinking made it sound like he called out my name, or if he was really coming to thoughts of me.

I didn't know what to do about either.

My house wasn't tiny, but small enough to be cozy—though, cozy wasn't necessarily a good thing for us right now. Upping the ante on the stifling sexual tension only made the crossroads we'd come to even worse.

When I'd watched Landon unpack the suitcases out of his truck, it finally hit me that he was staying—and how much I'd always wanted him to stay. Our goodbyes were always sad whenever he'd have to go back to Charlotte, and Nate had called me out a few times for moping a bit for a day or two after he left. I'd tell Nate I was just missing my best friend and nothing more, but I'd been questioning every piece of our history lately, trying to pinpoint the moment when everything had changed.

If I looked back with an honest perspective, Nate wasn't that wrong. It would be Landon, not Nate or anyone I was involved with at the time, whom I'd run to with good news first. When I was sick and kept it from Landon, it made the fear and anguish that much worse because—even though it was all my doing—I didn't have my best friend to lean on when I needed him the most.

The lack of shock from Landon's father that his son had married me, as if it was an inevitability, shook me into consciousness. My feelings for Landon ran so deep, I'd somehow managed to keep them a secret from even myself for years, yet others could clearly see.

I'd leaped into Landon's arms on instinct and clutched on to him like the lifeline he always was to me. Not because of the bad turns my life had taken as of late, but because I always needed him, plain and simple—and so fucking complicated.

I'd asked him to put me down, even though it was the opposite of what I wanted. I couldn't think with his body pressed so close, or the mix of wonder and lust in his gaze as his eyes had locked on mine. The flutters in my belly had become a zing of desire that shot straight to my core.

In the long minute he'd taken to set me down on the floor, my body had grazed his, sparking all kinds of fantasies. Landon pinning me against the wall as he plundered my mouth—and other places. I wanted to make him scream my name like I wanted to believe I'd heard in my shower and watch him come, knowing I'd done that to him.

I'd tossed and turned most of the night. Thoughts of his body sliding against mine at my door and of him pumping his probably huge cock in his hand in my shower as he might or might not have called my name played in my dreams during the short amount of sleep I'd managed to get.

I woke up tempted to crawl next to him, even though his body would have taken up all the futon space. But if he'd rolled on top of me—

When I dropped my empty mug into my kitchen sink in frustration, the clatter of the ceramic against the spoon was loud enough for me to wince. I'd plowed through half a day's work in two hours, trying to distract myself from heading upstairs and getting into bed with my best friend. Now, I had nothing else to do but think of what I'd heard last night, what it made me want, and what the hell to do about it.

If I'd thought marrying him would be dangerous, living with him was about to do me in and he'd only just gotten here.

I rubbed the knot at the back of my neck when my phone buzzed on my kitchen counter.

Karen: *Are you in a meeting? I have the good bagels, and I'll leave them on your doorknob if you can't come to the door.*

I trudged over to the door and found Karen just as she was about to run off.

"Hey girl," she said, smiling as she raked a hand through her short platinum-blond hair. "I was off today and thought

I'd take a walk over to Empire Bagels before the line got too long."

"You're a good neighbor," I said, sliding the handle of the plastic bag off the doorknob.

"And," she whispered and nodded to where Landon's SUV was parked behind mine in my driveway. "I thought if you had an overnight guest, warm bagels would be nice."

I laughed when her brows jumped.

"So the bagels were for intel?"

"I'm a nosy neighbor, and I own it." She shrugged. "Plus, I've told you more about Oliver and me than he would ever want you to know. I thought I'd drop the bagels off now and get the scoop later."

I hadn't told a soul that Landon and I had gotten married in Vegas for insurance's sake—or about my avalanche of feelings for him since. Karen wouldn't judge, and while she knew I had a best friend Landon who lived in Charlotte, she didn't know how our relationship had changed and progressed into the potential clusterfuck of lust that it was now.

"How about in exchange for bagels"—I held up the bag—"I'll make you a cup of coffee and give you the short version of it all."

"The short version?" Her blue eyes lit up. "Lead the way."

"But we have to be quiet." I pressed my finger to my lips. "Landon is asleep upstairs."

"Landon?" Her brows pulled together as she stepped inside. "Your best friend Landon who lives in North Carolina?"

I nodded and shooed her in, shutting the door behind her.

Was a short version even possible? I guessed the main points didn't need a lot of detail.

Landon and I had been best friends since college.

He'd married me so I could have his insurance.

We'd kissed at an Elvis chapel, and it had unleashed years of repressed desire we couldn't rein back in.

And now he was staying in my house.

Maybe there *was* a CliffsNotes pocket version of it all.

I made another pot of coffee while she set up the bagels, cream cheese containers, knives, and plates. It was eight thirty but seemed so much later after working since six, and I wasn't sure what time Landon would get up. I hoped a long day of driving would knock him out until at least nine, but I didn't have much time to spill my guts.

I went through it all as quickly as I could, Karen saying nothing as I went on, and I glanced behind me every minute or so to check if Landon was coming down the stairs.

"That's...a lot. Are you ready for when all this explodes?" She bunched her shoulders as if she was about to squeal. "This is so hot."

I scoffed and gulped my last mouthful of coffee. "I'm glad my life entertains you."

"Oh come on, appreciate this. You love all those forced-proximity books." She pointed to my small romance novel collection on the tiny bookcase by my desk.

My love of romance novels had gotten me through the worst of my illness when I didn't have the energy to do anything else but read. I'd found solace in a good love story with a dependable happy ending since I had no clue what reality was going to bring on a daily basis.

"Well," she said, tapping her chin. "You started out with marriage of convenience, and now you added forced proximity. A twist."

I kicked her under the table.

"Morning, Jules."

My head snapped up to the sexy grumble behind me. Landon held his glasses in one hand as he rubbed his eyes. His black sweatshorts clung to his muscular thighs the same way his T-shirt pulled across his chest. His dark hair was tousled all over the place, and my fingers itched to sift through it. That, with the extra stubble dusting his cheeks, almost made me swallow my tongue.

This was not good. Karen was right. Either this thing between us would explode or I would.

"Oh my God," Karen mouthed as her gaze raked up and down his body.

"Oh, I'm sorry," Landon said, shooting Karen a wide grin after he slid his glasses on. "I'm Landon, Julie's best friend and squatter for a few weeks."

"Karen," she said as she stood to take his extended hand. "Friend, neighbor, and bagel messenger."

"Nice to meet all of you," he said with a chuckle. "A bagel sounds amazing."

"The bag is on the counter, and I just made a pot of coffee," I said, darting my eyes everywhere but his mouth. I laughed at my attempt to shake off what had started brewing between us in Vegas. A sleepy-eyed Landon trudging around my kitchen was walking temptation.

"Julie said you just moved from North Carolina," Karen said as Landon came to the table to scoop up the container of cream cheese.

"I did. My best friend was nice enough to put me up for a while when my sublet fell through." He shot me a smile. "Plates are in that cabinet?" He pointed behind him.

"Yes, sorry." I stood and joined him at the counter. "I'm

not being a very good host." He framed my waist when I reached up to open the cabinet.

"You're fine," he whispered into my hair as he reached over me, the heat from his front against my back almost liquefying my knees. I was breathless by the time he grabbed a plate and went back to the counter.

I could've moved to the side, and he could have reached across, not over me. His sexy rasp in my ear made my toes tingle, along with other places below my waist, and my feet rooted to my kitchen tiles until he backed away.

Karen looked between us, obviously loving the show we were putting on. Had it been that long ago that Landon was just my friend who happened to be a guy? I wanted to believe this crush was because I was affection-starved and vulnerable, but the only thing I was starved for was the man in my kitchen.

"So, you guys have been friends since college?" Karen asked, smirking at me when Landon poured creamer into his coffee.

"That's right. Since freshman year." He looped his arm around my shoulder as he took a sip. "I used to come visit more, but in the past few months, I've been too damn busy." He yanked me closer. "But now that I've moved here, Jules gets me all the time." He kissed my temple. "She's thrilled, right?"

"Ecstatic." I shook my head and tried for a scowl as he peeked at me over the rim of his coffee mug. This was normal banter between us and how we teased back and forth. The flirting and the rubbing and the lifting, *that* wasn't our usual, and I shouldn't have wanted so much more of it.

I fell back into my chair at the kitchen table, taking a

bite out of my bagel and ignoring Karen's widened eyes in my periphery.

"Please don't think I'm rude. I slept longer than I wanted to and have to log on to work for a little bit. It's okay if I eat in the spare room?"

"Of course. And I forgot to tell you there's weights and a treadmill in the basement if you want to work out."

He turned to open the refrigerator, and my eyes roamed down his back. Black pants framed his ass perfectly, but those shorts hugging his backside made it almost sing. Again, I'd seen Landon in shorts and tank tops plenty of times, and I'd never had to check the side of my mouth for drool. The struggle not to pant over him now was as ridiculous as it was exhausting.

"I was going to jog around the neighborhood, but that's better." He flashed us both a wide grin. "Are you working all day?"

"No, I was up early and got everything done. Not much to do until I get assets for the next phase, which would be at the earliest tomorrow. But I'll keep busy and won't bother you."

"Actually, I wanted to head into the city and check out the office space, if you wanted to come along. It's not fully ready yet, but I thought we could make a day of it. Maybe get some lunch." He shrugged. "It's not a big place. We're renting three offices on one floor."

Technically, the Bronx was a borough of New York City, but if you were from anywhere in the tri-state area, you never said "head into Manhattan." Manhattan was "the city," and the other boroughs were referred to by name. I'd grown up thinking it was a given until I'd had to explain it to someone.

"We could do that," I said, relieved that we'd be out in

public for a day and I could stop thinking of my big, hot best friend in my tiny house and what other sounds he made when he came. Yes, out was a spectacular idea.

"Great, we can take the six right there and walk around a little. Maybe we can play tourist for a couple of hours."

"I grew up here, so *you'd* be the tourist," I teased, even though that wasn't totally true. The last times I'd visited any New York landmarks were on school field trips.

"Right, because Wallingford, Connecticut, is up in the sticks." His lip curled as he grabbed his plate.

"You're in trouble," Karen sang, her shoulders shaking with a chuckle after Landon headed upstairs.

"I am," I sighed. "I really thought it was the emotion of the weekend and the fake wedding and not seeing him for so long, but—"

"But when he came up behind you to get a plate out of the cabinet, I thought he was about to spin you around and back you against the wall."

"And if you weren't here, I probably would have let him. This is bad, Karen."

"Okay, that is what I don't understand." She scooted her chair closer to the table. "He's gorgeous and, from what I just saw, is pretty damn into you."

"He's my best friend."

That excuse was getting so old, it fell from my lips with no affect or emotion. It was a fact that I used to use to attempt to explain us, but that wasn't us anymore—or wasn't the only thing about us. We were so much more, more than I knew what to do with.

She rolled her eyes. "My best friend doesn't press herself against my ass and take more than a minute to back away. Again, I don't understand what's making you hesitate so much."

I let my head drop to my hands and pinched the bridge of my nose.

"What if we try, and it doesn't work out? And I lose him?"

She huffed out a sigh.

"He married you to make sure you had health insurance, and he didn't think twice about it from what you said."

"He called it a solution." I scoffed, rubbing my eyelids. "He worries about me, which was why I was so hesitant to tell him I was sick."

"I caught how he was looking at you, whether you want to face it or not. Offering marriage to make sure you have insurance like it's nothing, is something. And you're smart enough to know that." She crossed her arms and leaned back, narrowing her eyes. "Please tell me that Nate doesn't have anything to do with this."

I scrunched my nose and shook my head. "Nate and I are very, very over. The only feelings I have for that asshole are those of disdain."

"That's not what I mean." The concern creasing her brow made me uneasy. She was a little too intuitive sometimes, and I didn't want to think about what I knew she was going to say. "You told me what he said to you before he moved out."

"What, when he told me that I was fine and needed to stop feeling sorry for myself or else no one will want to be around me? When I got sick, I got on his nerves. He didn't say it, but he more than showed it. He couldn't handle it or understand it, and if he'd loved me, that wouldn't have mattered."

"No, it wouldn't have. But I think he made you think of yourself as baggage."

"Aren't I?" I huffed out a laugh. "I feel good at the

moment, but that can all change tomorrow. Maybe it's not fair to put that burden on Landon."

"You are not a burden. And while I don't know him or your history that well, from what you've said about him and after all he's done to make sure you stay healthy, I doubt he'd ever think of you that way. Talk to him if you're so concerned about what will happen when temptation finally gets the better of both of you."

"It's not a foregone conclusion. I can find a way to control myself."

"Right," she scoffed. "You're living in a *Three's Company* episode. Your tongue was practically hanging out of your mouth when he came downstairs, and his eyes tracked you from the second he saw you. All this sexual tension between the two of you is crackling all over the place." She rolled her shoulders in an exaggerated shiver. "Wait until you catch him in a towel. *If* you can find one that covers him," she said, throwing a forlorn glance toward the stairway. "Seriously, twenty years of knowing that guy, and *this* is the first time you've realized that you're attracted to him?"

"No, I've noticed him. He was just...Landon. I mean, he still is, but now..." I trailed off, no clue how to finish that sentence. "Maybe it's just been a while for me. Nate and I hadn't been *together* for a very long time before we split."

"Or..." she began, setting her elbows onto the table. "Or maybe this was brewing all along, and you both ignored it for the same reason of not wanting to lose each other. And in a weird way, maybe your diagnosis gave you both a push to see each other differently." She leaned over and squeezed my hand. "Sometimes the worst things in life bring the best perspective."

I'd never thought of a silver lining to anything when it came to getting sick, but maybe there were a few. Everything was different, and so was I. While this diagnosis filled my life with a fear and trepidation I still wasn't used to, it made some of the little things I'd taken for granted blessings.

"Life is short" was always a cheap expression to me, but having a chronic illness truly made it feel finite, like a stop-watch I'd never paid attention to until it started to tick.

Was it the same for him? The thought of losing me someday made him realize how much he wanted me? A mean voice in my head said he felt sorry for me, and while I knew that would never be Landon, maybe Nate had messed with my self-worth enough that pity was easier to believe than love.

After Karen left, I headed upstairs, avoiding a glance at the closed spare room door, to search for something to wear, my cheeks flushing hot when I walked past my own bathroom.

I blamed Karen for adding to it with the torturous visions of him in a towel.

I rummaged through my closet and settled on black leggings that could pass for pants and a light green sweater. I hadn't gone jean shopping yet, and shoehorning myself into an old pair, no matter how many times I'd jump, would exhaust and depress me.

I fluffed my hair and smoothed some product over the stubborn baby hairs from regrowth. As annoying as it was, pinning them down was better than figuring out how to hide a bald spot. As I swiped on some mascara, my gaze drifted to the photo on my dresser of the four of us from graduation. Dean and Maria were on either side of Landon and me, still in the enemies stage of their love story, all of us beaming at the camera.

Landon and I had leaned in close, his arm looped around my neck as if he were yanking me closer. My head rested against his chin—clean-shaven and smooth back then—as if there was nowhere else I'd wanted to be.

We'd both been dating other people at the time, but we looked like a couple happy to be together. We'd laugh when we'd often get mistaken for boyfriend and girlfriend, but maybe we were the fools, too dense to see what was obvious to everyone's eyes but ours.

I grabbed a lipstick to shove into my purse, trying to get accustomed to all this clarity hitting me from every direction. When I opened my bedroom door, I found Landon in the hallway in jeans and a gray T-shirt with his unruly hair now combed and slicked back, highlighting the longer bristles of his beard.

How had I spent two decades knowing this man and managed to ignore how beautiful he was? Karen was right, but it wasn't only the perfect face and body that drove me to the point of distraction. Under that broad chest was a gorgeous heart and soul, a man who had always thought of me first since the moment we'd met.

I wanted all of him to be mine, but after glancing at a picture of us from almost the beginning, maybe he always had been, and I was too foolish to realize it.

"I don't know where you wanted to go for lunch, but I hope this is okay." I glanced down at myself and lifted my head to his slow smile.

"Gorgeous," he said, dragging his gaze up and down my body. "Nice pants."

"Thanks." I pivoted back and forth. "God bless black stretchy pants."

"They help with the view from the back."

My head snapped up to Landon's wicked grin.

I exhaled a loud sigh and reached out to nudge his arm,

my cheeks aching from the wide smile blooming on my face.

"You look okay, I guess." I flicked my eyes up and down. "Embracing the scruff?"

"Too lazy to shave. And there is nothing going on, so I figured we could leave earlier if you want."

I laughed at his shrug and headed down the stairs. The subway station was a short walk from my house. We rode the train mostly in silence as I focused my attention out the window. The six train ride in the Bronx was mostly above ground, and I always enjoyed watching the buildings whiz by against the horizon. I'd seen many sunrises and sunsets from here, and after not taking the train for a long time and heading to do something fun instead of work, I appreciated the beauty of it all.

Things like a subway ride, even though I'd been doing it twice daily for many years, seemed different and new. When Landon draped his arm over the back of my seat, I dropped my head to his shoulder and let him draw me closer. When the car dipped underground, I allowed my eyes to shut and let the sway of the subway car soothe me, enjoying what was new between Landon and me, even if it had always been there.

I'd spend the afternoon with my favorite person, appreciating the simple joys and worry about what I'd tell myself about it later.

"You don't hate it, do you?" Landon asked, his nose crinkling as he sat across from me at Serra, Eataly's rooftop restaurant in the Flatiron District. The restaurant was set up like a greenhouse, enclosed by screens and under a skylight. Trees lined the middle of the dining area, and flowers hung from the ceiling. It was a sunny day with temperatures in the sixties, higher than usual for October in New York. The afternoon was pleasantly cool, but the sun streaming in from the open skylight above our table made it warm enough to peel our jackets off.

His office space was on Madison and Thirty-Fourth, right in the heart of Midtown Manhattan. I'd suggested walking to Twenty-Third Street for lunch. The way the city's atmosphere could change by traveling only ten streets always fascinated me. I'd worked around this neighborhood for years and always loved it. The streets were less crowded, and the vibe was more laid-back than corporate.

I'd suggested lunch on the rooftop so that we could enjoy the sunshine. After spending all that time at the beginning with legs sore enough not to want to even walk to the bathroom, I savored what felt like the new privilege of pain-free joints, at least for today.

Plus, the frosé machine behind their bar dispensed a sublime frozen concoction of rosé wine and vodka.

"I don't hate your office. Why would you think that? It's in a great location, and you said you didn't need to worry about much space, right?"

"There are only five of us." He shrugged and perused the menu. "The office is really just a home base for the moment to pick something up before we see a client. We'll probably never be there at the same time, but"—I had to hold back a laugh at his adorable sigh—"it's fine. Just not what I'm used to."

"It's different from your office suite in Charlotte, yes."

"I didn't have an office suite. It was just a regular office."

"Right," I said. "A *regular* corner office with big windows, a couch, and a sick view. This is more functional since you said you're all mostly remote, but it's not bad. No lush greenery when you peek outside in this office, but you'll manage." I patted his hand, glancing at my menu to make sure they still had the cheese plates I was dreaming about. Steroids still kicked up my appetite and I tried to keep it in check most days, but today was a special day and I'd spread as much Brie as I wanted on a cracker with no guilt.

"Greenery?" He snickered.

"You know what I mean. You lived there a while. I'm sure you miss it."

"I do and I don't. I'll miss the agreeable weather in a couple of months, I'm sure."

"I'm sure the women will all miss *you*," I teased.

"No," he chuckled, taking a sip of water. "I wasn't attached enough to anyone to make them miss me, especially since the only all-nighters I had were with work the past few months."

"Something you're not doing up here."

"I know, I know."

I stared at Landon, still scanning the laminated sheet in his hand.

"Do you ever hear from Shayla?"

He shook his head. "I ran into her once or twice. It was fine. We were so young when we got married. What she did sucked, don't get me wrong. But both of us were swept up in something we weren't ready for. I wish her the best."

"I'll never forgive her for what she did to you, but you have the right attitude. I tried to connect with her the few times I met her, but I always got the impression she didn't like me very much."

"She didn't," Landon said, not lifting his head.

"Not that it matters now, but did I do something to offend her?"

"It wasn't you. Well, it was," he said, chuckling to himself.

"Are you speaking in code? I don't know what that means."

"It means, it wasn't what you did, but it was you. She never understood or liked how close we were, and she even threw it in my face when I found out she was cheating on me. That I had something going on with you all along."

"Yeah, I don't know what that's like." I scoffed with a good amount of sarcasm as I searched for the waitress over his shoulder.

"Nate thought we were having an affair?" he asked, arching his brow.

"If I had a dollar for every fight we had because of you." I laughed. "He didn't get it either."

"Shayla and I didn't fight, but when you'd call, I'd get a look. She'd shoot daggers at me with her eyes until we'd hang up."

"No one understands us, do they?" I said, my chuckle dying on my lips when he lifted his head, his eyes boring into mine with an intensity that sucked all the mirth out of the conversation.

"No one has to. Anyone in my life who has a problem with how much you mean to me doesn't need to be there." He fell back in his seat, his expression turned wistful. "You're before everyone, Jules, and you should know that."

"I do, and same for you." I smiled despite the burn in my nose.

The waitress came to take our order, and we went back to normal, or normal as it could be for us now that this undercurrent pulsed between us.

After lunch, we settled onto a bench in Madison Square Park near the fountains. The park was full of dog walkers and, now that it was after three p.m., kids running back and forth in the playground.

"I used to like to eat lunch here, although not as often as I would have liked as the day always got away from me and I'd end up eating at my desk." I sat back and slurped the iced coffee we'd picked up on our way back from Eataly.

"And you talk about me."

"Yes, I was guilty of working too much sometimes as well, but I drew the line at weekends and late nights." I shrugged, scanning the park and remembering much simpler times. "I used to people watch and make up stories in my head about who they were." I slid closer to Landon on the bench. "Like, see those two?" I motioned to the young couple across from us, backpacks slung over their shoulders as they searched for a place to sit. There were several colleges in the area, so I guessed they were students.

"What do you think their story is?" I asked Landon.

"I think he likes her and wants to ask her out, but he's afraid she'll say no."

I whipped my head to Landon.

"That's awfully specific." I squinted back at him. "How do you know that?"

He scooted closer to whisper in my ear. "See how he's staring at her when she's not looking. It's like something is on the tip of his tongue, and he doesn't know how to say it."

"Not bad. Maybe he wants to tell her to back off, but he's trying to be nice about it."

He shook his head. "That's not it at all. Watch when she turns around and smiles at him. His whole face lights up as if he just won the lottery."

Sure enough, the girl turned around, giggling at something, and a wide smile spread on the boy's face.

"You're good."

"I'm used to reading people. Comes in handy at my job." He turned his head as he rested his elbows on his knees.

"And twenty-something years ago in the Fordham cafeteria, I was that stupid kid, wanting to ask you out but stopping himself."

My cheeks heated as I spied the wide grin on Landon's face.

"You should give him some pointers."

"Ha, right." He chuckled as he jiggled the ice in his empty cup. "I could have used some back then. Hopefully he doesn't lose his chance."

Something in Landon's gaze made me squirm on the bench. Neither of us ever held back from each other, but for the past couple of months, as often as we'd spoken, it'd always seemed like there was something we wanted to say but just couldn't come out with it. Living with him would either bring it out or bury it. I wasn't sure which yet.

Fatigue hit me hard at the end of a day sometimes, and with the rise and fall of adrenaline from the time Landon arrived last night and all the walking we'd done, the crash was even harder. My legs felt heavy when we climbed down the stairs to the subway station, and when the train pulled in and we found a seat, I conked out on Landon's shoulder.

"Hey." I woke up to Landon's whisper as he squeezed my knee. "Two more stops and we're home. Are you okay?"

I nodded on a yawn. "I was up early, and we did a lot of walking. It catches up to me sometimes."

"Please don't fall asleep on the train when you're alone. I know I'm not supposed to worry about you, but—"

"I don't plan on going back to an office anytime soon, but if I do, I promise I won't. I guess having you next to me made me relax." I slipped my arm into the crook of his elbow as I peered up at him, his brows pulled together as he looked me over.

"Stop," I said, tapping at the space between his brows.

"Remember the wrinkles." I rested my head on his chest and smiled at his long exhale against my cheek.

When we got home, Landon headed upstairs to change, and I plopped down on my couch, my eyes already heavy again when I dropped my head on the oversized pillow by the arm.

"Are you sure nothing is wrong?"

When my eyes fluttered open, I found Landon looming over me.

"This happens." I pushed off the couch to sit. "I was going to cook dinner for us later, but would you mind pizza?"

"I was about to ask you what takeout I could treat you to tonight, but pizza sounds fine by me." He rubbed slow circles over my back. I could feel the calluses on his fingertips as he grazed my neck, too tired to deny the delicious shiver from his touch.

"A late-night house guest I'm sure didn't help. Sorry about that."

"Please don't be." I turned my head, a smile pulling across my mouth despite my exhaustion. "I'm glad you're here."

"Me too." He grinned as he moved closer. "We could have a movie night when the pizza gets here."

"We could," I said on a yawn. "But you'll probably have to tell me how it ends." I gave him a wry grin. "I'm a barrel of fun," I said, rubbing my eyes and feeling the weight of what I was sure would be a concerned stare when I looked up.

"You're perfect," he whispered, brushing his lips against my cheek, the scratch of his stubble grazing against my jaw as he pulled away.

I dropped my head to his shoulder. "You're a good squatter."

His laugh rumbled against my cheek. Cuddling with him on my couch felt too perfect to dissect any whys or what-ifs, and it felt good to go with it and not question anything today.

After we ate and decided what movie to watch, the next thing I remembered was burrowing my head between the pillows on my mattress.

"How did I get up here?" I asked as I sank my head deeper into the pillow.

"Hey." I was awake enough to register Landon's raspy whisper. "You fell asleep, so I brought you upstairs."

"You carried me?" I asked, blinking at him as my eyes cleared.

"I did. Slow so I wouldn't wake you, but I guess I set you down a little too hard." He laughed, sitting on the edge of the bed.

"I'm sorry. You should've woken me up."

He shook his head. My eyes were still hazy, but the adoration in his gaze caught me right in the chest. My room was dark, but I could make out his soft smile as he swept my hair off my forehead.

"I was happy to do it. And I carried you the right way over a threshold. So we solidified this fake marriage thing."

I smiled through the twinge in my stomach. Joking about our fake marriage wasn't so funny anymore. I didn't want anything fake with Landon when it all felt too real to joke about.

"I hope that achievement didn't pull your back," I joked. "I'm no lightweight."

He shook his head. "Please stop saying things like that. You're cute when you sleep." His smile grew as he came closer. "Like I told you before, you're perfect." He ran his thumb back and forth over my jaw and brought my hand to his lips.

There was so much I wanted to say. All I felt and all I wanted scratched at the back of my throat as I tried to will my heart back into my chest.

The only word that came to the tip of my tongue was *stay*.

"Get some sleep," he whispered before pushing off the bed. I melted into a puddle on my sheets as he stepped out and closed my door behind him.

You didn't ask friends to crawl into bed with you. But we weren't friends. Not anymore and not for a while.

And now it was time to do something about it.

18

JULIE

How do you tell your best friend of two decades that you're in love with him?

I spent half the night after Landon put me in bed trying to figure out just that, and I still had no clue. After hitting the snooze button ten times, I finally rolled out of bed an hour later than usual. I tiptoed out of my bedroom, but the spare room door was open and his bed was made.

I took a quick shower and headed down the stairs, still rehearsing in my head what I'd say or how I'd even bring it up. To be this afraid to talk to Landon was ridiculous, especially since, at this point, what was there to lose? We were too old to play these games. At least, *I* felt too old and too exhausted to dance around this anymore.

I was almost sure he felt the same way, but if I was wrong, I'd deal with it. I'd been through a lot in the past six months, and I could handle an uncomfortable conversation with my best friend of twenty years.

The best friend I was in love with and who was staying in my house.

Mom was right. Landon would always be in my life. But he deserved to know where he stood. We both did.

I let out a grateful gust of air when I found a full coffeepot. I fished my favorite oversized mug out of the cabinet and heard the basement door creak behind me.

"Morning, sleepyhead." I heard the smile in Landon's voice before I turned around.

Jesus. Karen had teased about running into each other in nothing but a towel, but finding Landon in a sweat-soaked tank top was far worse. The cotton stuck to every sinew of muscle, highlighting every hard ridge and ripple of his torso. I spotted veins trailing up his forearms as he tipped back his water bottle, and my eyes followed the roll of his throat as he swallowed. His dark hair was slicked back, almost black, as a piece fell over his forehead.

I wanted to blow off work, logic, and self-preservation to attack his mouth, peel off his shirt, and drag him into the shower with me to get him dirty in a whole different way.

My house had become a powder keg, and I was ready to blow.

"Morning," I croaked out. "I guess you found everything down there okay?"

"Yeah, that's a nice setup for a home gym. Do you use it at all?"

"I do now. For the past few weeks, at least," I said, stirring the creamer a little too long to distract my eyes from where they really wanted to go. "I do low-impact weight workouts for my joints and yoga. Glad you're getting some use out of it."

"This hotel definitely has some sweet amenities," he teased, wiping his face with a towel. I stole one last look at the flex of his biceps. "If you're up for it, I'd like to take you out to dinner tonight."

"You don't have to do that," I said, the fight to keep my eyes on his and not drift lower making my head ache. "You treated to lunch yesterday and pizza last night."

"And I'm staying in your house, so dinners are the least I can do. Pick the place, and we'll go." He slung the towel over his shoulder. "I better get ready to log on by nine." He dipped his head, the corner of his perfect mouth twitching with a smirk. "You okay over there, Jules?"

"Fine," I said, my attempt to sound indignant falling flat when my reply came out breathless. "Why?"

"I don't think you've blinked in the past minute. Sure you're okay?"

"I'm just making sure you don't drip sweat on my kitchen floor."

I didn't know whether to kiss or slap the smirk off his face.

"Heading to the shower right now, darlin'." He held up his hands. "I won't mess up your floor."

I narrowed my eyes and stalked over to him. His smile shrank a bit as I came closer, stopping at less than a half inch between us. "You may want to shave while you're in there." I flicked my eyes to the long bristles of stubble covering his chin.

"You don't like it? I thought since I'm working remotely for a while and not seeing any clients for a couple of weeks, why not let loose." He rubbed his jaw. "But if my *wife* doesn't like my beard, maybe I should reconsider."

His eyes roamed up and down my body like a caress, heat singeing my skin along the path of his gaze, but it was the dip in his voice when he said *wife* that almost made my knees give out.

"Do what you want." I shrugged, even more pissed off at my breathy reply.

He eased closer, almost closing the distance between us. His soft chuckle settled deep in my belly as heat pooled between my legs.

"Have a good day at work," he said, tapping his knuckle under my chin and disappearing up the stairs.

I missed the days of sparring with Landon that didn't end with my head spinning and my panties ruined.

I settled into my office chair, hoping for a few hours of distraction before dinner, when my phone buzzed on my desk.

Karen: *Oliver will be over to cut the grass today, so tell him if you need anything else. Unless your new tenant is planning to flex his muscles around the house ;)*

Me: *Landon just came up from a workout in the basement soaked in sweat, and I almost attacked him. This is your fault.*

Karen: *Almost? And how is it my fault?*

Me: *You put the whole towel thing out into the universe. I had a restless night of sleep because I need to tell him I love him, and he's being all sweet and sexy and I can't think.*

Karen: *I hope you're still doing yoga in the mornings. Because your best buddy is going to break you in half soon. I am so happy for you I'm giddy as fuck. I'll tell Oliver if he hears furniture crashing around inside not to call his cop buddies.*

Karen: *And I'm glad you're going to tell him you love him. It's a good thing when you realize you're in love with your husband.*

We would see about that tonight.

After I shut down my computer and logged in my hours, I sifted through my closet for something to wear, examining each piece to see if it would fit my new size. My daily uniform was leggings and a T-shirt, and I still wouldn't venture into my jeans drawer.

I stopped at a black sleeveless dress with an elastic empire waist, the tags still hanging off it. I remembered buying it and finding that it was too big, then forgetting about it long enough to not be able to return it. When I slipped it over my head, procrastination paid off. It fit like a glove, complementing my full chest and hips without putting them on display. I'd have to wear a little jacket over it, but as I twirled back and forth in my mirror, I liked what I saw.

Maybe noticing how much Landon liked what *he* saw when he looked at me helped, but so what if there was more of me? More of me meant I was still here. When I met my gaze in the mirror, I looked different but familiar. I smiled, happy and grateful for the woman staring back at me, who was still standing when she thought she'd never get up again.

"Jules?" Landon called out from the hallway before he knocked.

"Yeah, come in."

"I'm officially off for the weekend, so let me know when you want to... Wow."

"I'll take that as a compliment," I said, flashing him a smile over my shoulder.

"You should," he said, leaning against the doorway as he ran his eyes up and down my body.

"You okay over there, doll?" I asked, stepping to Landon with my arms crossed over my chest, knowing how it would plump my breasts over the neckline. When his gaze flicked to my cleavage as I came closer, I bit back a smile.

"Very okay," he said, his husky whisper sending a shiver down my spine and right to my toes. "Although it may be a little hard to concentrate on dinner with you in that dress." He shifted, resting his forearm on the opposite side of the doorway and right over my head, boxing me in.

"I bet you can manage. We can leave in a half hour or so if that's good for you."

"Sure." He ran his tongue along his bottom lip as he held my eyes. I wanted to pull him inside and let him peel off my dress, but as much as I wanted to forget about dinner, we needed to talk first.

"Then get dressed and let me finish getting ready." I pushed his chest, leaning into it when he wouldn't budge.

"Fine," he sighed. "Should I dress up if you look like that?"

"No. Just giving this dress a night out. Move. I'm starving."

"I'm going," he grumbled, his eyes never leaving mine until he shut the door.

I turned my head and checked out the back of my dress in the mirror. New me was doing all right for herself, and it was time to give her a little credit.

When we sat down to dinner, we were back to us, mostly. Landon wore a gray Henley and black jeans, and I appreciated the stretch across his chest every time he shifted in his seat. Considering how nervous I was to talk to him tonight, the conversation was easy.

Maybe because we talked about everything except how much in love I realized I was with him and how I needed to know if he either felt the same way or if we were just in a lust spiral. By the time our meals were almost done, I'd already chickened out and resolved to wait to tell him until after we went back to my house, not wanting to ruin this amazing moment we were having by bringing the complications of reality into it.

I loved the food in this restaurant, but it was too loud for deep conversations about feelings. Parties and weddings were held in the back rooms, and a few times I'd had dinner a couple of tables away from one of the Yankees. The walls were plastered with signed photographs from all the New York teams and Bronx-born celebrities who would stop by.

Before my mother moved, we'd come here for special occasions, and although Landon and I couldn't have the serious talk we needed, I wanted to celebrate having him here with me—and being well enough to appreciate it.

"Is it weird to be back for good?" I asked Landon as I sipped my cappuccino.

"Before the last few months, I came back and forth enough for it not to be weird." He scanned the space. "Although not having NASCAR or the Panthers all over the walls in a place like this definitely makes it different."

"So, good news. They told us today that our project was extended, and I am treating you tonight."

"No, you're not." He narrowed his eyes and shook his head. "I told you. Dinners are on me for putting me up in your spare room for however long it's going to take me to find my own place."

My stomach sank at the thought. He'd eventually leave when he found his own place, whether it was a few weeks or a few months. He'd only been here for a couple of days and I didn't want him to go, but I wanted to try us out as a couple before he officially moved in, even though we were married already.

I laughed to myself at the very strange trajectory Landon and I had found ourselves on.

"We'll see. I need to use the restroom for a moment. I'll be right back." I grabbed my bag and headed toward the bar, not the bathrooms, to find our waitress so I could pay before he could try to stop me once the check came. Not having a rock in my stomach every time I checked my bank balance was sadly new, and while I didn't want to say to hell with it and run up my charge card, I could afford dinner with a friend, or whatever Landon would be after we talked tonight.

"Julie? I thought that was you."

I pivoted and spotted Nate sitting at the bar. He used to like coming here to watch the Giants games on Sundays, but I had no idea now if he'd actually come here all those times he'd said he had or if he'd spent the afternoon at his assistant's apartment. But I was no longer curious, so I didn't care.

He looked the same, his dirty-blond hair cropped a little shorter, and his face was clean-shaven as usual, highlighting the sharp jaw I'd always found so attractive. Now, I felt nothing when I looked him over, other than regret for how much time I'd wasted on someone who wasn't worth it.

"Hi," I said, not bothering to encourage conversation after that. I craned my neck to find our waitress taking orders at the end of the bar. She wouldn't see or hear me if I waved, and I tried to will her over to get the check and go. I didn't want to talk to Nate or have Landon find him here.

"You look great. I've been thinking about you a lot lately. I wanted to call you a million times."

My head snapped to him. "What? Why?"

A slow smile spread on his lips as he stood. *Shit, this wasn't good.* What the hell could he want to talk to me about after all this time? I didn't know, and I didn't have the inclination or the time to find out.

"I miss you. Come sit."

"No. I'm here with someone and just wanted to pay the check."

"Come on, Jules. Look, I'm sorry. I shouldn't have done what I did. I was under a lot of pressure."

"Pressure?" I squinted at him, taking a step back for each one he took toward me. "You had a months-long affair with your assistant because you felt *pressure*?"

He exhaled with a groan and shut his eyes. "It was all moving so fast. The house, setting a date. Then you started to change."

"I got *sick*. So yes, that changes a person." I glanced over his shoulder to our waitress who'd already moved on to the next customer. I needed that check and needed to get us out of here, but Nate wouldn't take the hint and back off.

"You fell into a depression, and I could've been more considerate. You just wouldn't listen and snap out of it."

My eyes bugged out so wide, pain shot across my temple.

"Nate, I have a chronic illness. Believe me, I wish I could snap out of it, but I can't. You couldn't handle that or have the decency to tell me that you weren't committed anymore. But it's water under the bridge that I truly couldn't care less about."

He stepped in front of me when I tried to leave.

"You look beautiful. Fine. This is what I mean. If you could just move past it, we could start over. I could move back in and try again—"

"Are you fucking kidding me?" Heads whipped around at the loud screech in my voice. "There is no starting over or moving back in to *my* house."

He stuffed his hands into his pockets and shrugged. "I didn't ask for my deposit back, so technically it's still my house too."

"No, it's not. You signed it over. Aww, did your little girlfriend break up with you, and you need a place to live? What are you doing in the Bronx anyway? I thought you hated *slumming* it here. Wait, you know what?" I held up a hand and shook my head. "I don't care. Just know that I have nothing to say to you, ever. There is nothing to talk about or snap out of or house to move back in to." I searched the bar, and the waitress was gone. Nate had ruined my nice gesture and my night.

I gave up and headed back to the dining area, hoping I could shake this off enough and not tip off Landon that something was wrong.

"Look." Nate grabbed my arm. "I said I was sorry. You were always like this. If you want to mope around the house all by yourself, fine, but there are legal ways I can get back in or take back my deposit."

"Get your hands off my wife!" Landon bellowed and pushed Nate against the edge of the bar. I stepped between them and leaned back into Landon to try to calm him down. His already hard body was rigid, and I could almost hear his teeth grinding from the sharp clench of his jaw.

"Your...wife?" Nate looked between us and burst out laughing. "Why am I not surprised? You were so mad about me sleeping with somebody else when you've been sleeping with this asshole for years. Did you think I was stupid?"

"Are you all right?" Landon asked me as he wrapped his arm around my waist and pulled me flush to his body, neither of us denying anything Nate said. While I hadn't slept with Landon while Nate and I were together, no matter who I was with, I'd always belonged to Landon—whether

I'd known it at the time or not. I was more than ready to own it.

"I paid the check and couldn't find you by the bathrooms, so I wanted to make sure you were okay."

"I'm fine, babe. Sorry I disappeared, but I was regrettably detained." I glared at Nate, biting back a smile at his eye roll when I said "babe."

"He wants to move back in and talk, and he thinks I should *snap* out of it all." I turned my head to Landon, who was narrowing his eyes to slits at Nate as if he was planning to rip him apart. "I was about to tell him to go fuck himself when you showed up."

Landon coughed out a humorless laugh. "Well, I see backup isn't necessary since she's already made it crystal clear to stay the fuck away. But come near my wife again and see what happens."

Goose bumps broke out across my body as Landon seethed behind me. I didn't know if he said "wife" for effect, but it was affecting the hell out of me.

Landon stepped to the side, his arm still around me, and loomed over Nate.

"And to think," Nate scoffed, losing a little bravado, "your *wife* called my girlfriend a whore when she was—"

"One more word," Landon told him in a low, menacing voice that was hot as all hell. "And you'll have to sip your beer through a straw because I'll break your fucking jaw. Got it?"

Landon didn't wait for him to answer before he pulled me past the bar and out of the side entrance, nor did he look back as he dragged me around the corner where his truck was parked. Rage emanated from every part of his body as he gripped my hand so tightly my palm was almost numb.

"Landon, stop. I know he's an asshole, but you need to calm—"

He turned around, the heat in his eyes still burning bright under the streetlights, and backed me against the brick wall, draping his hand over my throat right under my jaw before he crashed his mouth into mine.

We'd only shared one kiss, and while it was hot enough for the memory to keep me up some nights, this kiss was not that. This was blistering heat that didn't stop, all the buildup over weeks and probably even years pouring out of us as he hooked my leg over his hip and ground against me, his erection huge and hard against my core. Tongues tangled and teeth scraped as we pawed at each other, tasting and devouring with no relief for this hunger that we'd been so damn clueless about all this time.

"You're mine," he panted when we broke apart. "You belong to me as much as I belong to you." He grazed his thumb over my swollen lips. "Say it, Jules," he whispered, his hooded eyes searching my face as he sifted his hand into my hair, weaving his fingers around a fistful and pulling until I lifted my head.

"I've been trying to say it all night." I slid my hands up his arms and grabbed his face. "I'm yours. God, we're so stupid."

"No kidding." He skated his hand down the side of my hip and squeezed when he landed on my ass. "I was waiting for you to catch up, but then I saw him put his hands on you and..." He nuzzled my neck, dragging open kisses down to my collarbone and across my throat.

I fell back against the wall, lolling my head to the side as Landon devoured my neck. It was dark but not late, early enough for anyone to pass by and see us groping each other against the wall. I was about to note that when Landon shut me up with another kiss, this one even more desperate than the first.

"Please," I begged and caught his mouth in another sloppy kiss as I rubbed my core against the hard bulge in his jeans.

"I think we need to go home before I slide my hand in between those gorgeous legs and make us both forget we're in public. And when I peel that dress off you, your beautiful body is for my eyes only." He pressed his forehead against mine. "Let's go. Twenty years is a long fucking time to wait."

19

LANDON

The restaurant was only fifteen minutes away from Julie's house, but the ride home took forever. The inside of my truck was silent other than my groan every time we hit a red light, which seemed to be every fucking one on the way.

I'd asked her out to dinner tonight to finally tell her I wanted to be more than just friends, but she looked so damn beautiful in that dress and we were having such a good time just being together, like we'd been since I arrived at her house the other night, I didn't want to put a wrench in any of it if she wasn't ready to talk.

I'd never shied away from a conversation—never mind, so damn many times—in my life. But there was never this much at stake. I wouldn't know how to function without Julie, and the very last thing I wanted was to spook her enough to make her put distance between us.

They'd tease me at work for being the rock from the north, the cool cucumber always in control. When I'd found out my ex-wife was cheating, it was a shock and a blow to my ego, but I'd never felt the need to punch the guy or even threaten him. My size had intimidated him enough not to have to use my hands or fists, and I'd been satisfied when he'd simply cowered away.

Then I saw Nate's hands on Julie and completely lost my shit.

I would have felt like decking the guy if I'd run into him anyway, as everything Julie had told me about what he'd done before he left sent me into a white-hot rage just thinking about it. I'd had no idea she was sick or that she'd been treated like that for so long, and if I let myself think about it too much, the anger coursing through me would almost cloud my vision. I was furious with him and at myself for being too damn busy to notice what she was going through for all that time.

She hadn't needed me to come to her rescue tonight, as she'd looked about as close to punching Nate as I was. I'd had to bite back a smile while I watched her in action. She was always strong and tough, but the thought of her sick and suffering alone made my stomach turn.

Realizing my feelings for Julie was a shock, but there'd been so many clues over the years—clues I'd missed or maybe ignored on purpose. Some were small, like the sketches I'd never thrown away for two decades. Others were huge enough to be embarrassed for overlooking them for so long. The thought of anything happening to Julie or anyone hurting her made me want to set the world on fire. Tonight might have been the first time I'd shown it, but nothing and no one had ever been more important to me than she was.

Then, instead of taking it slow, I'd backed her against the wall and plundered her mouth. Had I not heard a car horn in the distance, I would have slipped my hand inside her panties and made her come all over my fingers, right there in the street.

Every time I snuck a glance at her in the passenger seat, I'd only see the back of her head as she gazed out the window. It was as if both of us were afraid to talk and break whatever spell fell over us outside the restaurant. We'd done the same thing by the Bellagio fountains, but our actions had said too much to talk each other out of it this time.

We were five minutes away from her house when we came to a stop. The street I had to turn on was blocked off as a sanitation truck loaded garbage bags into the back.

"You've got to be fucking kidding me," I groaned and let my head fall back on the seat, frustration simmering in my gut as I white-knuckled the steering wheel.

"Impatient?" Julie asked as she looped her arms around my neck.

"Maybe a little," I whispered, cupping her cheek. Her mouth was still swollen from my kisses as it curved into a smile.

"I've been afraid to look at you the whole drive." Her gaze landed on my mouth. "After fighting this hard not to touch you for so long, I'm about to explode." Our heads whipped around at the beep of the truck, now backing up in front of another house but not vacating the street. Julie's hand sinking down my chest was the only thing preventing my brain from short-circuiting.

I ran my mouth down her neck, swirling my tongue around the tiny patch of skin behind her ear that'd made her slump against me when I'd pinned her to the wall.

"Save that for later, darlin'," I rasped, skating my hand up her leg and inching it across the inside of her thigh, teasing the wet cotton between her legs. "If we ever get back to your house, this is the first thing I want to taste." I moved the soaked material to the side and traced her slit with the tip of my finger.

"Jesus, Landon," she said, gasping as she dug her nails into my shoulder.

"Open a little wider for me, baby. Just like that... *Fuck, Julie.*" I slid my finger inside her, pinching her clit as I pumped in and out at a slow pace that tortured us both.

Her legs fell open, and she whimpered into my neck as her hips bucked off the seat, riding my hand.

"Feel good, darlin'? Tell me."

A long moan fell from her lips as she buried her head into my neck.

"I'll take that as a yes," I chuckled. "You're so wet, so fucking tight. I'm ruined once I sink inside you tonight. My sweet Julie." My voice was nothing but gravelly need. Fingering her in the front seat wasn't much better than doing it outside the restaurant, but nothing short of death would have made me pull away now. I was about to unbuckle my seat belt and bury my face in her sweet, wet heat right here, with cars behind us and in front of us. The louder she'd scream, the more everyone would know she belonged to me.

Maybe this was why I'd resisted Julie for this long. Somewhere deep inside me knew that once my hands and mouth were on her, I'd be too hooked to ever stop.

She clenched her legs together, squeezing my wrist as she fluttered on my fingers.

"There's my girl. Look at me."

I clamped my other hand behind her neck when she lifted her head, her eyes so hooded they were almost closed as her hips quivered against my palm.

"Eyes on me when I make you come. I don't want to miss a thing." She clasped her knees together even tighter, gasping a shuddering breath as she held my eyes, pressing her forehead into mine.

"That's a good girl," I whispered against her mouth before I took it in a bruising kiss. I jerked against Julie's hand as she wrapped it around the aching bulge in my jeans. I was hard to the point of pain and ready to burst through the zipper. "So fucking beautiful when you come," I murmured, tearing my lips away from hers to drag kisses over her throat and down her chest, tracing a line along the swells of her breasts with the tip of my tongue.

We broke apart at the blaring of a horn behind us. It was the second time tonight a car horn had brought me back to reality, where I shouldn't have been the guy pawing his girl in public. Julie covered her face as I stepped on the gas and finally turned onto her block.

My eyes flicked to hers after I put my truck in park behind her car in the driveway. She laughed until I sucked my finger inside my mouth and inched it out. My eyes fluttered as her taste melted on my tongue like sugar.

"So damn sweet," I said, running my tongue along my bottom lip as I stepped out of the seat.

I rushed around my truck to open her door, chuckling when she climbed out on shaky legs.

"Need help, baby?" I took her hand and pulled her flush to me when she stood, loving this new novelty of touching her whenever the hell I wanted, which was all the time. "You're wobbling a little."

She tilted her head and shot me a glare. "You just made me come behind a sanitation truck. My legs are jelly, and my brain is scrambled." She scrubbed a hand down her face.

"Shit, that's hot when you say it like that." I slanted my

mouth over hers. She whimpered into my mouth but tore away when her back hit the side of my truck.

"We need to get inside before one of us gets arrested." She grabbed my hand and dragged me toward her front stoop as she fished inside her purse with her other hand for her keys.

"Landon, please stop," she said, slumped against me after I swept her hair off her shoulder and painted kisses down her neck. Every time she tried to insert the key in the lock, I dove in harder, sucking on her earlobe as an aroused but frustrated groan escaped her.

"Here," she said on a breathy moan as she dangled her keys. "Open the fucking door if you're going to make it impossible."

I cupped her chin and turned her face toward me. "Impatient to get your hands on me, darlin'?" I brushed her lips, nibbling on her bottom one as I pulled away. "You have me all night long."

And the rest of my fucking life. Julie was all I'd ever want. She was it for me, and I knew it with a bone-deep certainty.

"I want to start all night as soon as possible." She jingled the keys in front of my face. "I need to get inside."

"Took the words right out of my mouth." I snatched her keys out of her hand, smirking as I opened the door and locked it quickly behind us once we stepped through.

I threw the keys on the table by the door and brought her back into my arms.

"You get cranky when you're hot and bothered, huh?"

She grabbed the back of my head and crushed her lips against mine, moaning into my mouth as I backed her against the wall.

"Here we are again," I said, coasting my hand down her hips and squeezing her ass with both hands as I pulled her against me.

"So this is it? We're doing this?" She drifted her hands down my chest, breathing heavily as she searched my gaze.

"Yeah, Jules. We are." I brushed my thumb over her lips. "I love you. I've always loved you, but I'm so *in* love with you I can barely see straight. Maybe I always have been but was too stupid or chicken to see it, but"—I draped my hand over the nape of her neck as her eyes glossed over—"I was waiting for you to catch up to tell you. But I think we've waited long enough, right?"

Her face crumpled as if she were about to sob as she dug her fingers into my biceps and darted her eyes around the room.

"Jules, you're scaring me. Talk to—"

"I love you. And not just how I've always loved you. Or maybe, like you said, we ignored it because we were afraid. But I love you so much. I've spent my life kissing strangers when *the one* was right there all along." She let out a watery chuckle. "So stupid, isn't it?"

"Very fucking stupid," I breathed out, my relieved exhale so deep and palpable my shoulders drooped. "Now that that's out of the way, give me back those lips, darlin'."

This kiss wasn't as frantic as the ones by the restaurant or in my truck. This was unhurried and deliberate, our lips moving slowly to savor and appreciate rather than devour. I pulled her away from the wall to slide her jacket off her shoulders and threw it behind me.

"So beautiful," I whispered. "And you really have no idea. You never did." I skated my hands down her arms and lifted them over her head. "Beautiful and mine." I slanted my mouth over hers as I pressed into her, hard enough against her to feel every inch of how much I wanted her.

We were sloppy and starved as we pawed at each other to get as close as possible. This kiss was a lot dirtier and full of all the primal need that had built up over the past couple of months—or maybe even decades, I still wasn't sure. All I knew was I had to have her right here and right now.

"Let me go so I can touch you."

I released her hands and dropped to my knees.

"Better?" My lip curled as I hooked my thumbs into the sides of her panties and dragged them down her legs.

She didn't answer but looked down at me with widened, pleading eyes.

"I'm still sensitive from before. Please..."

She trailed off when I painted tiny kisses over her clit, swirling my tongue around the hard little bump as her hips jerked against my face.

"I've wanted to do this from the minute I saw you in this dress." I hooked her leg over my shoulder. "I dreamed of this so many times. Look at you, so fucking pretty." She trembled when I dragged my tongue back and forth before diving in and snaking my tongue inside her.

Julie let out a sound that was somewhere between a moan and a mewl as her head fell back against the wall with a thump. She wove her hand into my hair and pulled, bucking her hips against my face as I lost myself in her. I needed to make her come in the next few minutes or I'd blow in my jeans. I knew exactly what she meant by kissing strangers for so long, now that I'd found out what home tasted like.

Julie. It would always be Julie.

I moved my mouth to her clit and sucked hard enough for her to fold against me as I slid two fingers inside her. She dug her heel into my back as she screamed, muttering my name and other words I couldn't understand as she pulsed against my fingers, squeezing them like a vise.

"I think you're going to kill me," she said, pressing her palm into her forehead as she chased her breath.

"You taste so damn good." I stood and drew her to me. "Get upstairs." I swatted her bare ass. "I'm not done."

Her eyes widened a moment before a huge grin split her mouth. She was the one who was about to kill me once I sank inside her. When she turned around, gripping the banister as she climbed the stairs, I was right behind her, ready to catch her in case her legs gave out.

The minute she opened the door to her bedroom, I spun her around and grabbed the hem of her dress. I peeled it over her head and stepped back, allowing my eyes to drink her in. I drifted my hands over the swells of her breasts and the lace of her bra, her soft stomach, and the sweet curve of her hips I always had to drag my eyes away from.

I flicked on the lamp sitting on her nightstand. The soft glow of the streetlights leaked through her window, but it wasn't enough. I needed to see all of her.

A blush filled her cheeks as she reached to turn it off.

"Don't you dare," I growled, grabbing her wrist and hauling her to me. I held her eyes as I reached behind her and unhooked her bra, smoothing my hands down her shoulders until it was off.

"What did I say about hiding from me?" I whispered in her ear before I dipped my head to kiss down her chest and sucked her nipple into my mouth.

"I'm not hiding... Ah, right there." She arched her back as I cupped her other breast, teasing her nipple with my thumb as I traced circles around the other with my tongue.

"Like that, wife?"

A guttural moan escaped her as I ran my tongue over the cluster of freckles across her hip. The marriage was supposed to be fake, but the rush of warmth spreading through my chest when I'd called her my wife today had felt real as hell.

"Please, Landon," she panted.

She tugged at the back of my shirt until I straightened.

"If you want me naked, all you have to do is ask, darlin'." I pulled off my shirt as she fumbled with my belt buckle.

"You have something, right?"

I nodded, digging my wallet out of my pocket before I let my jeans drop, and I kicked them to the side. Before I could search for what I needed, Julie fell to her knees in front of me, skimming her hands down my chest as she sank to the carpet.

"My God, you're perfect." She bit her lip and pulled down my boxers until my cock sprang free and bounced against my stomach.

"Jules, please. If you put your mouth on me, I'm not going to—"

I dropped my head back with a growl as she swallowed me whole, digging her nails into my backside as her head bobbed up and down, moaning around my dick as she took me to the back of her throat. I yanked a fistful of her hair as I fought to keep my balance, my brain cells lost in Julie's mouth as she sucked me even harder.

I pulled her head back, and watching myself slip out of her mouth with a wet pop almost did me in.

"Time for that later. On the bed and spread your legs."

She stood and did what she was told, smirking at me as she propped herself up on her elbows, her trepidation over showing me her naked body gone as she spread her legs and tipped her head back. I salivated at the gorgeous sight in front of me and couldn't rip the foil packet open fast enough.

She was a goddess, and I planned to worship at her feet for the rest of my days. I was so done for. She had me in a way no one else had or ever would.

After I rolled on the condom and climbed on top of her, I hovered for a moment, resting my forearms on either side of her.

"What is it?" Julie asked, her voice strangled with the same need coursing through me.

"I just like looking at you." I pressed my lips against hers, slow and sensual, as I eased inside her. She dragged her hands up and down my back as I inched in and out, making sure she was used to me before I pounded into her like I wanted.

"Please do something for me," she croaked out in a hoarse whisper, her eyes fluttering every time I went deeper.

"I'd do anything for you." I draped my hand over her cheek.

"Go harder. Don't treat me like I'm made of glass." She clutched the back of my neck. "I'm all yours, so just take me."

I caught her mouth in a sloppy kiss as I did exactly what she asked, the mattress creaking under us as I hooked her leg over my hip, driving into her as deep and as hard as I could.

Her leg shook as she pulsed around my cock, and I lost it. I spilled into her, giving her all I had as my release ripped through me.

I dropped my head into the crook of her shoulder, my body spent and sated in a way I'd never found or thought possible with anyone.

"How was that?" I teased when I lifted my head.

She laughed as I swept kisses over her eyelids, down her cheeks, and along her jaw until I got to her mouth.

"That, husband," she said, clasping her legs around my waist, "was perfect."

20

JULIE

I fluttered my eyes open, squinting to make out the time on the alarm clock on my nightstand. Panic shot through me as I sat up and tried to swing my legs over the side of the bed until I remembered it was Saturday.

When was the last time I'd slept so well that I'd forgotten what day it was? Even when I was exhausted, my sleep was restless and I never slept straight through, or at least not enough to cause my brain to reset once I woke up.

"Where's the fire?" a grumbly voice said from behind me as I was yanked back into bed by a hard arm against an even harder body.

Ah, right. That was why I'd slept like the dead. Soul-deep confessions and multiple orgasms took a lot out of a person.

"I forgot what day of the week it was. Something knocked me out pretty hard." I sighed into the pillow as he lifted my hair off my neck and dragged kisses along my nape.

"Oh yeah?"

I squirmed against his mouth as he ran his lips down my

back, moaning at the silk of his tongue and scratch of his stubble as he moved lower.

"I love these three little freckles." He traced the cluster of dots on my hip bone with the tip of his finger.

"Freckles do it for you…" I trailed off when he followed the path of his fingers with his tongue.

"When they're on you." He painted kisses down the back of my thigh. "What else can I find?" I giggled when he nipped at the sensitive skin on the back of my knee.

"I think you found everything last night." I rolled onto my back as Landon peered down at me, his dark eyes full of heat as he raked them over my still-naked body.

"I'll keep exploring to make sure. Wouldn't want to miss anything." My legs fell open as he climbed on top of me. "Good morning, gorgeous."

"Back at you, doll," I said, gliding my nails up and down his back.

"Mmm…this is a nice way to wake up," he said, smoothing my hair off my forehead. "I could get used to this."

"Me too." I lolled my head to the side as he nuzzled my neck. "Can we just stay like this the whole day?"

"Naked and in bed? I may have to run to the store for condoms later, but we can absolutely do that." A smile broke out on his ridiculously handsome face. "I love you. And I love having you like this." He lifted my leg onto his hip and ran his thumb over the smattering of freckles. "I love knowing little things like this, where your freckles are, how your legs shake right before you come, what you taste like."

"You're a dirty romantic, babe," I said, rolling my hips against him. He was already hard and huge, and although I was sore from last night's repeat invasion, I was ready for much more. This was a good kind of sore, a *great* kind of sore.

"When it comes to you, I'm a lot of things. Just managed to ignore them for, like, twenty years or so."

I laughed at his exaggerated shrug.

"And not that I don't like when you call me doll, but babe gives me a rush." He popped his brow, a wide grin splitting his lips.

"You got it bad, Clark."

"I do," he said with a slow nod. "And it feels so fucking good to show it."

"I love you too." I lifted my head and pressed my lips against his. "Sorry I said it on a delay."

He chuckled against my lips and ran his fingers through my hair. I'd been having sex for more years than I wanted to tally up, but it had never been like this. Even in the dirtiest moments last night, I'd felt worshipped and connected to Landon in a way I hadn't been with anyone else. I'd woken up with an innate and pure satisfaction.

"Can I ask you something?"

Landon pulled back, squinting at me.

"Of course."

"The first night you came here." I chewed on my bottom lip. "I shouldn't have been listening and I'm sorry, but in the shower, were you..."

A bashful smile played on his lips, and he dropped his chin to his chest.

"I was." He nodded. "And you don't need to apologize. It's hot knowing that you were listening."

I pushed his shoulders back when he went for another kiss.

"There's a second part to my question."

He narrowed his eyes. "Okay."

"Did you...say my name?"

He dropped his head back as a laugh rumbled through his chest.

"Are you really asking me that, Jules?"

"I just...didn't know if I was hearing things out of wishful thinking. Stop laughing at me." I shoved his chest as he laughed even harder. "I shouldn't have asked."

He pinned me back down when I tried to roll away.

"I didn't say 'Julie.'"

"Oh," I said, my cheeks heating with humiliation and jealousy that he'd come with someone else on his mind, but it was my fault for asking the question and eavesdropping when I shouldn't have been.

He cupped my chin and turned my head to face him when I looked away.

"I said '*my* Julie.' I came with you—and only you—on my mind and only *your* name on my lips. So, any other questions?"

"Your Julie?" I repeated around the sudden lump in the back of my throat.

"Damn fucking right, *my* Julie." He took my mouth in a slow kiss, curling his tongue around mine as he snaked his arm under my waist to lift me closer.

"You're a swoony bastard, husband," I breathed out when we broke apart.

"We can head in there now." He nodded toward the hallway. "You can make all my dreams come true. I can eat you for breakfast before I fuck you against the tiles."

"I'm your dream come true," I teased and kissed his chin.

"Yeah, Jules." He cupped my cheek, skimming his thumb back and forth along my jaw. "You're exactly that."

His mouth came down on mine again as my head spun

from everything that had happened last night and all it meant for us in the light of day. I'd never known this kind of happiness, and while it frightened me a little, I was enjoying every moment of being right where I—where *we*—were always meant to be.

"I'm up for it if you are. Although, there may not be room for two of us." I scrunched my nose.

"That's half the fun. Come on." He popped off the bed and held out his hand.

If anyone had told me a year ago I'd be strolling naked down my upstairs hallway with Landon to get into my shower together, I would have said that was impossible because Landon and I weren't like that.

At the time, I would have been telling the truth. We weren't then, but we sure as hell were now—and there was no going back.

I'd been so afraid of taking a chance on us, but just on the other side of fear was something glorious. And the only thing I regretted now was not leaping over that line I was so terrified of crossing much sooner.

A morbid voice in the back of my head taunted me, asking how I could commit an uncertain lifetime to anyone. But today, that voice, and the monster around the corner, weren't going to ruin a thing.

My joints were stiff on some mornings, although the intensity and duration weren't nearly as bad as a few months ago. Today, I was sore from good old exertion as I put muscles to use that had been dormant for a lot longer than I'd been sick.

Sex with Landon was the best kind of shock to my system.

I pulled back the curtain to run the water, drifting my hand over the spray until it was hot enough to steam, and climbed into the tub. Even before my goal was to loosen up in the shower, I preferred it just short of scalding.

"I didn't know you liked bathing in liquid lava," Landon said as he stepped in behind me and reached over me to adjust the temperature. "I don't mind steaming it up in here, but I'd like to have skin when we're done."

"So dramatic," I sighed, pivoting toward Landon as I tipped my head back to wet my hair. I wasn't concerned with any rolls or ripples along my body as I stepped under the spray. Instead, I tilted my head back more, smiling at the tortured groan erupting from Landon's throat as I let the water run over me.

After hating what had happened to my body for the past few months, and a moment of panic when Landon had stopped me from turning off the light, I felt beautiful and powerful.

"You know what you're doing," he rasped, grabbing my waist to haul me closer. "Don't tease me, baby."

"Isn't that the point?" I raked my wet hands through his dark hair, scraping my nails back and forth along his scalp. "You wanted the fantasy, right?"

"I did. But I'll tell you a secret." He dipped his head under the spray and slicked his hair back with his hand. My eyes followed the drops of water over the smattering of hair on his chest, over his abs, and dripping off his cock. My tongue tingled, yearning to trace along the same path.

"What's the secret?" I asked as I reached for the body wash and squirted some into the palm of my hand.

"What you heard the other night, that wasn't the first time I'd called out your name with my dick in my hand, wishing it were you."

"Landon Michael Clark, I'm shocked." I pressed a hand to my chest in mock horror. "Turn around."

His brow furrowed.

"But then I can't see you."

"You'll feel me, I promise." I pressed my mouth against his, sucking on his bottom lip as I pulled back. "You said you wanted the dream. Turn around, babe."

He groaned and slowly turned around.

I rubbed my hands together and glided the soap up his back and across his shoulders, pressing my fingers into the muscle as I drifted my hands down his torso and kneaded the globes of his ass.

"How many squats do you do a day? It's like a rock back here." I dug my fingers deeper, smiling at his hiss when I skated my hand across and up and down.

"Let me turn around and I'll show you what's a *rock*."

"Poor baby, are you getting frustrated?" I wrapped my arms around him and worked my hands over his chest, skimming down his pecs, over his abs, and down his muscular thighs. "Have a little patience, doll. We're doing my fantasy first, and then we'll do yours." I dragged kisses across his shoulder blades. "You're so perfect," I whispered as I smoothed my hand across his stomach.

He truly was gorgeous perfection, and I still couldn't believe he was mine.

"Perfect and beautiful," I said as I took his cock in my soapy hand, pumping up and down as Landon pressed his hands against the wall.

"That's my line... Fuck," he hissed. "That's good, baby."

"Yeah?" I whispered into his ear as I cupped his balls with my other hand. He banged his hand against the wall when I squeezed, his cock jerking in my palm.

"Jules, enough," he gritted out, the muscles in his back constricting as his gorgeous body went rigid from head to toe.

I shifted him toward the water, kissing down his arm as I rinsed him off and maneuvered my way around until we were face-to-face.

"There's more room in here than I thought." I trailed my tongue across and down his chest, biting his nipple as I made my way down to the floor of the tub and onto my knees.

"Time to finish what I started," I said, peering up at him as I wrapped my mouth around his cock. His eyes widened as I took him to the back of my throat and inched him out, circling my tongue around the tip and along the vein trailing up the side, smiling as his whimpers and moans reverberated around my tiny bathroom.

The porcelain of the tub bit into my sore knees, but I didn't care. Landon grew harder in my mouth as I continued sucking, kissing, and teasing every inch until he tapped the back of my head.

I hummed around his dick in approval right before he spilled down my throat with a roar.

"Fuck, Julie," he cried out as he dug his fingers into my hair and yanked on a fistful, swaying his hips into me as I swallowed every last drop.

"My Julie," he whispered as he cupped my chin, gazing down at me with hooded eyes and a hazy smile.

"Dream come true?" I asked, a smirk tickling the side of my mouth despite the scratching at the back of my throat from all the love in his eyes.

He grabbed my wrist and pulled me up to stand as he crushed his lips against mine, pinning me against the tiles.

He laughed when he tore his lips away, sifting both his hands into my wet locks.

"You have no idea."

21

LANDON

"You're a fucking show-off."

I laughed as Will smirked at me on-screen.

"I was lucky. Sullivan asked if he could bring some friends with him to lunch at the 21 Club, and I thought it was just his staff, not friends from other firms."

"So the New York office tripled their revenue before they even *have* an office." He raised his soda can in salute. "And being so damn humble is the worst kind of showing off."

"Maybe I'm just used to being awesome." I shrugged and leaned back in my chair. "And we have an office, just not the NameTech complex in Charlotte."

I mostly worked from Julie's spare room, only using the Manhattan office when I needed to see a client. Even then, for the past two weeks, I'd taken the six train into the city, seen who I wanted to see, and come home.

I kept my stuff in her spare room but climbed into bed with her every night—and some afternoons. We never discussed whether my staying at Julie's house was a permanent arrangement, but I'd already told the apartment broker that I'd found a place and would let her know if I wanted to look again in the future.

As far as I was concerned, I was home, in this house and with this woman. But while we were in love and married on paper, we were still getting used to the new us. Most couples didn't marry, move in together, and then start dating, but when it felt this right, rules weren't needed.

"Hey—oh, sorry." Julie brought her voice down to a whisper as she cringed by the doorway, her adorable face twisted in a grimace. "You usually close the door when you're in a meeting."

"It's not a real meeting. It's Will," I said, waving her over. "You remember Julie, right?"

"I do." I held in a growl at the seductive dip in his voice. "Nice to see you again."

"You too," she said, angling her head toward the screen. I pulled her onto my lap, stifling a laugh at her widened eyes when she swiveled her head around.

"Ah, so Sullivan isn't the only luck you're having in New York, then?" Will arched a brow at us. "Congrats on that too."

"Thanks. New York definitely doesn't suck." I wrapped my arms around her waist, kissing her cheek as I held Will's gaze.

Julie pursed her lips at me when I shrugged.

"Will and I were just catching up," I told her as I lifted her arm and placed it around my neck.

"And your man was showing off earlier about how much he's already killing it in New York." Will shut his eyes and shook his head. "And he may be showing off a little now for my sake, but I'm glad he's happy."

"I would agree on all of that." Julie chuckled, holding my gaze. "And I hope he is."

"Oh, he is." I dropped a kiss to her shoulder and turned back to the screen. "We can catch up on the rest when I'm there."

"I look forward to it," Will said, flashing us a genuine smile. He was a pain in the ass but a decent guy and a good friend.

I smirked at Julie's raised brow after I ended the call.

"I've never been claimed over Zoom before." Julie turned in my lap and draped her legs over my thighs. "I'm surprised you hadn't told him about us already."

I shifted her around until she straddled me.

"I was waiting until I went back to Charlotte in a few weeks and he made another crack about how hot you are."

I rubbed my palms along her thighs and squeezed her ass with both hands.

She tilted her head to the side and narrowed her eyes at me.

"Seriously?"

I lifted a shoulder. "I like making it crystal clear that you're mine. And I'll probably do that a lot." I shrugged and pulled her closer. "Sorry if that's a problem."

"Are you going to do that at Dean and Maria's later?" She pushed off my chest. "I'm kind of looking forward to the shock."

"I feel like we're going to get a lot of *finallys* thrown back in our faces tonight." I skimmed my thumb along her jaw.

"Either that or *but we knew this already*. Nana will probably think she worked her magic on us in Vegas."

"We seemed to be the last to know." I ran my hands up and down her back. "All done with work?"

"I am."

I groaned when she rubbed herself against me.

"I like knowing you're right upstairs. It's going to be hard to function when you go back."

"It's only for a week, and this time when I come back , we can have all the happy reunion sex." I nuzzled her neck and ran my lips along her collarbone.

"You really are kicking ass in New York," she said, dropping her head back to give me more access. "Plus, watching you leave for the subway in a suit is serious eye candy." My chest pinched at her wide smile as she dug her fingers into my hair. "I'm so proud of you."

"There is a lot more to do before I can say I'm kicking ass here, but it's a good start." I brushed her hair off her shoulder. "It's all falling into place, darlin'." I dipped my head and trailed kisses above the neckline of her T-shirt.

"Camera is off, right?" she asked on a breathy moan.

"It is," I rasped, leaning forward to slap my laptop shut. "We have an hour, you said?"

She pulled her T-shirt over her head and threw it off to the side.

"They have enough extended family coming. We don't have to be the first ones there," she said, her eyes on mine as she reached behind her to unhook her bra, slipping it off her shoulders. My mouth was on her nipple like a magnet as she writhed against me. I rolled it between my teeth, both of us moaning as it pebbled on my tongue.

"Let's hope we're not the last ones," I murmured, grabbing her thighs to bring her closer. I lifted my hips off my chair as I positioned her right where I wanted her. Dry humping my wife as I buried my head in her perfect tits was my idea of heaven, and I never wanted to leave.

We pulled up to Dean and Maria's house only a half hour late, mostly due to Julie's search for another shirt after I'd left a bite mark on her chest.

"You and I are like two horny teenagers," she said,

looking down her shirt. "I haven't had a hickey since high school."

"We had a long buildup, Jules." I reached over the console to pinch the inside of her thigh. "There's a trail of scratches down my back too. Animal."

A sweet laugh fell from her lips as I shut off the engine.

"What's wrong?" I asked when I noticed her flexing her fingers.

"My hands are sore. Happens when I work a lot. Usually, ibuprofen helps, but it's been nonstop all week. It sucks to be a creative with bad hands." She hissed as she pulled her fingers into a slow fist.

"You have beautiful, talented hands." I picked up her hand and kissed her palm. "You need to tell me when something hurts."

"Babe, something *always* hurts," she said with a soft chuckle. "But I can manage."

My stomach sank as she climbed out of the cab. Sometimes, it was easy to forget about Julie's condition. I hadn't seen her symptoms at their worst, but for the past few weeks, I'd catch her wincing in pain in the mornings or how she'd be full of energy one day and have trouble getting off the couch the next. She asked me to trust her enough to let me know when something was really wrong, but I hated thinking that pain every day was something she shrugged off as normal.

"Hey, guys!" Maria gave us quick hello hugs after she answered the door. "Come in," she said as she held the door open behind her.

We made our way past the oversized 4 and 0 balloons to go inside.

"These are courtesy of my niece," Maria said as she picked up the weights holding down the strings and put them in a corner. “Dean didn’t want a lot of forty decorations, but Lila is hard to refuse.”

“There they are!” Dean rushed over to us and pulled us both into a hug. “Glad you could make it.”

“Sorry we’re late,” Julie said. I held in a laugh when she adjusted her shirt to move the collar up. Maybe we were animals, but I was loving every second.

“You’re fine. The trays of food are in the kitchen, so you can help yourselves.” He leaned in to whisper to us. “And this is why a real wedding would have been a circus.”

I laughed as I swept my gaze over his living room. I recognized Dean’s aunts and uncles and Maria’s sister playing with a little girl on the floor. I heard Mr. Calabrese’s voice drift in from the kitchen and others I wasn’t familiar with. Their house seemed big, but extended family was in every corner.

“And this isn’t even everyone who was supposed to come. Go get a plate before the last two folding chairs are gone.”

“Uncle Dean, why are your balloons hiding?”

Dean laughed at the little girl pulling at the hem of his shirt.

“Because, Li,” he said, lifting her up. “The balloons are great but they’re big, so they may get in the way of people trying to eat. This is Lila.” Dean turned toward us. “Our niece and decorator.” He dipped his head to meet her gaze. “Lila, this is Landon and Julie. They’ve been friends with me and Titi Maria for a long time.”

“Nice to meet you,” Julie said behind me. “Wow, you look just like your aunt.”

Lila had the same long, dark hair pulled back into pigtails and olive skin.

“Hi,” she said and stuck out her bottom lip at Dean in an

unhappy pout.

"But how is anyone supposed to know you're forty?"

"Oh, we know, sweetheart," I said, cracking up at Dean's scowl when he lifted his head.

"You're next, buddy, so stop being so damn smug."

Lila gasped in his arms. "Isn't that a bad word?"

"Low-level bad word, kiddo." He kissed the top of her head before setting her down. She took one last glance at the balloons in the corner and went back into the living room.

"We meant to have you over earlier, but since the wedding, it's been a whirlwind. How is it already three months since we've seen either one of you?" Maria said.

"Let them get something to eat," Dean's grandmother said as she came up behind him. "Before there's nothing left." She put her hand in the crook of Dean's elbow and motioned to the kitchen.

"Looking good, Nana," I said, kissing her cheek.

"I manage. Do I look old enough to have a forty-year-old grandson?"

"Not even close," Julie said.

"Your friends are nice kids." Nana patted Dean's hand. "I told you that at the wedding a few months ago."

I snuck a look at Julie behind me. Her eyes widened for a second when they met mine. We'd been married just as long, but it was still—mostly—a secret only between us. She hadn't mentioned telling anyone, and the only ones I'd told were my father and the HR department at work.

Dean nodded to the kitchen behind him. "Help yourselves. Anything you want to drink is in the cooler on the side."

"What can I get you, darlin'?" I asked Julie, stifling a grin when I spotted Dean's furrowed brow in my periphery.

"Just water for now. I'll have some wine after I eat." Julie's lips twitched as her eyes met mine. "Thanks, babe."

I wrapped my arm around her waist and pressed my lips against hers. We both smiled into the kiss when Maria gasped.

"For real?" she asked, clasping her hands under her chin as her eyes darted between us.

"For real." I drew Julie closer and kissed the top of her head.

"Holy shit," Dean said, his eyes wide. "I mean, it's a shock, yet it's not. But...wow, I feel like this needs a toast or something."

"I knew it," Nana said, slapping Dean's chest. "Now they can get going on those babies." Nana smiled at us as she ambled back into the living room.

"I don't know about that yet." I grinned at Julie but felt her stiffen next to me.

Julie smiled back, but something was off. I knew her well enough to know the difference between a genuine smile and one she pushed across her lips to pretend. She'd done that for most of the weekend in Vegas, and now that I lived with her, I watched for it all the time. She'd said her hands hurt, but she'd made her way inside without limping.

It was easy to fall into a spiral of panic and worry when it came to Julie, but I would fight to keep it in check and trust her to tell me whatever was bothering her later.

"I am going to need details," Maria said. "Like, when did this happen?"

"I must be missing a step," Dean said, laughing as he rubbed at his neck. "When you said you were staying with Julie, I didn't think anything of it. I guess you moved in since you were..." He tilted his head from side to side.

"Well, yes and no," I said with a shrug. "We haven't been

together for long, but it's been brewing for a while."

"Almost twenty years is a while?" Dean snickered. "You're lucky I'm too happy for you guys to give you shit about that tonight."

"Wait, did this happen in Vegas?" Maria squinted at us. "I thought I picked up on something between you guys."

Julie looked up at me and shrugged. I didn't know where to begin either. I'd gone on that trip to celebrate Dean and Maria's wedding and spend time with my best friend. I'd ended up marrying her and then slowly realizing I was in love with her.

It was too complicated to think about, much less explain.

Dean scoffed. "Go get some food and sit. We need to talk."

"What would they say if they found out we got married too?" Julie whispered to me after we filled our plates.

"That we stole their thunder, probably."

"That may be a little too much for tonight." She chuckled and motioned to where Dean and Maria were waiting for us on the couch, Dean tapping his foot when he caught our gaze. "Maybe just say we had a good time in Vegas together, and we didn't want it to end."

"I guess it's good to start with the truth." I slid my arm around her waist. "Then I realized I was crazy and hopelessly in love with you and eventually landed on your doorstep."

"Crazy and hopelessly?" She smiled, but it was another one that didn't make it up to her eyes.

"Oh yeah, darlin'," I whispered, leaning in to give her a kiss.

"All right, enough," Dean called out to us. "Details, kids," he said as he patted the empty seat next to him.

"But before you start—here." Dean handed me a bottle

of beer. "To the long road to happiness and its glorious destination."

"I'll drink to that," I said, clinking the neck of my bottle to his before I took a long pull.

We were together in all the ways that mattered and permanent as far as I was concerned, but our marriage was still just on paper. I had plans to make it official in every sense, but I was waiting for the right time. We threw around the words husband and wife for a joke and sometimes for foreplay, but the day I finally made her my wife for real wouldn't be in secret.

We took Dean and Maria through the shortest version possible, and I was thankful when cake time gave us a reprieve from questions.

"I want to point out," Dean said as he handed me a piece of cake, "that I didn't say *finally* once."

"I'm honestly a little disappointed," I said as I passed the first piece of cake to Julie.

"Nah, I'll save it for your wedding toast." Dean jabbed my arm.

"It's okay. Titi Maria will clean it up."

We turned to Maria's niece, tears streaming down her cheeks as she clutched on to an empty cake plate. Her mother was trying to calm her down, but she only cried louder as Maria wiped the cake remnants off the kitchen tile.

"Here, sweetheart." I went over to her with my piece of cake and a fork. "Don't cry. See?" I pointed behind me. "There's plenty of cake."

Her big brown eyes studied me before they darted from me to her mother.

"What do you say, *mija*?"

"Thank you," she said, eyeing me as she took the plate

from my hand. A tiny smile pulled across her lips as her sniffles ceased. I hated seeing kids cry, which would probably make me a wimp as a parent.

When I turned around, Julie was already in the living room, settled into an empty corner of the couch as she sipped from her paper coffee cup with an empty gaze, ticking up my concern from the beginning of the night.

I turned to go join her and figure out what was bothering her when I felt a tap on my leg.

"Since you gave me your cake, do you want a cookie? Titi bought them for me, but you could have one." Lila handed me a paper plate with an oversized chocolate chip cookie.

"Thank you, Lila." She smiled widely when I took the plate out of her hand. "That's very nice of you."

"I think my niece is trying to steal your man," Maria said to Julie as she squeezed my arm.

"She is beautiful, but my heart belongs to the brunette on the couch."

Julie's smile was tight when she lifted her head, tempting me to say a quick goodbye and get her out of here so she could tell me what was wrong.

"You guys can stay later," Dean said, pulling me out of my panic for a moment. "We can give you a tour."

"No, we'll head home in a little while. Next time."

"Head *home*?" He chuckled and dropped his hand to my shoulder. "So, tell me something," he whispered. "It's new, but is it serious?"

I glanced back at Julie, a bit of relief flooding through me when she gave me a real smile this time.

"Fuck yes."

And I meant that with every bit of my soul.

"Everything okay?" I asked Julie once we were almost home. She'd been quiet since we'd gotten into my truck, but

I didn't press, hoping she'd open up on her own. "You seemed a little quiet tonight."

"I'm fine. Just a crazy few months, I guess."

"You get mad at me when I worry, but I know you well enough to tell when something is bothering you. So, talk to me."

She shrugged without turning around.

"A lot of my friends are having babies in their forties. Comes with a little risk, but it's common and usually okay. But for me..." she said on a long sigh. "My doctor told me that some women have a big risk of flaring post-pregnancy, and that combined with the risk that already comes with age...well, she didn't say no but didn't seem to be a big advocate for it, considering my test numbers go up and down each visit."

I nodded, waiting until she got it all out before I figured out what to say.

"I decided that day it was too big of a chance to take. Not only for me, but for a baby I may not be able to take care of after it's here. I had just broken up with Nate, so it wasn't like it was a real option for me at that point anyway. I was disappointed but was mostly okay with being a cool aunt to my friends' babies. It's not that I can't have kids, it's that I won't. And I can't in good conscience change my mind." She let out a long exhale and shrugged. "Maybe it was a selfish decision, but I never doubted it was the right one."

"Until now?" I asked as I pulled into her driveway.

"We've been so deliriously happy lately, that at times, I almost forget that I'm...me." She uttered a sad chuckle and rubbed the back of my neck. "I was okay with my decision not to have kids when it was just me, but you are this wonderful man with all these gorgeous and brilliant genes to pass along to a baby." She sucked in a long breath. "What

Nana said got to me a little, and then watching you with Lila and how good you were with her... I felt awful keeping you from that. Not that we've talked about anything that far into the future, but it's not fair for you to miss out on being a father because of me."

I sucked in a long breath and stretched my arm along the back of her seat.

"No, we haven't talked about the future too much since we only just figured out the present."

Her shoulders shook with a chuckle.

"There are other ways to have kids if we decide that's what we want. My cousins were adopted, and I only found out when I was in high school. They were just my family, and that's how it would be if we adopted. And if kids aren't in the future, even though I have all this awesome DNA I'll have to keep to myself"—I picked up her hand and laced our fingers together—"the only thing I'm sure I want is you." I brought her hand to my lips. "As long as I have you, I'm flexible with everything else."

"Flexible?" She gave me a soggy smile.

"I've told you before, but I guess I have to say it again. Nothing matters to me more than you do. That's always been true. You're the only thing I could never live without."

"I just—" she sniffled and rubbed her eyes "—I don't want you to have regrets because of me."

"I already do."

Her head snapped up. "You do?"

"I do," I said. "I regret not asking the beautiful girl in philosophy class to go out with me out of consideration for a guy I didn't speak to after sophomore year." I leaned over and kissed her, close-mouthed but lingering longer every time I touched her lips. "And now that I finally have you, you're stuck because I'm never letting you go."

22

LANDON

"I know you're up to something," I said, eyeing Julie as I pulled my jacket on over my suit.

She tightened the belt around her robe and rolled her eyes.

"You said that you didn't want to do anything for your birthday, so I have made no birthday plans as per your request." She held up her hands as she met me by the front door. "Well, I did give you a gift in the shower," she said, slipping her arms around my waist. "But you didn't seem to object."

"I would never object to that pretty mouth around my cock any day of the year." I lifted her chin and brushed my thumb over her kiss-swollen lips. "Forty is just a number. No need to make a big deal over it."

"Really?" She squinted at me. "Because I turn forty in December, and I expect a big deal."

"You're different. I don't mind celebrating you." I yanked her closer, slipping my hand under the silk of her robe to squeeze her ass.

"So I can't celebrate you? That's unfair." She glowered at me as she ran her fingers over the lapel of my jacket. "I ordered you a cake for today. Do I have to cancel it?"

"Not if you feed it to me naked later. But I have a meeting this morning and a couple this afternoon, so I'll have to continue this argument later. I love you, and I'll be back around three."

"I love you too." She took my face in her hands and gave me a soft, slow kiss that had me going back in for another on instinct. "I should be back by then."

I stilled after I opened the door.

"Today is your day off."

"And I have plans." She shrugged.

"Julie..." I grumbled. "I told you—"

"You won't come home to everyone hiding behind the furniture and yelling surprise. My God, you're such a grumpy old man already. Go." She pressed her hands against my chest and pushed me toward the door.

I tripped onto her stoop and headed for the subway, a grin pulling at my lips all the way down the block. I didn't doubt that Julie was up to something, but I wouldn't fight her anymore. I wasn't grumpy, but I never liked a whole lot of attention focused on me. Birthdays in college were an excuse to drink more, but after that, I was never into the fancy dinners that Shayla dragged me to when we were together. They always felt like a show, and that was exactly what they turned out to be.

I was okay with a private celebration with just Julie and me, and I truly hoped she hadn't planned anything beyond that. She was all the gift I needed, but I'd go along with whatever I walked into later.

My office still felt like an oversized locker when I opened

the door, but I'd grown accustomed to it for the little use I needed it for. I had a breakfast meeting with my boss, who'd flown in to meet with some of our senior clients, and then I'd scheduled a couple of client visits downtown before I'd head back to the Bronx.

It was funny how I'd always thought long hours and weekends were unavoidable at this level, but when I found someone worth sharing my life with, I'd discovered the motivation to keep work within the workday. It was also a big reason I did most of my virtual meetings in Julie's spare room. I wanted to update the desk and the furniture, mostly to get rid of any remnants Nate had left behind, but whenever I thought of suggesting it, something stopped me.

Julie and I were in a weird in-between. I still said I was staying with her, not living with her, even though the thought of leaving and staying alone somewhere else and away from her twisted my insides. I was afraid to push and burst the bubble we'd been nestled in since that night we'd crossed all the lines.

I still hadn't shaken the trepidation from when I first realized I was in love with her. She knew, and I knew she loved me too, but I wanted to be married for real, not just keep the ring in my toiletries bag as a souvenir. I loved her so much it paralyzed me, and the hesitation I couldn't seem to move past was frustrating the shit out of me.

"This looks good."

I lifted my head to my boss's voice as I gathered the PowerPoint printouts for my meetings this afternoon.

"Hey, Damian." I rose from my seat to greet him. "It's functional, like the pictures I sent you. It's more of a way point for us anyway."

"Maybe we can move you in to somewhere bigger in the

next year," he mused, shaking my hand. Damian had been my boss for the past five years, and he'd led the recommendation for me to become a partner. He'd become a mentor of sorts over the years, but despite having a wife and three kids at home, he kept longer hours than I did. I'd aspired to that kind of life, a C-suite position and high salary, but the only life I seemed to want these days was the one I had after five p.m.

"It's not necessary. At least not anytime soon. Keep the profits and save on the overhead." I grinned and slid the decks into my messenger bag.

"We can talk about that later." He waved a hand. "Right now, I need some breakfast."

I locked my office door behind me and followed him to the elevators. The floor housed a few different companies, but we were the only suits on the elevator. I spotted him eyeing the workers getting on and off the elevator in casual attire, some in jeans and sneakers. I had the impression that his mention of a bigger New York office space was more for status than our functionality.

"I knew you'd be the right choice to run this branch," Damian mused after we found a table at the diner around the corner. "Not only because you're from here, but I always knew the New York clients would invest more if we were local. And you knew how to capitalize on that right away."

"Well, I'm not exactly from here. I grew up in Connecticut and went to college in the Bronx. But I spent enough time in Manhattan to know my way around."

"I get the feeling not having a Southern drawl may work in your favor, though." He chuckled as he lifted his coffee cup. "I think in a few years, when this branch takes off, maybe we can bring you back down to Charlotte. Maybe into a much bigger office than we're paying for up here—with a C-suite position."

I nodded as I poured sugar into my own coffee. A year ago, hearing that would have been a dream come true. It was what I'd been working toward since the beginning, or so I'd thought. I'd worked hard to even be considered for an offer like that, but I didn't want to be married to my job.

I wanted to be married to Julie, and I couldn't leave her or ask her to uproot her life and move to a city where I'd be too busy to even see her, like all the other executives I'd seen.

"Landon? Are you okay? I thought that was your goal all along."

"I did too," I whispered, more to myself. "To be honest, I'm happy here. I'm building the client base and am comfortable where I am. I'm not saying no, but for right now, I want to see this through before I make any greater plans."

And I wanted to stay in the pretend marriage with the woman I wanted to claim but was too chickenshit to make that final move.

"I heard you got married before you came here. I was surprised you didn't say anything."

"It...happened sort of fast. And then the move for the New York office started, and I didn't have time to discuss anything about my personal life."

He nodded slowly, assessing me with narrowed eyes.

"What's her name?"

"Julie," I told him, a smile running across my lips before I could help it.

"And you live with her here, right?"

"Yes, in the Bronx. Quick train ride into Manhattan."

"I guess that's part of the reason you were so quick to accept this new position?" He arched a brow.

"Not the only reason, but yes. And we're happy here. Not that I'm saying no for a move in the far future, but for now—"

"I get it," he said, a chuckle shaking his shoulders. "Enjoy this time. The honeymoon period doesn't last long, trust me."

It didn't seem like a honeymoon period to me. It just seemed...permanent. Like I was where I was supposed to be. I'd spent too much time without Julie, and I wasn't going to Charlotte or anywhere else without her.

It was the second time an epiphany that seemed so obvious hit me when I wasn't looking. I wanted to live with my wife, not just stay with her while my stuff was in her spare room. I wanted her to have my last name and my ring on her finger. I wanted to stay in that house with her for the rest of my life if that was where she wanted to be.

The chickenshit phase of my life was finally over, and all I wanted for my birthday, or any other day, was Julie, forever.

I made it through my meetings downtown on autopilot. Closing deals with clients was as easy as breathing to me, almost too easy, as with every meeting, my client base seemed to multiply.

I grabbed lunch at the lower-level mall of my client's building and meandered around after, people watching as Julie said she liked to do. Couples ate lunch together on the marble steps, while kids surrounded the children's store kiosk in the middle of the floor. A buzzing in my pocket interrupted my musings, and I glanced at my father's name on the screen.

"Happy birthday, baby boy."

I snickered at his immediate greeting.

"Your forty-year-old baby boy, huh?"

"You know you'll always be baby boy to us."

My gait slowed at the reference to my mother as if she were still here.

"I suppose. You caught me at a good time. My meetings just ended for the day."

"You worked on your birthday?"

"You know me, Dad. I don't make my birthdays a big deal. I told Julie I didn't want anything, but I got the feeling she was up to something today."

"I'm sure she is. Let her do it."

"I am," I said as I spotted a jewelry store near the building exit. A large engagement ring was spinning in the middle of the display, the square diamond twinkling under all the different light angles.

"Are you going to let us take you out to dinner next week? I'll try not to mention anything about milestone birthdays."

"Yes, that's fine," I said as I stepped closer to the window. "Can you bring something for me?"

"Sure, what?"

"You still have Mom's engagement ring, right?"

"I do," he said slowly. "Are you asking me because of why I think you're asking me?"

"I am. I know it's a little backward."

"Yes," he said with a chuckle. "But who cares? I remember that you didn't ask for it the last time."

I shook my head at my reflection in the glass.

"No, I didn't."

When I'd asked Shayla to marry me, I'd brought her to the local jewelry store to pick out a ring. She'd always hinted at how pretty her friends' princess cut or emerald-shaped rings were, and I didn't want to get her anything that she didn't like, knowing how particular she was. My mother's ring had never even crossed my mind. Maybe even then I'd known Shayla wasn't the one, the one I wanted to give my past, present, and every bit of future to—because I already was giving it to Julie without ever realizing it.

"I want to ask my wife to marry me. And I want to do it with Mom's ring. If it's okay with you."

Dad's deep chuckle filled my ear. "It's very okay with me, son. I'm thrilled to give it to you. Congratulations and happy birthday, kiddo."

"Thanks, Dad."

"I love you, Landon. And do something for me this year. Just be happy, and don't waste any more time. Julie's yours. She always was."

"Yes, she was. She is. And I love you too."

After I ended the call, I made my way over to the Fulton Street train station and pulled out my phone before heading down the stairs.

Me: *I love you.*

Julie: *You're home already? You're early.*

Me: *Tell me again how you have nothing planned for today...*

Julie: *Sorry for trying to do something special for my husband. Geez.*

Julie: *And I love you too. Are you okay?*

Me: *Very okay. I'll be home soon. Unless I need to linger somewhere so I don't walk in early on whatever you're not doing for me today.*

Julie: *Very funny. See you soon, doll. xoxo*

I rushed down the flight of stairs to the subway platform. Now that I'd figured out the rest of my life, I wanted to start it as soon as possible.

23

JULIE

"I still can't believe you talked me into this," I told Karen as I stared at the framed eleven by fourteen photo on my kitchen counter.

"Landon's heart is healthy under all that muscle, right?" She laughed as she leaned against the sink. "Because that may be enough to—"

"Stop it," I said, a flush burning my cheeks a bit as I slid a large gift bag over it. "His heart is fine. I hope. But I don't know where he's going to keep this, and I don't know why I chose such a big size to frame. I blame the Fireball shots."

"I told you to take the shots they offered you. Jeannine said you were a natural."

"She did?" I crinkled my nose as I shoved Landon's birthday cake into the refrigerator. "I felt a little silly with all those poses she put me in."

"That's the whole point. To let go. She said once she got you talking about Landon and you had a buzz, you were very fun to work with."

"That's nice of her. It was weird. I went there as a gift for

Landon, but it ended up sort of being for me." I peeked inside the gift bag.

"It's oddly empowering, right?"

"Absolutely," I said as I angled my head inside for another glance at the photo. Jeannine was a magical genius because I seemed to look good from every angle. "What made you do it?"

Her smile faded for a moment.

"After my hysterectomy, I fell into a spiral. I had a kid in college, so I wasn't looking to use my uterus again, but I had a big scar across my stomach and my entire body changed. Oliver was great throughout the whole thing, but it was my perceptions that were fucked up, you know what I mean?"

"Oh yeah," I breathed out. "When you look in the mirror and morph into someone you don't recognize, and the old you doesn't come back."

"Exactly." She pointed a finger at me. "I knew Jeannine from when our kids went to school together, and she told me about her new business and asked if I knew anyone who'd be interested, and I said why not?"

She bunched her shoulders in a shrug.

"I thought that we could laugh about it later, but, to my shock, I loved every shot." Her grin was wistful as she came over to the counter. "Instead of making fun of my body, I was honoring it for all it went through. Maybe you could understand that, too."

"I can," I said, a wide grin breaking out across my face. "I never thanked you."

"For what?" Her brow crinkled. "Introducing you to Jeannine? I'm thrilled you went through with it."

"No, well that. But..." I shrugged. "If I didn't have you across the street at the beginning. If I didn't have you checking on me every day, sending your poor husband to do my yardwork."

We shared a laugh.

"He's happy to do it. I told you, staying home all the time isn't good for him."

I tilted my head and shot her a wry grin.

"You were there when I didn't have anyone else because I wouldn't go to anyone else. It helped." I swallowed, a lump poking the back of my throat. "A lot."

Dean and Maria were my oldest friends and still didn't know my diagnosis. I'd told my work friends out of necessity, but Karen was a safe space. Someone I could be a sickly mess in front of without worrying about how *they'd* worry. It was an invaluable gift that I didn't believe I could have lived without.

"I'm proud of you," she said. "And I'm very happy for you. You've been through a lot, kid. Enjoy the victory spoils." She cracked a sneaky grin. "Like that big, sexy giant who's getting off the train any minute."

After I walked her to the door, I glanced up the block to see if I could spot Landon coming from the train station. I ran upstairs to change into the underwear I'd kept from the photo shoot and shrugged into my silk robe. It still knocked the wind out of me sometimes that we were here and together like this. It seemed surreal and yet as if it had always been like this at the same time.

I had never been happier with anyone or thought being this happy was even possible, but I was afraid to put a label on us when everything was so perfect. Graduating from best friends to lovers was a big deal, but while we still liked to joke about being married, we weren't. Not in the way I wanted to be.

I wanted him here with me for good, not just living out

of his suitcase in my spare room. I wanted this to be his home. *I* wanted to be his home.

But for today, I'd celebrate the us that we were instead of wondering what we could be.

"Honey, I'm home."

I laughed at Landon's greeting wafting up my stairs. I was excited to give him the photo but nervous at the same time. It was a side of me I wasn't even aware of, and since he had me in a way no one else ever had, it seemed perfect. I tried to keep that in mind as I wiped my sweaty palms along my robe.

"Am I allowed to say happy birthday?" I asked as I ambled down the stairs. "And don't worry, I'm the only one here."

He did a double take in my direction as he hung his jacket on the coatrack by the door.

"With you dressed like that, you better be." His gaze roamed my body, my skin flushing hot along its path.

"Take it easy, caveman," I said as I came up to him and wrapped my arms around his waist. "There's stuffed chicken parm in the oven and tiramisu cake from Zeppieri's in the fridge. I didn't even get candles."

"It's okay. We can celebrate however you want to." He dug his hand into my hair and yanked me closer, tugging at the knot on my robe with his other hand. "I'd like to open my presents now."

"Wait," I said, grabbing his hand. "Not yet. I have something better for you."

"Better than you naked?" He bent his head, grazing his bottom lip over mine. "Not possible."

"You'll see," I said, holding in a laugh at his crestfallen expression as I pushed my hands against his chest. "Come with me," I said, cringing when I turned around to lead him into the kitchen.

"This is for you." I lifted the gift bag off the counter. "I think you'll find this better than the crappy sketches I gave you sophomore year."

He pursed his lips as he slid the frame out of the bag.

"Your sketches were awesome, that's why I kept them. So stop that—"

He held up the frame, a deep crinkle in his brow as he fell back against the counter.

"Karen knows someone who does boudoir photography and suggested this when I told her I didn't know what to get you, even though you wanted me to ignore your birthday altogether."

He gave me a tiny, almost indiscernible nod, still studying the picture. I'd worn a black push-up bra and matching lacy bikini underwear with thigh-high stockings and heels. I hadn't had to stand up other than to lean against a wall a few times, so I was able to tolerate the pain enough to be able to still act sexy. My hair was curled in waves, and I stared at the camera with smoky eyes. The pose Jeannine and I had settled on was me sprawled out on a bed, my arms flung over my head with my back arched and knees bent.

"It's big, so I don't know where you'd put it. The photographer gave me a couple of Fireball shots to loosen me up, and it may have clouded my judgment a little when I chose the size. I have the proof outtakes if you want to see." I stepped closer as he grazed a finger over the glass. "You can file it with the sketches for the next twenty years."

I'd thought he'd either tease me or tear my clothes off once he saw the photo, but the look on his face was hard to decipher. I did spot heat in his eyes as they traveled up and down the photo, but what I registered the most as he traced along the frame with the tip of his middle finger was something I hadn't expected.

Reverence.

That I hadn't anticipated or didn't know what to do with.

"Okay, could you maybe blink or something? Or did I short-circuit your brain?" I sputtered out a nervous chuckle.

When he finally looked up, his eyes were wide as they darted from me to the frame still clutched in his hands.

"Jesus Christ, Jules," he finally breathed out, chuckling to himself as he shook his head. "How are you mine?" he whispered and set the frame back down on the counter. "So fucking beautiful," he said, his voice a low, husky rasp as he took my face in his hands.

"So, you like it?" I croaked out, a rush of unexpected emotion scratching at the back of my throat when I tried to find my voice.

"Like it?" He scoffed, glancing at the photo before turning back to me. "I never want to look at anything else for the rest of my life." He skated his thumb over the seam of my lips. "I'm so goddamn lucky. Give me that mouth, baby."

Our mouths fused together, a mess of tongues and lips and desperation as he untied my robe.

"Fuck, Julie." His low rumble came out like a growl when the silk pooled at my feet. "Was your plan for my birthday to kill me?" He peeled off his suit jacket, dropping it to the floor next to my robe as he nodded toward the table. "Get on the table and spread your legs."

I stared at him, not moving an inch as he tore off his tie. His eyes had a feral gleam I'd never seen before. A chill ran up my spine as he stalked toward me and lifted me up by the waist, setting me down on the edge of the table.

"You're so fucking incredible." He grabbed the back of

my neck and brought my mouth back to his. The kiss was hard and thorough, his tongue making long strokes inside my mouth as he clutched the back of my head, like he was trying to tell me something. I whimpered when he broke the kiss and ran his mouth down my neck and over the swells of my breasts, already spilling out of the tiny cups.

With one yank, his mouth was on my nipple, sucking and rolling it between his teeth. He drifted his mouth across my chest, repeating all the same torturous movements and trailing openmouthed kisses over my stomach, dragging my panties down my legs as he moved lower.

He flicked his eyes up to mine, a smile playing at the corner of his lips as he held my gaze and licked a path along the inside of my thigh.

"Don't tease," I begged, arching my back as he continued the torture on my other leg.

"It's my birthday. I'll celebrate however I want."

I cried out when he dragged his tongue back and forth over my slit and then sucked my clit into his mouth.

I dug my heels into Landon's back, rocking my hips against his face as he gripped his fingers into my thighs to pull me closer, holding me in place as my legs shook.

"Close, darlin'?" he murmured, coasting his hands up my stomach and cupping my breasts, my body jerking when he traced my nipples with his thumbs.

I didn't have time to answer as all the sensations from everywhere hit me and my body went rigid from the waist down. I squirmed against his mouth, but he wouldn't let up, torturing me with tiny kisses until I rolled up to sit.

"Whose birthday is it again?" I joked and dragged a hand down my face.

"Mine," he said, dragging his tongue across his soaked bottom lip. "Or it will be once I'm inside you." He held my gaze as he fumbled with his belt buckle, smiling wide when the whir of his zipper filled the silence.

"I guess I'm staying put—" I yelped when he brought me closer.

"Yeah," he whispered, picking up my hand to kiss the inside of my palm before he settled in between my legs. "Come closer, baby," he crooned as he eased inside me.

I looped my arm around his neck as he inched in and out, a wide grin stretching across his lips before he brought his mouth back to mine.

It wasn't the most comfortable position, but we moved together in slow waves, Landon's hand in my hair and his arm still holding tight around my waist, as if he was afraid I'd disappear. I pressed my hand into the table behind me as I bucked my hips against him, meeting him thrust for thrust and trying to tell him, despite the words that wouldn't come out, that I was here to stay.

Because I was his—from the beginning and for all those years after, whether I'd known it or not.

"I love you," he grunted into the crook of my neck as he picked up the pace. "I love you so fucking much."

He lifted my leg over his hip, changing the angle and the friction just enough for me to fall apart in his arms. He slumped against me, his own release hitting him hard as he dropped his head to my chest.

"I really hope I didn't burn your dinner."

His shoulders shook with a chuckle as he lifted his head.

"And I love you too," I said, clearing my throat when my voice cracked. "So much, you couldn't imagine."

He shot me a dazed smile and pressed his forehead against mine.

"How about we clean up for dinner, and then bring dessert upstairs to bed?"

"Can I sing happy birthday then?"

"You can sing whatever you want as long as you don't put any clothes on. Come on, wife." He lifted me off the table and set me down on the floor.

Come on, wife.

I'd be his wife, wear his ring and take his name and him, forever.

All he had to do was say the word.

24

LANDON

Travel had always been a part of my job. Since I'd made partner, I could count the full weeks I'd spent sleeping in my apartment and not in a hotel for at least a night on one hand. I'd lived alone, with no pets or plants to take care of, and could come and go as I pleased with no obligations. While I was never a fan of weeks of back-to-back travel, it never really bothered me.

But as I packed my suitcase for a week in Charlotte, I dreaded everything about this trip, beginning with getting on a plane and leaving Julie for seven days.

Being this torn up about leaving was ridiculous. I'd always known I'd have to fly back and forth at least once a quarter to meet with my bosses at NameTech, but I'd gotten too used to sleeping in my own bed every night.

Or, sleeping in the bed I shared with Julie.

I had inquiries with clients for potential meetings in other states too, and if all went as I intended it, I had some overnight trips to New Hampshire and Maine in the upcoming weeks. It was all part of my job and how I'd done it from the beginning.

So why did my dopey heart feel so damn heavy as I zipped up my bags and set them in the hallway for tomorrow morning?

"I don't mind driving you to the airport. You don't need to take an Uber," Julie said as she leaned against the wall in the upstairs hallway, the frown pulling at her lips mimicking the lousy twinge in the pit of my stomach.

"My flight is at seven. It's stupid to get up that early to drive back and forth when I could take a cab and be at LaGuardia in less than thirty minutes."

I smiled at her defeated sigh as she averted her gaze from mine to the carpet.

"Listen to me," I said, taking her face in my hands. "There is no need for you to take me to the airport for a drawn-out goodbye, especially when they don't even let you park at the terminal for more than five minutes."

"I know," she said with a long sigh. "I'm being ridiculous and clingy. This is like all those other times you went back to Charlotte, and I need to get over it."

"No, Jules. It's not." I dropped my hands to her waist and drew her closer. "This time, I'm coming back in a week. I live *here* now—with you." A tiny smile pulled across her mouth when I dipped my head to meet her gaze. "Just think about all that reunion sex."

I skimmed my hands over her hips, squeezing her perfect ass as I pulled her flush to my body.

"And after being without you for seven days...well..." I pressed my lips to hers, nibbling on her bottom lip as I slowly pulled away. "You better rest up *all* week for when I get back."

She chuckled and dropped her head to my chest.

"I hate leaving you just as much," I whispered as I kissed the top of her head. "So, we're both being ridiculous."

"You know, every time you'd visit and go back, I'd get a little withdrawn and sad for a couple of days. Mopey." She shrugged, wrapping her arms around my waist. "Nate and I used to fight about it. I told him that you were my best friend, and it was just hard to see you leave. But looking back...I think that may have been one of those clues I didn't pick up on."

"It's actually pretty funny. Or sad, but I'm going with funny." I cupped her neck. "At the time, I figured you were always my first thought because you were my best friend. I'd tell Shayla the same thing when she'd call me out on it. But looking back?" I shrugged, shaking my head. "All the puzzle pieces were there, we just didn't know to put them together."

"Very true," she said, her gaze drifting over my shoulder. "Are you all packed?"

"I am. I'd take you with me, but I'm in meetings all week, and there's an off-site company outing for a whole day. I'll miss you every fucking minute." I pecked her lips. "Believe me."

"I do, and although I've lived alone for a while, this house is going to be empty as hell without you." I shut my eyes as she rubbed soft circles on my back. "And I couldn't have gone with you anyway. Every single deliverable we have on this project is due over the next week." She drifted her hand along my jaw. "Before we have to sleep alone and miss each other for the next week, want to get into bed early?"

"Hell yes," I whispered before I slanted my mouth over hers, backing her against the wall with a bruising kiss. I was already counting the days until I landed back in New York. Not only because of how much I'd miss her, but because of the plans I had for us when I returned.

My mother's engagement ring was burning a hole in my

briefcase. My plan was to ask her to really marry me the minute I got home. I hadn't worked out exactly how—if I was just going to collapse to one knee the minute I came through the door or take her somewhere. I didn't want to do it before I left and have to head out of town right after, when all I'd want to do would be to celebrate the rest of our lives together.

I'd always expected to be with Julie forever. Finding out that my best friend was the love of my life was the best kind of surprise, even if it was an obvious given. We'd taken the long way, but we were here, and that was all that would ever matter.

She squealed when I lifted her legs off the floor and carried her into the bedroom.

"That's *how* many times you've carried me in here?" She laughed against my lips.

"Not enough," I told her before I set her on the bed and climbed over her.

"What are you staring at?" She shot me a playful grin as she pulled at the hem of my T-shirt.

"Like I keep telling you, I just like looking at you, Jules." I ran my thumb over her lips and hissed when she sucked it into her mouth.

"Lose the shirt." Her voice dropped to a sultry whisper as she slid her hand under my shirt and lifted it up my back. I peeled it over my head and threw it behind me.

"God, you're beautiful," she breathed out, skimming her hands down my chest.

"Yeah?" I said, hooking my thumbs into the waistband of her yoga pants. "You're a fucking goddess." I caught her eye roll as I dragged them down her legs.

"I created a monster with that photo, didn't I?"

"I'd say so." I ran my mouth up the inside of her thigh,

painting tiny kisses over the wet scrap of cotton between her legs. "I took a shot of it with my phone so I can look at you every night, even though you sprawled on that bed is all I can ever think about."

"Right there, babe," she groaned, bucking her hips off the bed when I slid the material aside and covered her with my mouth. I wanted to tear her panties off and devour her like usual, but I took my time to tease and memorize every inch for the next six nights when all I would have was that photo and my hand on my dick, wishing I were back here already.

"My sweet Julie," I murmured against her soaked skin as I pulled her panties down and dove back in, fucking her with my tongue as she clenched her thighs around my face. I was drowning in her and loving every damn second.

I loved that photo for so many reasons. Not only because of how goddamn breathtaking she was, so much to the point that I couldn't think or speak for the first minute after she'd shown it to me, but because I knew the guts it took for her to do it. She'd come such a long way from the woman who wouldn't even get on a video call a few months ago because she didn't want me to see how she'd changed.

She'd always be the most beautiful woman in the world to me, and now she was all mine.

"Landon, stop."

I lifted my head, flicking my eyes to hers.

"What's wrong?"

"Nothing," she said, panting as her skin flushed from her cheeks down to her chest. She peeled her panties off from where they hung around her knees and sat up. "It's very right, but—" her hooded eyes danced when they met mine "—I want to ride."

My brows shot up as I climbed back onto the bed and leaned against the headboard.

"Do whatever you want to me, baby. I'm all yours."

A slow grin split her mouth as she tore off her tank top and tugged my sweatpants down until my cock sprang free. She held my gaze, licking her lips before swirling her tongue around the tip.

"*Fuck*. Baby, please. I want to come inside you, not down your throat."

"You will," she whispered, dragging kisses across my stomach and up my neck. "I just wanted it like this." She took my cock in her hand and straddled my hips, guiding me in until I slid all the way inside her.

Julie had been on the pill for the past month, so condoms weren't needed. I could take her bare every night, and I did, each time more mind-blowing than the one before, even though I swore it couldn't get any better. She'd never asked to get on top before, and I thought it was because her knees and hips were sore at the end of a day—something she'd never tell me, but I'd notice.

From this position, she was so tight and I could get so much deeper, but I wanted it to be just as amazing for her too. Her body rolled against mine, and the only words between us were low moans as she sank down on me harder with every thrust, her eyes fluttering as she circled her hips.

I jackknifed off the bed, grabbing the back of her head, and took her mouth in a sloppy kiss as I met her halfway, pumping into her as hard as she was thrusting against me. I searched her gaze when our lips broke apart, relieved to see winces of pleasure, not pain. I slipped my hand between us and traced slow circles on her clit. She sucked in a loud gasp, rocking into me harder and faster.

"Let go, darlin'. I'm right here," I whispered as a drop of sweat poured down my temple. "I've got you, baby."

She cried out, scratching her nails down my back as her legs quivered. I held her tighter, my own release hitting me hard as she pulsed around me, drawing out all I had as I spilled into her.

We clutched on to each other for a long minute, our hearts racing together as we sat chest to chest. I was still inside her and didn't want to pull out or let go—or leave this house or this room.

Julie lifted her head, raking a hand through her sweaty hair, and sputtered out a breathless laugh.

"We are so damn dramatic."

I burst out laughing before I could help it.

"We sure are." I brushed her tangled locks off her damp shoulder. "And now we'll clean up, and you'll sleep naked in my arms. Tomorrow morning, I'll kiss you goodbye and then come right back. Okay?"

"Okay," she said, smiling despite the crack in her voice.

We were ridiculous and dramatic, and when I got back to New York, we'd be husband and wife.

For real this time.

25

LANDON

"Like you never left, right?" Will mused as we sat at the bar by my old office after a long day of meetings. I'd arrived at the office fifteen minutes before the first one, and they'd been back-to-back ever since. I'd booked the Hilton across the street from the complex, and my first chance to check in and drop off my luggage hadn't been until almost five.

"I've been spoiled," I sighed, and I took a long pull from my beer bottle. I was exhausted but wired enough not to refuse Will when he suggested we get a drink at the end of the day. "I can honestly say I didn't miss this at all. I like meeting with clients all day and checking in via email most of the time."

I also liked sneaking down to the kitchen during the workday to give my girl a kiss—or more, depending on how busy we were. I'd expected to miss Julie to the point of distraction, but ever since I'd landed, it was as if I were missing a limb. Other than our sleepy kiss goodbye at the crack of dawn this morning, we'd only spoken in sporadic texts between meetings.

I planned on downing the one beer and heading across the street to FaceTime her before she went to sleep.

"If they promote you again, I'm sure this will be you all the time again soon enough." He snickered around the rim of the bottle.

"Hell no. I already told Damian I'm happy where I am. Growing the New York branch and living in the Bronx. I'll come for a visit, but my plan is to stay put."

"With your wife?"

My head whipped up to see his smug grin. "Word gets around, I guess."

"Honestly, I didn't know until after we spoke a couple of weeks ago. I'm just surprised you didn't tell me. Unless it was the fun of watching me put my foot in my mouth every time I said your wife was hot." He arched a brow as he set the empty bottle down on the bar.

"Maybe a little." I shrugged, a laugh slipping out when he scowled back at me. "Honestly, the whole thing started out too complicated to explain."

"Looked pretty simple to me. Even over video, I was blinded by the stars in your eyes." He looked me over with a smirk. "I'm guessing it's good."

"It's..." I trailed off, checking my phone under the table just to peek at Julie's photo on my home screen wallpaper. "It's *really* fucking good."

"That's awesome," Will said, slapping my back. "I'm happy for you, man. Want to hear the other rumor I heard?"

"Sure, why not?" I pushed the empty bottle away and reached for my wallet.

"The annual awards banquet with the holding company? It's in New York this year, and they're nominating you for the achievement award."

"What?" I narrowed my eyes at Will. "Where did you hear that?"

"Kerri, the new HR manager, asked me if I was still friends with you after you moved. It's pretty much a done deal, she said. They just have to add you to the roster. I bet they'll tell you on the golf course tomorrow."

"Are you sure? I'm not saying I'm not good," I chuckled. "But I just took over New York. Seems a little early."

"Are you fucking serious?" Will rolled his eyes." You've been here your entire career. And you've only been in New York a short time, and they're already talking about moving you guys in to a bigger office. Plus, no one works as hard as you. You make us all look bad."

"Well, thank you. I'll take all of that as a compliment." I scrubbed a hand down my face as I stifled a yawn. "I guess if I want good intel, I should come to you since you have an in."

"An in?" His brows drew together.

"I saw the glint in your eye when you said Kerri's name."

"Ugh," he groaned, scrunching his nose in disgust. "Just because you're all happy and domestic, don't project that shit on me."

I pushed his hand away when he tried to leave cash on the bar. "I got it. And I am going to call it a night so I can FaceTime with my girl." I threw two twenties onto the bar. "See you on the green tomorrow."

"Don't remind me." A smirk curled the side of his lip. "Thanks for coming out. I miss giving you shit. Not the same over video."

"Same, man. You should come see us in New York. We could all double date."

I cracked up when he shot me a glare over his shoulder as we stepped outside. As Will headed to his car, I went to the corner to make my way to the hotel entrance, rubbing at my eyes. I hoped to be able to keep them open enough not to pass out on Julie tonight.

"Landon? I thought that was you."

I turned to a familiar, pixie-like voice. I'd placed it right as I spotted Shayla behind me, a wistful smile curving her lips when her gaze slid to mine.

"It's me," I said, stuffing my hand in my pocket. It had been five years since I'd last run into her, but she looked exactly the same. Long blond hair brushing her petite shoulders, the simple yet fancy black dress hugging her slender frame. Her head barely cleared my shoulders, but when I studied her from half a block away, she seemed even smaller.

She was still beautiful, but although I had been married to her at one time, I felt nothing for her now. There was no bitterness or nostalgia, only regret. Shayla shouldn't have cheated, but she'd never compared to Julie for me. And while I hadn't realized that consciously at the time, I was sure part of her had always known.

And just like that, all the anger festering for her all those years evaporated into a dull guilt over what my oversight had done to both of us.

"I'm surprised to see you," she said, crossing her arms over her torso and taking a tentative step toward me. "I heard you moved to New York."

"I did," I said, sticking to my part of the sidewalk. "I'm back for some meetings this week."

"I heard you got married too." Her lips curved up. "Congratulations."

"Thanks." I nodded as I tried to figure out how she could have found out. Any mutual friends we'd had after we split I'd lost touch with, but I was sure word of me getting married ripped through everyone we knew as soon as my coworkers found out. This city and industry were borderline incestuous when it came to degrees of separation.

"It's Julie, right? Who you married."

"Is that what you heard?" I asked, now taking a step closer.

"No," she chuckled. "But I figured, and I'm not surprised. I'm happy for you. You deserve to be happy."

A smile snuck across my mouth as I made my way over to her.

"Thank you. I truly appreciate that. You look great. Everything is good?"

"It is," she told me with a slow nod. "I met my friend Kerri for drinks. She just started at NameTech a few weeks ago. I spotted you leaving, and I wanted to come say hi."

And there was the link. I never cared if anyone found out, but our marriage wasn't the ruse for functional purposes that we'd written it off as at the beginning. I'd make it officially real when I went home, but whenever my mind drifted to Julie, I already considered her my wife. Shayla had been my wife before I'd realized the weight of the word and what it was supposed to mean.

"I'm glad you did," I said as I stepped closer. "Take care of yourself."

She leaned in, hesitating for a second before brushing a light kiss on my cheek. Marrying Julie wasn't just a solution. It was what was always supposed to happen. With that realization, I could let the missteps of the past go—both Shayla's and mine. We'd been two kids with good intentions who didn't know how to make sense of a reality that wasn't meant for us.

"You too," I said, pressing a kiss to her temple. I caught

the curve of a sad smile as I pulled away and shifted back toward the hotel.

I went through the hotel entrance and blew out a long breath as a surprising relief filtered through me. My marriage to Shayla had been years ago and didn't last very long, but the remnants of it had weighed on me more than I'd realized. I'd thought what had happened with us had soured me on all things marriage and commitment, but now that I was content in the present with the person I was always supposed to be with, it was easier to let the past go.

I trudged upstairs and changed as fast as I could to get into bed, setting my phone on the nightstand as I called Julie.

"Hey, big shot," she said as her face filled my screen. I cringed at her raspy whisper.

"Did I wake you? I'm sorry, darlin'. I had a drink with Will after a very long fucking day of back-to-back meetings, and I didn't realize the time."

I slid my glasses on to get a better look at her. She was lying on her side, hugging the pillow with a sleepy grin pulling at her mouth. From the angle, it looked like she'd propped her phone on my side of the bed. The thought made my smile grow wider.

"It's not that late. It's just been a long day for me too. My team got a little screwed, so we have to take on more work than we thought." She turned her head to yawn into the pillow. "I got up early and have been at it all day too. I finally had enough and climbed into bed."

"What happened? Everything okay?"

"Yeah, long story. And not one I want to waste time on when I finally get to talk to you. I'd ask how it was to be back, but if you had meetings all day, I guess it sucked."

"It did, but it was fine. Word is out that I'm a married man."

"Oh?" Julie propped her elbow on the pillow and rested her chin against her palm. "Sorry if that cuts into your social life while you're down there."

"Yeah, it's a hardship," I teased. "My boss knew when I saw him in New York. I guess once stuff like that is out, it gets around fast." I sat up against the headboard to get a better look at the screen. "I have no issues with everyone knowing I'm taken as fuck."

"Taken as fuck?" She arched an eyebrow. "That is actually kind of romantic—" My stomach dropped when a sudden coughing fit cut her off.

"Are you feeling okay, babe?"

"I'm fine," she said as she shifted on the bed. "Allergy drip. It's probably worse because I'm so damn exhausted." She leaned in and pursed her lips at the screen. "I'm fine, babe. I see the crease in your forehead. Tell me about the rest of your day."

"I ran into Shayla tonight."

"You did?" The smile faded from her lips as she squinted at the screen.

"She spotted me leaving the bar and came up to say hello. And congratulations since she's friends with one of our HR managers and heard I was married. She assumed it was to you."

"Did she now?"

"Yes. And you are so fucking hot when you're jealous."

"I'm not jealous at all that I've been in bed since eight p.m. while you were having drinks at what is probably a swanky bar in Charlotte with your ex-wife." She tried to scowl, but I spied her mouth twitch.

"No drink. Just a short but actually good conversation.

We both ended up where we're supposed to be. I wish her the same happiness as I finally have."

A slow grin split her cheeks. "When you say things like that, I can see why you're taken as fuck."

"You know it, baby." I pointed at the screen. "Even though you swiped the shirt I sleep in. That explains why I couldn't find it when I was packing."

"I swiped it from the laundry last week to wear it while you were gone." She glanced down at the NY in white block letters. "You just didn't notice because you usually sleep shirtless."

I cracked up when she waggled her eyebrows.

"I've had that shirt since freshman year at Fordham. It somehow managed to stretch with me all these years."

"I remember. Dean told me to buy it for you to wear because he wasn't letting you sit with us at the Yankees game if you wore a Red Sox shirt. He knew if I bought a Yankees shirt for you, you'd actually wear it."

"Makes sense. But you both knew I never really cared about baseball either way. My dad just happened to be a Boston fan."

"Which makes me sad, but thank God we got you away from that." She dipped her nose under the collar and shut her eyes as she inhaled. "Smells like you. I'm surprised you kept it for so long if you didn't care."

"I kept it because of the girl who gave it to me. The same way I kept everything else from you."

She darted her eyes away from the screen, a bashful smile pulling at her mouth. Five more nights now seemed like years.

"You sexy, giant sap. I had big plans for FaceTime sex, but I'm fading, and we both have a long day tomorrow. I love you."

"I love you so much, you have no idea. Take it easy tomorrow, okay?"

"I'm fine. Don't be a nagging husband." She glowered at me as she set the phone down next to her and shimmied back under the covers.

"I can't help it if I love my wife."

She stilled as she was cuddling into the pillow, her brown eyes glossy as they stayed on mine.

"Good night, doll." She kissed the tip of her finger and trailed it down the screen.

I blew her a kiss before I ended the call.

"Sweet dreams, darlin'."

26

JULIE

"Do you think voodoo dolls really work? Because if so, I kept one from a trip to New Orleans as a joke, and I'll give it a try."

Kaitie and I cracked up at Sierra's playful scowl on-screen. Thanks to Elyse doing the bare minimum since the beginning and then ghosting us without a word once she found a full-time job, we all had to split what she was supposed to do and had to cram to get everything done on time.

"If I weren't afraid that kind of stuff boomerangs back to you, I'd say go for it." I chuckled. "And I'd start with a pin right between her eyes to alleviate all that negative energy she said was hindering her creativity."

We all burst out laughing until I lapsed into another coughing fit. We'd been putting in twelve-hour days all week long, and when I could no longer deny that my allergy drip had turned into a chest cold, I had barely enough time to go to the bathroom, much less the doctor. I hoped once everything was delivered tonight, I could sleep it all off this weekend.

Not exactly the reunion I'd wanted when Landon came home, but I'd make it up to him. I missed him like crazy, and feeling like shit while being so damn busy only made it worse.

"Are you okay, Julie?" Kaitie asked as she leaned closer to the screen. "That cough doesn't sound good."

"I'm fine," I said once the hacking slowed. "Let's get this all done today, and I'll keep guzzling cough medicine in between."

There was a time I'd thrived on this. A big project with a load of different facets and watching it come together at the end was always such a great feeling of accomplishment. It was great to be part of something like that again, but my body was too exhausted to appreciate the end results.

I just wanted it to be over so I could get into bed. But if I wanted more freelance work, I had to give this project my best. I couldn't and wouldn't make it even harder for Kaitie and Sierra by passing along my work to them too. I'd get through it and enjoy passing out after.

My doorbell rang just as we ended the call. I was thrilled that we just had to upload assets and not present each to the client like Frank had originally thought we had to do. The only reason I'd showered over the past few days was to break up the congestion enough to be able to breathe, and I had no energy to fix myself up after.

When I opened the door, I found Karen leveling me with a glare as she held a paper bag.

"You look like shit."

"Oh good, the outside matches the inside, then." Another cough rumbled through my chest as I stepped to the side. "Come in."

"Here is the Greek chicken soup you asked for. Once you have some, I'm taking you to urgent care."

"Thank you," I said, grabbing the bag from her hand. "I can't go now. Everything is due today, and I'll be working until tonight. I may be able to go tomorrow."

"You can take off for an afternoon," Karen said, shaking her head as she passed me into the kitchen.

"It's just a chest cold," I tried to say after my next coughing fit made me wheeze.

"Honey, nothing is just a chest cold when you have an autoimmune disease. That was the first thing they told you, and you're smarter than that."

"Karen, trust me. There is nothing I want to do more than go to the doctor and pass out in bed for the next two days." My voice trailed off as my lungs ran out of air.

"At least sit down and take a break." She nodded to my kitchen table. "I'm not leaving until I see you get one bowl of soup into you."

I nodded, plopping onto one of my dining room chairs as the fight seeped out of me. "There's a bowl in the sink." I cringed when I heard my voice rasp.

"You worry me here alone. When is Landon coming back?" She set the bowl and spoon down in front of me, eyeing me with a concern I didn't want to acknowledge. I needed to keep going, and I was afraid if I stopped, I wouldn't get back up again.

"Day after tomorrow," I said, stirring my crackers into the soup. I'd lived on this soup at "the beginning," when climbing up and down my stairs was all the activity I could handle. It was creamy with a spicy kick, and I hoped it would clear my sinuses enough for the afternoon.

"You wouldn't be this sick if he were here."

"I wouldn't be upright if he were here. He wouldn't let me out of bed, and not in a fun way." I met her gaze with a weak smile. "He worries about me too much as it is. If he saw or heard me like this, he'd drop everything to fly home and hover over me."

We'd both been so busy, we'd only spoken via text for the past couple of days, and I'd been passing out right after we'd finished working for the day and missing his phone calls.

"Why are you rubbing your chest?" Karen asked as she sat down next to me.

"It's sore from coughing. Just like my ribs. Maybe I'll get abs," I joked, another cough rumbling through my chest as I tried to swallow more soup. My stomach muscles were sore, but the pain in my chest was more piercing, like someone had punched me.

"I'll check in on you later." Karen rose from the chair, exhaling a long breath as she shook her head at me. "You're going to the doctor tomorrow morning. If Oliver and I have to force you into the back seat like one of his perps, we will. So don't make us embarrass you in front of the whole block."

"Don't make me laugh," I said when my chuckle turned into another coughing fit. "As soon as this is all done, I will go to the doctor and rest. I'll be between jobs anyway once this is over, so I'll have nothing else to do." I trudged behind her to my front door, already dreading having to think about what my next move would be. Maybe it would be a blessing that I'd be too tired to think about it.

I ran out of steam at seven p.m. and took my phone over to my couch just to lie down for a few minutes. I blinked my eyes open an hour later and could barely move. Every joint in my body was screaming at me as I tried to sit up. Another fit of coughing hit me as I tried to take in a breath, and it wouldn't stop. After it finally subsided, I couldn't catch my breath. Every gulp of air I attempted wasn't getting into my lungs and amplified the pain in my chest.

Once I was able to get my eyes to focus and my hands to stop shaking, I picked up my phone to message an apology to Sierra and Kaitie and noticed a voice mail notification from Landon.

"Hey, babe. I guess you're still working. I hate that I haven't heard your voice in days, but I have good news. I'm coming home early. They're giving me an award tomorrow night at a company dinner in Midtown, and I'd like you to be my date. The award isn't a big deal, but I made plans for us after. I'm flying out tonight, but I'll tell you all about it when I get home. And if you wore the green dress from Dean and Maria's wedding tomorrow night, I wouldn't hate it."

His soft chuckle made hot tears spring to my eyes. He was winning an award, and I was going to miss it. I was so damn proud of him, whatever it was for, but I couldn't leave the house like this, much less go to an awards dinner. I didn't know what made me feel worse, disappointing him or the anticipation of how he'd react when I told him I was sick.

"Sorry for the last-minute ask, but I promise it will be worth it. I love you so much. See you soon, darlin'."

My living room spun around me when I pushed off my couch. I shivered despite the drops of sweat dripping down my neck as I made my way back to my alcove office. The walk from my couch to my desk winded me so much, I had to stop three times.

Frustrated tears streamed down my flushed cheeks as I finally made it to my chair. The only work message I'd missed was an email from Frank giving us an extension until tomorrow afternoon. My relief was short-lived, as it was all too clear that I wasn't making this deadline when the thought of heading back to my couch made me want to cry. I mustered up the strength to upload everything I'd been working on and sent an email apology to my team for being too ill to complete my part by tomorrow afternoon. I was far enough along in what I had to do for them to be able to wrap up what I'd done without too much of a hassle, although I still felt as if I were letting them down. But as much as I wanted to keep going, I was no good to them like this, regardless of the extra time we had been given.

Karen was right. I knew better than this. I'd thought if I could just push through, I could prove to myself that I could still do it, but I had nothing left now. Not for me or for anyone else. A sob rolled through me, my chest on fire as I hiccupped.

My cheeks burned, but I had no idea how high my temperature was since my thermometer was in my upstairs bathroom, and upstairs was a no-go for me right now. My house was so quiet, other than the whoosh of the six train coming and going and the wail of sirens in the distance, typical city sounds that were like white noise to me. It was quiet enough inside for every gasp and wheeze to echo in my ears.

I couldn't be there for Landon, my job, or myself. I'd been doing so well for so long, I'd forgotten how everything could turn on a dime until it had.

I shut my eyes and tried to will myself to calm down. I was sick because I was too busy to get to a doctor, and I'd compromised my already half-assed immune system. I'd get the medicine I needed and be fine.

Probably.

But what if I wasn't? What if I'd let it go too far and couldn't come back? It was a fear always in the back of my mind, of the monster constantly lurking just around the corner that would pounce when I wasn't looking or became cocky enough to think I could pull long hours with a cold and be fine just like everyone else.

I wasn't everyone else, and I dreaded how much I would pay for that oversight.

I almost laughed to myself at the sick irony of it all. Three days ago, I'd had an annoying allergy cough. Now, I was rocking back and forth on my couch, bargaining with God for me to please be okay. That I'd just go to the doctor and be able to laugh later about how I'd burned myself out over a project when Landon wasn't home to watch me.

The months before my diagnosis were a never-ending flu, but this was something different. Something bad enough to make my blood run as cold as my skin felt, as goose bumps burst over my arms.

I took slow breaths in and out, but as much as I tried to gulp it in, I couldn't take in any air. I crumpled into a ball each time pain shot across my chest, and I was ready to admit defeat and finally ask for help.

Me: *Are you up?*

Karen: *I am. Are you all right?*

Me: *I think I have a fever, and I can't breathe.*

My phone buzzed with an incoming call just as I was about to set it down.

"Can you make it outside, or do I need to come in to get you? We're going to the ER."

27

LANDON

I scrolled through my phone and looked over the hotel reservation confirmation sent to my email. It wasn't the Plaza, but the best I could get on short notice when the plan to propose had come to me. I'd been to the NameTech awards dinner a few times and it was boring as all hell, but I wanted her to be there. I wanted her there for everything for the rest of my life, and I was done waiting to make it official.

Tonight, we'd be husband and wife for real. If she wanted a wedding for the sake of our family and friends, I'd go along with it, but this was it. We were forever from the beginning, and I didn't care about the award or anything else that happened today as long as it ended with me slipping my mother's ring on her finger.

My last-minute trip back was brutal, thanks to a storm heading up the Eastern Seaboard. I'd been on my way to the airport for a late-night flight when I'd called Julie, but we'd ended up stuck on the runway for three hours when we finally boarded. Once we were in the air, I tried to get enough sleep to function at my client meetings later today, but adrenaline had made it almost impossible to shut my eyes.

As I waited in the taxi line outside the airline terminal, I scrolled through my notifications. No text or call back from Julie. She'd been working all hours this week and had probably been sleeping when I'd left her a voice message last night, but she should have been up by now.

I let out a relieved breath when my phone buzzed in my hand with Julie's photo on the screen. I smiled, prepping for the questions she was about to pummel me with about the plans I wasn't telling her about.

"Good morning, dar—"

"Landon?"

Julie's voice was strained, almost an inaudible whisper, and sent my heart straight into my stomach.

"What's wrong, Jules?"

"Karen took me to the ER last night. They think I have pneumonia." Her weak voice cracked between sniffles. "I'm so proud of you, but I can't come tonight. They're running a bunch of tests, and I don't know if I have to be admitted."

"I don't care about the award. Where are you? What hospital?" I craned my neck to the front of the line. I still had three people in front of me and was about to plow through them all to get into a cab and get to Julie. "Why didn't you call me last night?"

Fuck. Fuck. Fuck. A week. I'd only left her for a week. How could she be this sick so fast? My hands shook and I cursed under my breath when the couple in the front of the line took their sweet fucking time to stuff their luggage in the trunk of the cab.

"Einstein. It's not too far from the house. I didn't want to leave you a voice mail when you were in the air and make you panic. And we had no service in the ER until they moved me to the other side."

"I'll find it. Is someone with you?"

"Karen had to leave, but she was here most of the night. My mother is in Florida and is trying to change her flight to come back today. I'm scared, babe. My chest hurts so much it's hard to breathe."

I raked my hand through my hair when she cried in my ear, trying like hell to calm myself down enough to calm *her* down. I'd read all about this. Small infections blowing up into pneumonia or worse because of a compromised immune system. I hadn't liked the sound of her cough at the beginning of the week, but she'd told me over and over again to trust her to tell me when something was wrong.

I didn't know what was worse. That she'd lied to me this week about being okay, or that this had turned this bad so fast. I'd worry about all that later, but for right now, all that mattered was getting to her as soon as I could.

"Okay, baby. I need you to calm down. It's all going to be okay. I'll be there as soon as I can." The fight to keep my voice even was exhausting me. Her tears only made the fear icing my veins grow colder.

"But you're going to miss the awards dinner—"

"Christ, Julie. Do you really think I'd be anywhere but with you right now? Don't bring that up again."

"Okay, I won't." I smiled when I heard a chuckle mixed in with her sniffles. "And good because I really need my husband."

"You have him, Jules. You've *always* had him. I love you. I'm getting a cab now, and I'll head right to the hospital."

She replied with a raspy okay and hung up.

I'd made it to the front of the line by the time I lifted my head, throwing my suitcase in the trunk once the cab pulled up and jumping inside.

"Einstein Hospital, the Bronx," I told the driver as I texted my boss that my wife was in the emergency room and I'd be unavailable for the rest of the day and wouldn't be able to make the dinner tonight. I emailed my clients to cancel my appointments for today and shoved my phone into my pocket. I didn't care about the replies or any questions they'd have about what was going on because it didn't matter.

Nothing mattered but Julie.

What would I do without Julie?

Jesus, I couldn't go there now. She'd see it all over my face. I'd keep my own terror in the back of my mind and be the man she needed, not the one scared to death of thinking about what life would be like without her.

It would be nothing. *I* would be nothing. So she'd beat this and be okay because I needed her too much to think of anything else.

The ride from LaGuardia Airport should have been less than thirty minutes, but thanks to an accident on the highway, it took over an hour. Once the cab pulled into the emergency room parking lot, I ran inside with my suitcase trailing behind me. I was breathless by the time I made it to the intake clerk.

"Can I help you, sir?" The clerk squinted at me from behind her glasses. I was sure I was a sight, still in the sweats I'd thrown on once I'd scheduled the last-minute flight and had to race to the airport. I hadn't bothered to look in a mirror since I'd boarded the plane.

"My wife is here. Julianne Robison."

The clerk nodded, tapping on her keyboard with long red fingernails before she raised her head.

"I'll buzz you in." She flicked her eyes to the double doors at the end of the hallway. "She's in curtain four."

"Thank you," I muttered before cursing the slowly opening doors and running inside.

I breathed a sigh of relief when I finally found the number four and ripped open the curtain.

My heart seized when I met Julie's gaze. Her skin wasn't only pale. It was gray. Her cheeks were wet as she took slow breaths in and out around the nose cannula giving her oxygen.

"Hey, darlin'," I whispered, leaning over the bed to kiss her forehead. Her face crumpled as I came closer. "Sorry it took me so long, but I'm here and I'm not going anywhere." I cupped her cheek and let my thumb drift back and forth to clean up the tears. "How does your chest feel now? Are you in pain?"

"Not as much," she said, reaching up to grab my wrist. "Just hard to take in a breath. I thought it was just a chest cold."

"There is no such thing as just a chest cold when it comes to you, but we'll talk about that later. How's the fever?" I asked her and cradled her cheek. Her skin was warm and clammy but not burning up.

"They gave me something for it, so it broke. But I'm tired." She ran a weak hand through my hair. "Did you just roll out of bed?" she teased with a hint of a tired smile.

"Sort of. I got a weird look from the ER clerk." I pulled the visitors chair closer to her bed.

"I shouldn't talk. I'm sure I look like death."

I shook my head. "You're always beautiful to me, Jules."

"Yeah, I'm gorgeous." She scrubbed a hand down her face.

"When did this turn?"

"Little by little, I guess," she said with a shrug. "Yesterday was the worst. I texted Karen when the room started to spin and I couldn't breathe."

"I'm sorry I wasn't there." I smoothed the hair off her forehead.

"Please don't be. You can't watch me all the time. I'm sorry I was stupid. I thought I could just power through, but I guess not." She popped up, clutching her chest as she coughed. It was deep and dry and scary as hell.

I rubbed her back when it finally stopped, shaking my head.

"Power through. Really?"

She laughed at my narrowed eyes.

"I know you're mad at me."

"Mad?" I coughed out a laugh. "I'd like to put you over my knee right now."

"Wait until I'm better so we can both enjoy it."

I glared at her and picked up her hand, lacing her fingers with mine as I watched her chest slowly rise and fall, a high-pitched wheeze escaping her every time she tried to suck in more air.

"I'd like to talk to the doctor. Can I get you anything?"

"Water would be nice," she croaked out. "My mouth is dry."

"Sure, babe." I brushed her lips and stood. I spotted a white coat at the nurses station and made my way over to start with him.

"Excuse me. I'm Julianne Robison's husband, and I just got here. Are you the doctor treating her?"

"Yes." He glanced at me for a moment while he signed something on a clipboard. "I was just looking over her chest X-ray."

My stomach dipped again when his gray brow furrowed.

"She said she may have pneumonia."

He shut his eyes and nodded.

"She has pleurisy too. Water on her lung. That's why she's having so much chest pain. I at least want to keep her overnight until the rest of the tests come back to rule out any other infections."

"Other infections?" My attempt to keep my voice calm was shit. Even I heard the shrill panic in my reply.

He nodded, an eerie sympathy in his gaze as he studied me.

"She presented with a very high fever last night. With autoimmune diseases, there are too many possibilities, I'm afraid. And I want to rule them all out."

"Sure," I said as I glanced back at Julie, clenching her eyes shut as she stirred on the bed. Watching her having this much trouble to breathe made me want to jump out of my fucking skin and scream.

"With lupus patients, the trajectory of illness and treatment is tricky. I don't want to send her home thinking it's just pneumonia when there's something more serious going on."

"Of course, I get it."

I got it too much. All those online rabbit holes I'd fallen into while researching lupus complications were always in the back of my mind, and now all my biggest fears were coming true. Julie was sick. Really sick. There could be a million reasons why, and until they narrowed it down, she couldn't fucking breathe. Rage and terror coursed through me, and all I could do was stand there and nod.

"I'm sure she wants to get out of here and into a regular room. We're working on that. In the meantime, keeping her calm and comfortable will help."

I nodded. "She said she was thirsty," I said, forcing my

voice past the lump I couldn't swallow away in the back of my throat.

"We'll get her some water. I know it's not what you want to hear, but all we can do now is sit tight and wait for answers."

He shot me a sad smile before huddling with one of the other doctors.

I wandered into the waiting area and fell into a chair. I pinched the bridge of my nose as a tear streamed down my cheek. I sniffled the rest back in and took slow breaths in and out to shake off the panic enough to go back to Julie.

My Julie.

I pulled my phone out of my pocket, ignoring all the messages littering my screen before I made a phone call.

"Landon? Hey, what's up? Is everything okay?"

"No, Dean. Not even close."

28

JULIE

I'd finally drifted off to sleep once the pain in my chest subsided enough to get sort of comfortable lying on my side. I pretended not to feel Landon's worried gaze as he stroked my hair. He grazed his fingertips along my scalp, calming me enough to breathe a little easier.

My entire body had relaxed when he arrived, but I couldn't hold his gaze without wanting to cry. He was always meant for great things, and now they were finally happening. I loved it for him but couldn't help feeling like an anchor around his neck. Granted, if I'd gone for treatment early, I might've avoided becoming this sick, but complications were always possible, no matter what. I'd been feeling good and doing well, riding so high on the new love we'd found—or old love we'd finally recognized—that I didn't want to taint any of my dreams about the future with harsh reality.

And now, I had no choice.

I'd never blamed Nate for not wanting the obligation of a sick partner. Not everyone was built for the ups and downs and frightening uncertainty. It took massive amounts of unconditional love to commit to someone with a chronic illness, and if the roles were reversed, I wouldn't have been so callous about it. But I understood the weight of extra responsibility.

I also knew that if I ever told Landon that I was a burden, he'd be furious and refuse to hear it. If he had an illness that meant I might have to take care of him someday, I wouldn't think twice about it. He was my person, as essential to me as the air in my lungs that I'd been trying to gulp in for the past day and the blood in my veins.

Landon was the one thing in my life that I couldn't live without. While it was beyond my control, I felt like the shittiest person alive for being the reason he was missing getting an award tonight and whatever he had planned for us after. I knew he'd never leave my side and would be angry if I ever suggested it, but I hated the concessions he was making now and the possibilities of what he might miss out on in the future because of me.

I opened my eyes, forgetting where I was for a minute when I wiped at my nose and almost dislodged my oxygen. I turned toward the whoosh of the IV in my arm and pressed my palm against the scratchy blanket to sit up.

"Hey, darlin'," Landon crooned, leaning over the bed rail. "Glad you got some sleep."

His warm smile still made me want to weep. I nodded, falling back when the room spun around me.

"Hey, take it easy." He grabbed my arm and eased me back on the mattress. "Want something to drink?"

"Okay," I rasped. My voice was still sandpaper but at least not as breathless. I lifted my head to Landon, his hair still a disheveled mess as he poured a cup of water.

"Here. Sip." He lifted a brow at me as he held the cup to

my lips. My chin quivered as I took small sips of water, the drops just enough to wet my tongue and cool my throat.

"Your bedside manner is stellar, husband," I joked, my voice laced with more tears.

I'd done so much crying since I'd been checked in, I was sure that was the cause of my dull headache. At first, it was fear, especially when I couldn't breathe and Landon and my mother were so far away. Once the doctor had found the water on my lungs and explained what was going on, it wasn't as frightening, but frustrating as fuck that I couldn't do something as simple as take in a breath without struggling.

"I'll give you a full examination when you're better." He winked and set down the cup.

"I'm so sorry," I blurted out as weak tears snaked down my cheeks. "I ruined everything—"

"What did I tell you about that?" The sly grin faded from his lips as he glowered at me. "I couldn't care less about the award right now."

"But you had something planned after, and you sounded so excited—"

"Babe, please stop this," he said, taking my face in his hands. "You got sick. It's not like you stood me up." His lips curled as he shook his head at me.

"I *am* sick. And it's a lot on you, and I hate making you miss out on—"

"Julie," he said, narrowing his eyes as his jaw clenched. "The only thing I care about or will *ever* care about is you. I don't think you understand how much I love you, or how fucking useless I'd be if..."

His throat worked as he held my gaze.

"You are everything to me, wife. Every. Fucking. Thing.

And all that matters is that you get better. I'm not going anywhere. Ever. I can't make it without you."

He swiped his cheek with the back of his hand.

"And my plans after aren't canceled. Just postponed. You didn't ruin a thing, so cut it out."

I turned my head and kissed the inside of his palm.

"Okay. If you say so." His lips curved up when I lifted my head. "You can at least go home and change. You must be exhausted."

"I'll get a ride home later to drop off my stuff and change and come right back."

"If my phone isn't dead, text Karen. She said she'd come back to take you home."

"I called someone else."

"Who?"

"Hey, guys! Are we interrupting anything?"

I whipped my head around to Dean's voice. Maria trailed behind him, looking me over with a watery smile.

"Jules, Jules, Jules," Dean said as he approached my bed, stuffing his hands into his jean pockets. "Any other secrets that your oldest friends should know about?"

I cut a look to Landon as Dean kissed my temple. Landon gave me a slow nod before Maria pulled me into a gentle hug.

"How much do you know?"

"Enough to know that your husband stole my idea." Dean scoffed and narrowed his eyes at Landon. "Asshole."

"We have the same anniversary," Maria said as she sat on the edge of my hospital bed. "We need to plan something big next year."

"As soon as I get out of here, we can make all the plans. If Landon ever lets me out of his sight."

"We'll see," Landon said, shooting me a scowl. "Dean is

going to drive me back to the house, and Maria is going to stay with you until I get back."

"You guys didn't have to drive down. I can stay alone while Landon goes home."

"Actually, I'm not leaving you alone for a while, but we'll talk about that another time." He jerked his chin at Dean and Maria. "They're mad at you too."

"But we love you and need you to get better before we tell you that." Maria squeezed my arm.

"I'm sorry." There went the tears again. "I didn't mean to lie. It was just that I was—"

"Stubborn? Unreasonable?" Dean teased as he nudged my blanket-covered foot. "Maria is right. We love you. I think what we all have is something special." Dean smiled as he gazed around the room. "How many people get to keep their best friends since college? You guys are family. If you needed us, regardless of if you didn't want to upset us or put a damper on something, you tell us. Let the people who love you be there for you."

"Yes," Maria said, studying me with glossy eyes. "Do you know when you can go home?"

"Tomorrow," Landon said. "All the tests should be back by then. She hasn't had a fever since I've been here, so they think she's moving in the right direction. She's going to have to rest once she's home, and I'm going to make damn sure that happens." He picked up my hand and brought it to his lips, raising a brow at me as he pressed a kiss to my wrist.

"Don't you have to work?" I asked, more tears pricking my eyes. I was exhausted and overwhelmed in every possible way, but the pinch in my chest squeezed my heart instead of my lungs this time.

"I have some time off coming to me. And I can work out

of the spare room when I need to. My wife is my priority and all I care about."

"You're married," Maria said in a loud whisper as she looked between us. "This is so *wild*."

"Seriously," Dean said, barking out a laugh. "Let's go. We can grab some dinner for all of us on the way back. And I never asked, did you do the Greatest Hits package?"

"We walked down the aisle to 'Can't Help Falling in Love,'" Landon said with a smirk twitching at his lips.

Dean's eyes thinned to slits as he glared at Landon.

"Fuck you, man."

Maria and I shared a laugh until I was knocked out by a coughing fit.

"I'll be back," Landon said and pressed a long kiss to my lips. "See? Everyone loves you and wants you to get better. And that is what we're all going to make sure of. Got it, darlin'?"

"Sure, doll." I draped my hand over his cheek as a wide smile spread over his perfect mouth.

"That's my girl."

"Yes, get better," Dean said, kissing my cheek. "There is a whole bunch of shit I'm waiting to give both of you, and I can't until you get well."

I smiled as they made their way out of my hospital room.

"I wish you would have told me."

Guilt coiled in my stomach when I spotted the regret in Maria's eyes.

"Not many people know. Landon had to drag it out of me in Vegas. I just wanted to celebrate with you both and not think about it."

"But we saw you after that. Dean is right, we've all been together for a long time. You lean on your friends."

I shut my eyes and nodded. "I'm sorry if I hurt you. It's just been a lot the past few months."

"Oh, I can see that." Her brows jumped as she scooted closer. "He has *always* been in love with you. I knew this day would come, and I am so thrilled for you guys."

"I know, and I've always loved him too. We've just been idiots and didn't realize it until now."

"Until you became husband and wife?"

I tilted my head from side to side when her brows popped. "We are, and we aren't."

"No, you *are*. You can't see how in love with you he is?"

"I know he loves me, but we started out married for insurance reasons, then fell into being lovers. I love him like crazy back, and we throw around the words husband and wife, but we never had the 'Are we really married?' conversation."

"Julie," she said, grabbing my wrists. "I don't know anyone more married than the two of you."

I shrugged and squeezed her hands back. "I'm sorry I wasn't honest with you. I'm relieved that you know. I'm sure you have questions, and I'll answer anything once I'm feeling better."

She shook her head. "I trust you to tell me what I need to know from now on. But like Dean said, please don't suffer alone ever again."

I nodded and let my head fall against her shoulder when she pulled me in for a hug. It was odd to feel cursed yet so blessed at the same time.

29

JULIE

THREE WEEKS LATER

"Again, I could have driven myself today," I told my mother's reflection in the rearview mirror of Sean's car from where I sat in the back seat. "You wouldn't have had to deal with all this traffic."

When I'd suggested coming to visit for the afternoon, Mom insisted they wanted to go for a drive and could pick me up for lunch out. I knew their ride home would be bumper-to-bumper, and they didn't have to double their time in the car just to baby me.

"You could have, but why if we can just come to get you and treat you to an early birthday lunch." She flashed a smile over her shoulder.

The residual effects from pneumonia took a lot out of me, but I was going stir-crazy in my house. I'd recovered from most of the symptoms, but I still got winded going up and down my stairs, and I wiped out a lot quicker at the end of the day. I regained a little more energy every day, enough to want to do things for myself and get into my car without someone offering to be *helpful* and take me instead.

I tried to keep in mind that I wasn't the only one who'd had a good scare, so I dug deep for more patience and reminded myself they were all driving me crazy out of love. At least Landon had started working in the spare room again. When I'd first come home from the hospital, he'd camped out with his laptop next to wherever I'd decided to lie down. My husband had meant it when he'd told Dean and Maria he wasn't going to leave me alone for a while.

As much as I'd tell him that I was fine and that he didn't have to watch me every second, I didn't hate snuggling into his side on the couch every afternoon. Landon was the one person I'd never get sick of. Since we'd first met in college, we could talk for hours and never be bored, and it had stayed like that between us ever since. It was one of those pesky clues that we kept stumbling on and more evidence of how we were always meant to be but somehow never picked up on it.

Falling in love with someone I liked so much was the best kind of surprise, even if it should have been a given after all this time.

"What time did we say we were bringing her back?" Sean asked my mother.

"What time did you say?" I asked as I scooted to the edge of the seat. "Back to whom?"

"He just means that...we have something else after this, so we need to make sure we have enough time," Mom stammered and cut a look to Sean. I held in a laugh at his apologetic shrug.

"Did Landon tell you to keep me out of the house until a certain time?"

That made sense since this was the first time I'd left the

house in a while without him peppering me with questions of how I was feeling and telling me not to overdo it. But *why* did he want me out of the house?

"I think he just wanted to make sure he was home."

"I have a key to my own house." I chuckled. "Why does he have to be home when I'm home?"

Mom groaned and shifted toward me. "Maybe he just doesn't want you to be home alone in case you need something."

"Is he afraid I'm going to get into the cabinets?" I scoffed. "I'm not a toddler, and I'm breathing fine—wait. Is this about my birthday? I'm not dressed for a party if that's what I'm walking into."

"It's not a party," Mom said, arching her brow when she met my gaze. "I can tell you that he'll be the only one home when we drop you off. So leave it alone, Julianne."

I sat back and nodded. Mom never pulled out my full name unless she meant the discussion was over. I met her eyes in the mirror again and pulled two fingers across my mouth, pretending to zip it shut.

"Enjoy the rest of your thirties," Sean quipped and reached back to tap my knee after he pulled up in front of my driveway.

"I will, Sean. All seventy-two hours of them," I said, squeezing his shoulder as I made my way out of the back seat. Forty had seemed like a daunting number before I was diagnosed with lupus, but aging meant something completely different now. It was something I hoped for rather than anticipated with dread.

I'd always loved birthdays, but now birthdays had more resonance than presents and cake. They meant I was still here, and I wanted to collect as many birthdays as possible. The extra lines around my eyes and growing gray roots that always irritated me when I glanced in the mirror seemed inconsequential now.

I had a good life, and I simply wanted more of it.

"Thanks for lunch," I said, and I stumbled back when my mother clobbered me with a tight hug.

"Are you okay?" I laughed as I rubbed her back. "I'm not working right now, so you can come back any afternoon you'd like."

I'd felt awful about being too sick to finalize my part, but Kaitie and Sierra had incorporated all my work into the project, creating a presentation the client had loved. Frank had called me the week after I'd come home from the hospital to both thank me for all my hard work and yell at me for making myself so sick in the process. He assured me that he would send more freelance projects my way in the new year—and that he'd never hire Elyse again.

"I'm fine," Mom whispered. I almost teared up at her watery smile, and now I was even more suspicious of what I was walking into. "And that sounds good. Happy early birthday, sweetheart."

"Thanks, Mom." I kissed her cheek and gave Sean one last wave before I headed back inside.

I unlocked the door slowly, scanning the living room and kitchen as I locked it behind me. Nothing seemed off, and the dining room and kitchen tables were empty. No bakery boxes or flowers and balloons. Maybe Landon really did ask my mother what time I was coming back so I wouldn't be home alone. That was fine, if a little disappointing. He needed to get over this fear eventually, but as with everyone else in my life at the moment, I'd let him fuss over me if it made him feel better.

For now.

I let out a long sigh as I shrugged off my coat and turned to hang it up on my coatrack.

I jumped when an arm wrapped around my waist and a hand went over my eyes.

"Don't turn around."

Landon's whisper fanned hot against my neck and triggered goose bumps down my arm. We'd made slow, careful love since I'd been sick, and I was very ready for hot and dirty again. That would beat the hell out of cake and flowers.

"Are you kidnapping me? I could be *so* into this." I held my wrists above my head. "Do you need to tie me up so I don't struggle?"

His gruff chuckle vibrated against my back.

"Not today, but I'll note that very good idea." He framed my waist and turned me around. "I'll let you go up the stairs with your eyes open, but you need to shut them before the last step, okay?"

He wore a tight black T-shirt and sweatpants, looking hot as hell, but he didn't appear to be taking me anywhere. I was confused—but excited and pretty turned on in anticipation of whatever secret he had upstairs.

"You got it, sir." I shot him a wry grin as I grazed my hand down his chest.

"Sir, huh?" His shoulders shook with a chuckle. "We'll explore this new kink of yours later, but come on." He grabbed my hand and pulled me toward the stairs. "Remember, eyes shut before the last step."

"Yes, I remember," I sighed, trying to crane my neck to see what was going on, but the upstairs light was off and I couldn't make out anything. I stopped at the next to last step and clenched my eyes shut.

"Okay. Eyes are closed," I said, slowly raising my foot to

feel around for the final step. Landon took my hands and led me to what I was sure was my bedroom, judging by the familiar dip in the carpet right before the threshold.

"All right, open your eyes."

When I blinked my eyes open, the first thing I noticed was a trail of rose petals leading to my bed and arranged into a heart on top of my comforter. A bottle of champagne was chilling on ice in a silver bucket on my nightstand.

"This is amazing," I croaked out, pressing my hand to my chest as I swept my gaze over the room. "What's this for? My birthday isn't for a few days."

"These are the plans I had after the awards dinner. I told you," Landon whispered, brushing my hair off my neck to press a kiss behind my ear. "Not ruined, just delayed. Plus, it's better to do it at home anyway."

"Do what at home?" I asked, even more confused, until I swiveled my head and found Landon on one knee behind me.

"Didn't we do this already?" I said, chuckling through the tears burning my nose.

"No. Not the way I want and not the way we deserve. I know it's backward, but—" he reached into his pocket and pulled out a bright pink box "—the last time I did this, I was offering you my insurance as a way to keep you healthy. Now, I'm offering you my life, every last second of it. I can't live without you. I never could."

A shy smile curved his lips as he popped the box open. The sparkle of a diamond was the only thing I could make out through the blur of tears.

"This is my mother's ring. I never gave it to anyone else because I never thought to, but I want you to have it. I think she would want you to have it, too. Even she knew before us. She'd always say how we made a good pair." He laughed and shook his head. "You're my heart and soul, Jules. My other half. Always were and always will be. I know I asked you to marry me already, but now I'm asking you to be my wife. For real."

"I'm already your wife." I sank down to my knees in front of him. "It's always been you, doll." My voice shook as I grabbed his face.

"Back at you, darlin'," he whispered, peeling one of my hands off his face to slip the ring on my finger. I recalled admiring this ring when I'd first spotted it on his mother's finger, the round diamond on a plain platinum band so simple yet stunning. Everything about it said classic love, and Landon and I had one for the ages that had already stood the test of time, sickness, and health.

Life was still a fuzzy path for me, but the one thing I was certain of was who I wanted by my side—the man who was there already and had been all along.

"Is that a yes?" Landon asked, his lips twitching as he laced our fingers together.

"It's an absolutely." I roped my arms around his neck and slanted my mouth over his. The kiss was slow, full of love and promise and relief, with all the same passion that had blinded us after an Elvis impersonator had told us that we were husband and wife.

"I actually wouldn't change anything about our wedding day, except for one thing," I said, tracing my finger across Landon's lips, still wet from our kiss.

"What's that?" he rasped, sliding his hand over the back of my neck.

I glanced back at our bed and popped my brow when I met his gaze.

"This time, we get a wedding night."

EPILOGUE

LANDON

FOUR MONTHS LATER

"Having trouble over there, Dad?" I teased as my father muttered to himself in the floor-length mirror.

He peered at me over his shoulder, rolling his eyes before he slid the tie he was fighting with off his collar.

"I wore a tie every day for thirty years and taught you. What the hell is wrong with me today?"

"You're allowed to be jumpy on your wedding day." I snatched the tie from his hands, tucking it under his collar before I made a quick knot.

"I taught you well," he said, studying me with a smirk.

"Nah, I just have more recent practice."

"Maybe it's all that mountain air thinning out my brain. We didn't want a big wedding since we've both been married before and thought a quaint little ceremony would be less stressful. We didn't want to make it a big deal." He dipped his head to tighten the knot I made.

Julie and I had flown out to Lake Tahoe to watch my

father marry Darlene. We'd already signed their marriage license as witnesses, and Dad had been on edge since this morning.

"Take it from me, it's always a big deal. Something like this, without the big party to distract you, gives the whole thing more weight."

"You were marrying the love of your life. No matter if it was in a cathedral or by Elvis, marrying Julie would have meant everything to you, son." He smiled, his shoulders less rigid as he adjusted his cuff links.

"I'm sure you're right," I said with a chuckle as I smoothed down the lapel of my suit jacket. "And that was when I was only marrying her for insurance. If we'd set out to do it for real that night, I probably would have passed out."

"I'm surprised you didn't anyway."

I couldn't do anything but nod as I followed him out of the dressing room next to the chapel.

"I'm happy for you, Dad." I squeezed his shoulder as we headed toward the small altar. "I'm glad you found someone to love."

"Me too," he said. "I never expected to. But—" he flicked his eyes to mine, the corner of his lips curving up "—Darlene is easy to love. It's not the same as..."

I nodded when he trailed off. Mom would've been happy for him today, but it still seemed odd saying her name out loud on the day my father was marrying someone else.

"It's quieter. Not as crazy. But still undeniable." He lifted a shoulder, nodding a hello at the officiant, and peered down the aisle with a wistful smile.

Julie headed down the aisle first, holding a small bouquet of lilies, not too unlike the fake ones she'd had when she married me. She'd been growing her hair longer, a couple of inches past her shoulders and closer to how she'd always had it, but no matter what length her hair was, she'd always be the most beautiful woman I'd ever seen. Her black sweater dress clung to all my favorite places, and I had plans for those knee-high boots in our suite later tonight. She flashed me a wide grin when she caught me staring, a flare of lust in her eyes as she did a quick sweep down my body.

Real marriage was damn good. Being at the first wedding since the Now or Never Chapel was already bringing back a ton of memories, although the dirty ways we'd reminisced last night were different from eating tacos on a bench after our ceremony that now seemed like a lifetime ago.

Dad was right. I'd known even then what marrying Julie meant as my heart had thundered in my ears the whole way down the aisle.

Darlene followed, beautiful in a long-sleeved gray dress, her spiked heels almost bringing her to my father's height. I didn't hear much of the ceremony as I was too busy flirting with my wife over my father's shoulder. I'd handed over the rings when asked and cheered loudly when they were announced as husband and wife.

"They're cute," Julie whispered to me as we followed them down the aisle. "I'm happy for them."

"Me too," I said, despite the twinge in my chest when Darlene slipped her hand out of the crook of Dad's elbow to drape her arm over the back of his waist. I liked Darlene a lot, but it would always be a little strange to see another woman at his side. Still, I was glad the woman he'd found had a big enough heart for all of us.

"You okay?" Julie asked as she slid her hand down my arm and entwined our fingers.

I replied with a slow nod and bent my head to brush a kiss to her lips. "I am. Getting married in Nevada is lucky. I'm sure they'll be very happy."

"It seems to be a trend for the people we know. And us."

I laughed as we followed them to the resort connected to the chapel and the wedding dinner they'd requested. The long table in the back had a two-tiered cake in the middle and four full champagne glasses.

"This is nice, right?" Darlene mused as her gaze drifted to the mountains outside. The restaurant was upscale but not too formal or crowded with other guests. "Five-course meal for all of us with no receiving line."

"I'll drink to that," Dad said, raising his glass. "To my new wife, and my kids." He smiled at Julie. "Love, health, and happiness for a hundred years."

"I will definitely drink to that," Julie said, clinking her glass with mine.

"Look," Darlene said after taking a long sip. "There's a jukebox in the corner."

We all turned to an almost antique-looking jukebox next to the bar.

"Feel like picking a wedding song?" She scanned the dining area. "Even though no one is dancing."

"It's our wedding day. We can do whatever the hell we want." Dad pushed off the table and stood, holding out his hand for Darlene before they sauntered over to the jukebox.

"Feeling okay?" I asked Julie as I drifted my hand back and forth across her back.

"Pretty good, actually. Cold mountain air seems not to anger my joints. Maybe we should move here."

"Maybe, except we don't ski, and that's a lot of snow to shovel." I followed Julie's gaze to where Dad and Darlene still swayed back and forth. "Sorry we didn't have a wedding dance?" I draped my arm over the back of her chair.

"We technically did," she said, meeting my gaze with a shrug. "We had a nice dance at Dean and Maria's wedding. Besides, I'd be too stressed out picking a song for us if I had to."

"Why would that stress you out?" I snickered and let my thumb drift back and forth over the nape of her neck.

"After twenty years with you, even though we've only been officially together for a short time, I'd want too many songs for too many reasons. I like the one we ended up with." She set down her glass and crossed her arms, squinting at me. "Do you remember what it was?"

"The song we danced to at someone else's wedding? I didn't think there'd be a test after."

"So, you don't remember, then."

"I didn't say that."

"Then what is it?" She tapped her foot, arching a brow at me.

"Ah, so you're issuing a challenge then, wife."

"Because I know you don't remember, husband."

"Everything all right?" Dad asked, laughing as he looked between us. "This is how they used to look in the basement during a ping-pong match when they were in college."

"Ooh, competition can be fun," Darlene said, resting her head on her hand as she grinned at us from the opposite side of the table.

"No competition. My wife doesn't think I remember the song we danced to the day we were married." I stood and set my napkin on the table. "If I pick right, you have to do something for me."

Julie's brow furrowed as she stood. "I don't make bets without knowing the stakes, Clark."

"You sound unsure of yourself, *Clark*," I teased as I led her over to the jukebox.

"Wow, this even still takes quarters," I said as I pulled out my wallet and fished out two. I surveyed the song choices and held back a fist pump when I found what I was looking for. I slipped the quarters in and pressed in the code.

Julie's head fell back at the beginning chords of "The Way You Look Tonight."

"I remember *everything* about that night, Jules." I grabbed her hand and pulled her flush to me. "That green dress, fighting the urge to kiss you all night, my world turning upside down once I did."

I picked up her hand and brought it to my chest. "So now you owe me."

She laughed and dropped her head against my shoulder. "I remember all that too. I also recall feeling so damn hopeless and never wanting to leave your arms and deal with my new shitty reality."

"Well, now *I'm* your reality. Forever."

"You always were." She peered up at me with a gorgeous, wide smile.

"I'll never understand how we were so stupid for so long."

"No one else will either," she said, shaking her head with a chuckle. "What bet did I lose, despite the fact that I didn't agree to it?"

"Ah, yes." I pressed my hand against the small of her back and pulled her even closer. "I want you to marry me."

Her brows drew together. "You're proposing a third time?"

"Sort of. I want this." I jutted my chin toward Dad and Darlene. "I want the walk down the aisle again and not to have to stop kissing you this time. I want the dance, and I want the wedding night."

"We had the wedding night. A few, actually," she said with a watery laugh.

"It's the marriage that matters, and we have a fucking great one, but I want the big deal. So, marry me. You know, again."

She roped her arms around my neck, shaking her head.

"You're crazy, husband."

I shrugged, bringing her in for a slow kiss as Frank Sinatra sang again about what he'd do when the world went cold. My world would never be cold because I'd have the woman I'd always wanted for the rest of my days.

"I can't help it if I love my wife."

BONUS EPILOGUE

JULIE

SIX MONTHS LATER

“We just love to see repeat customers,” Mandy gushed when Landon and I came up to the front counter of the Now or Never Chapel of Bliss for the second time. Her eyes sparkled around her already frosted eye shadow as she looked between us. “Of course,” she said, leaning in to whisper, “it’s nice to see repeat customers with the same bride and groom. That only happens half the time.”

I peered up at Landon, who was holding in the same laugh I was.

“My wife isn’t replaceable.” He brought our joined hands to his mouth. “I wouldn’t be here with anyone else.”

“I love being in the business of love.” She clasped her hands under her chin. “I knew from that kiss you both were destined to be together. This will be quicker since you don’t need the paperwork, but what song would you like to walk down the aisle to? I’ll even throw in the Greatest Hits package for free.”

“Man,” Dean groaned behind us.

"We had a nice wedding," Maria told him in an irritated loud whisper. "It's our first anniversary, so stop sulking."

"That would be great," Landon said as he draped his arm over my shoulder. "We'd like to walk down to 'Can't Help Falling In Love' again, but we'd like them to walk down the aisle before us and meet us there. It's okay if it's extra."

We glanced back at Dean and Maria. I had to bite my lip to keep from laughing when Dean's eyes lit up.

"You can be here for when we say vows and get part of the wedding dream you can't seem to let go of. Our anniversary gift to you."

"We're in," Dean said, holding out his elbow for Maria. "You're all right, Landon. For a thief." He narrowed his eyes at us but couldn't help the smile that broke out across his face. My eyes burned when I met Maria's gaze. Coming back here for our first anniversary had seemed a little ridiculous when Landon had suggested it, but having our oldest friends here as we said vows as a real husband and wife felt very right and poignant.

"Perfect, and no extra charge. It's wonderful to see lasting love. As you can imagine, it doesn't come easy in this town." We chuckled at her raised eyebrow. "Come with me. I'll set Hal up."

"You guys must have been something if she remembered you," Dean mused as we waited for the music to start.

"I'm sure Mandy isn't used to seeing sober couples in love," I said, eyeing the fake lilies in my hand.

"Or maybe she's not used to seeing couples so hopelessly gone for each other," Maria said with a wide grin.

"Now she'll see two." Dean cupped Maria's chin and turned her head toward his for a kiss. "Our wedding was nice, and I got to leave with you, so it was perfect."

He swiveled his head as his gaze drifted down the aisle. Hal had donned a black jumpsuit this time, and his sideburns were even thicker.

"This is just really fucking cool."

"Never change, man," Landon said, tapping his shoulder.

"I hope I never do. I hope we all stay the same." Dean swept his gaze over us, a wistful smile lifting his mouth. "We all took the long way here, but I don't think I'd change a thing."

"Hard same, my friend," I said, squeezing his shoulder.

The music flowed out of the speakers, Mandy once again singing about fools rushing in.

"That's our cue. Come on, Mrs. Calabrese. Let's live the dream."

Maria laughed, burrowing into his side as they made their way down the aisle.

"So here we are again," I said, flicking my eyes up to Landon.

"We are. Although this time, my heart isn't quite as loud in my ears."

We headed to the altar once Dean and Maria took their places on the opposite sides of Hal's pulpit.

"I didn't know you were so nervous," I whispered.

"Maybe not nervous. It was a big deal to marry you, I just didn't fully figure out why until we kissed. And even then, I tried to reason it away."

"I remember. I'm glad they got a picture."

Landon nodded, a wicked grin curling his lips. Our first kiss was framed on our bedroom wall, right next to my boudoir photo. Anyone who came up to our bedroom would linger on both once they noticed. Some would blush, but no one had said a word about it. After denying the passion we didn't understand for so long, neither of us minded showing it off.

"We love repeats," Hal said, his belly jiggling as he laughed and still fighting with the seams of his jumpsuit. "We are gathered here today to celebrate the marriage of Landon and Julianne. Who has the rings?"

"That would be me," Dean stepped forward and dropped the same rings we'd purchased from this chapel a year ago into Landon's palm. He passed me his and picked up my other hand.

"Do you take Julianne to be your lawfully wedded wife?"

"I absolutely do. With all that I am and all that I have. I belong to her." Landon held my gaze as he slipped the ring onto my finger.

"Do you take Landon to be your lawfully wedded husband?"

"I do. He's my best friend and the other half of my soul. Always and forever." The tiny smile on Landon's face sped up my pulse as I slipped the ring on to his finger.

"Jesus," Dean whispered behind us. I caught him wiping his cheek with the back of his hand. "Desert sand in my eyes." He waved a hand at us. "Go on."

"By the power vested in me by the state of Nevada, I pronounce you husband and wife. Again."

Landon slipped his hand over the back of my neck, easing in slowly before he slanted his mouth over mine. The kiss wasn't new or the life-altering surprise it had been that night, but it was hot enough to make my toes curl in my low-heeled shoes when his tongue tangled around mine, and the groan rising from his throat made me drop the bouquet again. I knew exactly why he'd asked me to do it for real this time. Because knowing I didn't have to reason away the thump in my chest and that I could kiss Landon for the rest of my life made it worth the redo.

"I got a shot of that one too."

We broke apart and turned toward Mandy's squeal.

"We can frame that one too," Landon whispered and sucked my earlobe into his mouth.

"People are going to start to think we're perverts," I said as Mandy set up her tablet for another picture.

"More like we're working off two decades of frustration." He raised a brow, cupping my cheek. "I'll always be hungry."

A shiver rolled up my spine at the wicked gleam in his eyes. I'd always crave him the same way. As Karen once told me, it's good when you realize you love your husband.

"Smile," Mandy sang as she lined up the picture. "Got it."

"Wait," I said, reaching out to touch her arm. "Can we get a second with all four of us? Hal, would you mind getting in the middle?"

"Why, I'd be honored." He ambled to the middle of the altar. "Sunglasses or no?"

"Definitely sunglasses," Dean said as he stepped next to Hal, pulling Maria behind him.

"Okay, everyone!" Mandy said as she came in front of us. "Say—"

"Viva Las Vegas," Maria called out.

"I love you so much," Dean gushed and wrapped his arms around her waist.

We were set up like a prom picture with an Elvis in the middle, and nothing could have been more perfect.

"I could get used to this," I sighed, leaning back against Landon's naked body in the Jacuzzi of our Bellagio honeymoon suite. We'd grabbed tacos outside the chapel and gelato on our way up, as per our new tradition. I flexed my hand back and forth over the jets, any soreness I'd had from the adrenaline of the day melting away with the bubbles.

"This is nice," Landon swiped the loose hairs escaping from my bun off my neck and peppered light kisses over my nape. "Feeling okay?" he asked as he reached under the water to massage my palm.

"Never better." I glanced back at him. "This tub works miracles."

"We should get one at home."

I shook my head. "We don't have the room for a Jacuzzi."

"Well, not now. We could plan some renovations when we get back. It wouldn't suck to have an excuse to get you naked and wet all the time."

"You don't need a Jacuzzi for that," I teased, squirming in his lap.

"Mrs. Clark, you have a filthy mind," he said, cupping my chin and covering my mouth with a slow but dirty kiss, dragging his tongue along the seam of my lips as he pulled away.

"I learned from my husband."

"Didn't I tell you marrying me was a perfect solution?" He shifted my hips until I was straddling him in the tub. I nodded when his brow furrowed.

"This is fine, feels good." I moaned as he trailed his hands up and down my back.

"That it does. I still can't believe you're mine. A whole year of being the luckiest bastard in the world."

"I don't know about—"

"Don't ruin this, Jules."

My test numbers had improved, although at a slow pace, over the past year. The fatigue didn't clobber me as it once did, but I'd learned an important lesson about rest and getting comfortable in seeking immediate treatment if anything felt off. The guilt over sharing my limitations with him would always be there, but I knew he loved me too much to care about any of it. He only worried if I was well—and he still worried all the time.

Hovering was his love language, and like everything else about him, I'd soak it up and enjoy it.

"So, I'm the other half of your soul?" He gathered me closer, a smile twitching on his lips.

"You're the other half of my everything."

And that was why it didn't matter how broken I felt sometimes. Thanks to my husband, I'd always be whole.

AUTHOR'S NOTE

Julie isn't my first heroine with lupus. In 2015, I wrote Only You, an emotional story about a woman who becomes ill after losing a close family member and keeps it to herself until it's almost too late. It's still my husband's favorite story of mine because even though it had plenty of steamy and lighthearted moments, I took things to a darker place than my readers may be used to from me. But, while everything was resolved and Paige got her HEA, I never showed how she lived with lupus after or how it affected her daily life, even when I brought her back as a side character. It's been almost nineteen years since my own lupus diagnosis, and I wanted to show someone actually *living* with a chronic illness.

Friends to lovers is my favorite trope to write, and I've wanted to create a marriage of convenience story for a long time. I had a ball showing Landon and Julie realizing how in love they were from the very beginning but somehow never knowing it, but as with all stories having do with illness, I had to work up to a black moment. As someone with lupus for a long time, I never forget about it but it's become routine for the most part. I know what to do when a flare pops up or I become sick. Right when I had to write the most difficult part, I caught my son's school virus. It was a chest cold that lingered until one night, I ran out of air while studying with my son. I tried not to panic until I woke up with a fever. It wasn't high, but fevers bring out a lot of scary memories for me, when, like Julie, I had a constant string of them at the beginning. When Julie compares lupus to the monster around the corner, moments like that are frightening reminders of how true that really is.

All my betas told me how scared they were for Julie when she became really sick, and how you truly could feel her fear. My low-grade fever was enough to bring out all my own fears and make that chapter so raw, it was a little difficult to edit for me as I read it all over.

What I wanted to show the most in The Marriage Solution other than an epic lifelong love story, was that having a chronic illness may make you different, but not less. That you can have the big love and a great life, even if it may not be the one you planned on. In the end, Julie got the guy and the HEA she deserved.

I hope that you enjoyed The Marriage Solution and loved Landon and Julie as much as I do.

Much love,

Steph

ACKNOWLEDGMENTS

To James and John, my husband and son and my biggest fans. I couldn't do this without your love and support, and hope I make you proud.

Mom, maybe someday you'll pick up a book of mine, but I hear the pride in your voice when you talk about this crazy gig I'm doing that you may not totally understand. Thanks for always having my back.

To my betas: Jodi, Lisa, Michelle, Lauren, Bianca, Jeannine, and Rachel. Thank you for sticking by me throughout all the rewrites, whining, and self-doubt. The reason this is a story that I'm proud of is because of all of you.

Jodi, I'll never be able to thank you for all you do for me, but for this book you went completely above and beyond. Your "nice work" and "well done" was worth a million five-star reviews. I'm beyond lucky to have you not only as my PA but as a close friend I consider family.

Rachel, I don't know what I did to deserve you, but I am never giving you up. Your love for Landon and Julie pushed me through when I was ready to give up. I can't thank you enough for loving me and my people.

Karen, the wise one, your friendship and voice messages brighten my life every day. There is a reason Julie has a wise friend named Karen who seems to know everything.

Lauren, my Bronx sister and the friend who organizes my chaos. Thanks for being my found family.

Bianca and Camille, thank you for sharing your experiences and being my sensitivity check. Bianca, you'll always be my soul sister.

To Lisa, my editor and friend. Thank you for not judging my lack of knowledge of English and polishing this story to the best it could be. I'm so glad I found you, and that I didn't have to spend hours de-gazing this story.

Najla Qamber, still a creative and patient genius. Thank you for making my first object cover a true work of art.

To Shanna, thank you for naming Landon's company! I think you may have meant it as a joke but it worked out perfectly. Thanks for keeping me smiling (and hydrated)!

To my That's What She Said Publishing family: Lucy, Tim, Rick, and Dan, who are responsible for the beautiful book in your hands. Thank you for all you've done for me.

Lucy, thank you for not only changing the trajectory of my author life by sliding into my DMs to ask me to join TWSS, but for your awesome cover idea that fits this story so perfectly.

LJ and Kathryn, thanks for being the best hype friends a girl could ever ask for. Thank you, Melanie Moreland, for being the best author idol and sister wife. I'm grateful for all my author friends who lift me up every day. After being in this industry for almost a decade, the cluster of genuine friends I've found mean everything to me.

I always mention how my measure of success when I first published was to have ten people not related to me buy my book. To be here now is a dream that was beyond my imagination. Thank you will never be enough to cover how grateful I will always be.

ABOUT THE AUTHOR

Stephanie Rose is a badass New Yorker, a wife, a mother, a former blogger and lover of all things chocolate. Most days you'll find her trying to avoid standing on discarded LEGO or deciding which book to read next. Her debut novel, Always You, released in 2015 and since then she's written several more—some of which will never see completion—and has ideas for hundred to come.

Stay in touch!
Join Stephanie's Rose Garden on Facebook and sign up for Stephanie Rose's newsletter at www.
authorstephanierose.com

BOOKS BY STEPHANIE

Second Chances

Always You

Only You

After You

Always Us, A Second Chances Novella

Second Chances Spinoffs

Finding Me

Think Twice

Never Too Late

Rewrite

Simmer

Pining

Ocean Cove

No Vacancy

No Reservations

Kelly Lakes

Standalones

Made in the USA
Monee, IL
29 August 2023